The Trainee
Jake England Thriller

Thomas M. Jardine

ISBN: 978-1-62420-884-3

Credits

Cover Artist: Design by Ms G
Editor: Amanda Armstrong

Dedication

To my dear friend, Mickie Coughran. Iggy and Jake's first fan. R.I.P. Mick.

Chapter One

For the fifth time in the past hour, Jake England wondered what the hell he was doing here, anyway. *Here* being the front door of the Bank of New Brunswick building in Chatham, N.B. at eight thirty on a Monday morning. The bank, of course, was currently closed to the public. He knew this, not from prior personal knowledge, but only because the door to the intimidating structure was locked. He had tried opening it, only to receive questioning glares from one or two of the employees inside.

He had never been in the building, knew very little about its business. In fact, he never even had a bank account at *any* bank, anywhere. He did not see the need. It was the fall of 1964, he had graduated with honors earlier in June and all he had on his mind since then was the weekly Saturday night dance at the Chatham Exhibition building where his rock band, The Esquires, played. Jake was the bass guitarist in the five-man group, and over the past year they had become quite popular in the area.

This morning Jake was at the bank for a job interview, more to appease his parents than any lofty plans that might involve banking. He recalled the initial discussion he had on Career Day in May when some dude from the Bank of New Brunswick had visited his school. He was there to speak with the graduating class about prospective employment with them, an annual thing the bank did to show they were part of the local community.

The guy who Jake was here to see was the son of the Doyles … friends of Jake's parents who had apparently given Jake's name to their son, since he had singled him out after his talk to the group during assembly. Jake had half-listened to him and he must have made some kind of commitment to meet with him, since he had called Jake at home last night to remind him of their scheduled meeting.

So here he was, dressed in a grey tweed sports jacket, a blue button-down dress shirt (no tie), black slacks, and freshly shined black shoes that he had only worn once, at his high school graduation three months ago.

He noticed some movement behind the bank's main entrance door and, finally, a lady was opening the door for him, welcoming him into their hallowed structure. *Wow, she is quite an attractive lady*, Jake thought. She introduced herself as Sharon Donovan. Maybe a few years older than Jake, she had brunette hair, cut in a short bob, beautiful sea-green eyes, a few freckles on her nose that enhanced a great summer tan, and a killer smile that, immediately in *his* mind, she managed to display only for him.

"I guess you would be Jacob England?" she asked.

"Uh yeah," Jake mumbled. *God, he was dumb struck.*

"I think you're here to see Ron Doyle?"

Jake frantically recalled the guy's name. "Ah, yeah. Ronnie. Good guy." *Jesus!* From the straight face Sharon displayed, he realized he was babbling, making an arse of himself. "Is he in?" *Damn! He did it again. Of course, he was in, this is where the guy works, fool!*

Sharon just gave him that fantastic smile and a small chuckle. "Follow me Jacob, I'll bring you to him."

Sharon led Jake into the bank where he saw eight or ten people busy behind desks sorting files, or teller wickets counting cash. There were three men sitting in what Jake took to be the manager's office. Two of them were sitting in front of a desk, apparently in a meeting, the boss behind it, taking a drink from his coffee cup, then grimacing as he placed the cup in front of himself. It was toward this office where Jake was led by Sharon.

"Excuse me, Mr. Crawford. This is Mr. Jacob England who is here for his appointment with Mr. Doyle." Crawford quickly placed his coffee in the side drawer of his desk which had been opened. Jake watched as Crawford scowled at Doyle who then got up and came out of the office, leaving the other man alone with the manager.

"Jacob, glad you could make it," Doyle said, extending his hand which Jake shook. "Let's go into our staff room and have a talk." Doyle looked at Sharon, giving her a wink. "That'll be all Miss Donovan. Right this way, Jacob."

They were seated at a table in a small room off a back hall that led to a washroom, and Doyle explained their company's commitment to the community by attempting to hire at least one young student from one of the town's three schools annually. He went on to reiterate the benefits to Jake: secure, steady employment; a competitive salary; good, clean working conditions; staff rates on things like car loans and home mortgages; and last, but not least, a great support staff here to help in the training process.

"In your case, Jacob, assuming you are interested in joining our firm, Miss Donovan will be your trainer. You've met Sharon already."

"Uh, yes sir. Sharon. She's beau __, I mean, she's great." He wanted to say, '*Sign me up, Ron, when do I start?*', but caught himself in time. From that point on, Jake was sold on his new job. The rest of his meeting with Doyle was a blur. He ended up having to give some personal info to an older lady, Viola, who opened an account for him, which at first Jake had declined. But then he was informed by Viola, with a frown, that it was a necessity, that is, if he wanted to get paid. After this, he was passed back to Sharon.

It was noon time. "Want to grab some lunch, Jacob?" suggested Sharon. They were on their way out the main entrance when they passed Ron's desk.

"Hey Sharon, what's up?" said Ron, giving her a big smile.

"Jacob and I were just going out for lunch, Ron. We'll be back by one. See you," and they were out the door. Jake noted a scowl that had appeared on Ron's face as they made their exit.

They sat across from each other in a window booth with a street view in the Mic Mac Restaurant, a popular diner for the younger set of the town. There were at least four dozen booths that each held room for six average-sized teenagers. That did not include another twenty or more singles stools that ran along the front counter of the large dining area.

There was always current pop music playing from hidden speakers. Songs that patrons would select from an array of choices available to them in glass-enclosed boxes in each booth. Song selections appeared on thirty or more pages of song lists that one could 'flip' through by turning metal clips attached to the top of each page; then one could push designated alphanumeric buttons relating to their selections…very similar to the 'juke boxes' that were introduced in the fifties.

At the moment, *B-9* was Jake's favorite which he now selected after depositing a dime in the proper slot. When the previous tune that had been playing was finished, the opening to Jake's selection commenced, *Oh, Pretty Woman* by Roy Orbison.

He watched Sharon as a waitress arrived and took her order for a burger with fries and a coke. Sharon tapped the tabletop in time to the heavy four/four beat produced by the snare drum, bass and lead guitar intro. He picked up on this and knew right away she was someone he could really get to like.

Sharon sensed she was being watched and she returned his stare, raising her eyebrows in question marks.

"My apologies for staring," he said. "I was just admiring your timing."

"My timing?"

"Yes. With this song. Your table taps. You'd make a good drummer," Jake said, nodding toward her hands, fingers, keeping time. She stopped tapping, and blushed.

"You got me, Jacob, I like that tune. And hey, my mother was a music teacher, then taught Literature in her later years, so maybe it comes naturally." Again, that smile.

"Okay, now I got it. Yes, Mrs. Donovan. She taught me English 1 last year. I like her. Why did Ron give you a mean look when we were leaving for lunch?" This question, out of the blue, took her aback.

"Well, Jacob, don't you think that's getting a little personal?"

"I'm sorry."

"It's okay. But just so you know, while you were speaking with him in the staff room, Mr. Crawford told me I would be responsible for your training. So, us coming to lunch together? I just wanted to get to know you better, seeing as how we will be working closely over the next few months." Just then the waitress arrived with their food. They both waited, then when the girl had left them, Sharon resumed.

"And, since you picked up on something, here is the situation: Ron and I dated for a while. I made a mistake, now it's history. Maybe he's still peed off, I really don't know, nor do I care. But a little advice: be careful with Doyle, okay?"

She was serious, and Jake didn't quite know what to make of this. He simply thanked her and nodded. There'd be lots of time later to get back into that part of their discussion. They ate their lunch in silence, and soon it was time to go back to work.

"Tell me Jacob, why do you want to work with the bank?" Sharon asked before they got up to leave.

"Ah, fair question," replied Jake. "Steady job, pay's not bad, indoor work, you know," he faltered.

"That sounds like something Ron Doyle would say at one of his recruitment sessions."

Jake just smiled at Sharon and nodded. She continued to talk to him.

"We've been here almost an hour, and you have not yet asked me one question about work."

"Well, there *is* one other perk that Doyle mentioned."

"Oh yeah?"

"Yep. He was high on the 'great support staff' that's available for training purposes. His words."

"Do you know Ron? You referred to him earlier as 'Ronnie', a 'good guy'."

Jake was now embarrassed by his stupid remark. He had trouble meeting her eyes as he spoke.

"No, Sharon, I don't know the guy from Adam. I was stupidly trying to act as if I had an *'in'* with you guys. His folks know my parents, that's all. I'm happy with what I'm doing at the moment. I play in a rock band."

"Yes, I've heard about your band from some girlfriends. They tell me you guys are pretty good. But how long will this last? And isn't music very *fickle*? I mean, styles and fads change quickly. If you really are into music, why not go to university and get a degree, become a music teacher?"

"All good points," he said. "And maybe I will, down the road. But this is the here and now. I feel it is like a kind of movement, not some fad, like, ah, hula hoops, or bell-bottom jeans. I think it's important, Sharon. And I have a chance to be part of it. Maybe I can do both, that is, work in the bank, *and* play in the band?"

"Maybe you can. But personally, I think your two pursuits will eventually clash. In the meantime, let's get back to this one. And remember what I said about Doyle. I think Ron has his own agenda, so watch what you say and do around him, okay?"

"Yes ma'am," Jake suddenly sounded all business. Then, as they left the Mic Mac, "But one thing, Sharon. Can you call me Jake?"

Their walk back to work took them through a back-alley short-cut where they ran into a couple of young punks whom Jake vaguely knew. They were not friends, just guys that hung around the dance hall, often causing the odd fight, either with young airmen from the Canadian Air Force base located in the town, college boys from St Thomas University, or other kids from Newcastle, a nearby rival community. Jake prepared himself for trouble. He recalled their names were Johnny Dorsey and Fred MacMillan.

"Hey Jake! Lookin' gooood!" the taller of the two said, basically leering at Sharon as they approached them. Jake could tell the guy was stoned, and it was mid-day, for God's sake.

"Hi John," Jake responded, not giving the guy a second look.

"Whoa, wait up, man. Don't suppose you could help out a friend with a five-spot, now that you got yourself a big job?"

"Can't help you today, John. Maybe next week," he continued on, but it was necessary to brush against the guy who had gotten too close to them. "Sorry, John. I'll see you later."

"Yeah, you will, Jake…" The guy's response was ominous, and it matched the glare he gave Jake. *What the hell is wrong with them?* Lately he had noticed a number of guys his age who seemed to be getting into some very serious drugs. Up until this point, Jake had experimented with a bit of pot a couple of times but that was where he drew the line.

"Come on, Sharon." Jake took her hand and led her out of the alley.

"Sorry about that," he said. "Not the most upstanding citizens in town."

Sharon had no response; she just kept her head down until they were back to the bank.

The remainder of the day was spent with Sharon while she introduced Jake to the rest of the staff at the branch. There were four cash tellers, two stenos, a Personal Loans Manager and his assistant, and finally, they went into the manager's office where she formally introduced the bank Manager, Mr. Ralph Crawford, whom Jake had only nodded to when he first came into the bank that morning. Now the man asked Jake to have a seat and Sharon left them alone.

"So, Jacob. You want to be a banker." It was a statement, and Jake was not inclined to debate the matter with the manager at this moment. "Look," said Crawford. "I don't have a lot of time. Do you have any questions?"

"Ah, no sir."

"Very well, then," and Crawford reached down and pulled an empty coffee cup from the bottom drawer of his desk. "Son, would you let the water run *really* cold from the tap for me," he instructed Jake, handing him the cup and pointing toward the washroom. "And I think it would be a good idea to get yourself a haircut."

So, Jake thought, *Ralph likes his vodka cold.* Good info to have. The first day at his new job had begun, and already he had mixed ideas about how long he'd be here. Certainly at least long enough though, to get to know a little more about Sharon Donovan.

The haircut could wait.

Chapter Two

The next morning, Sharon introduced Jake to a routine part of his training that he would be undertaking. She sat beside him in the staff room and explained the new function.

"The first of your daily duties, Jacob, will be to deliver drafts around town." This statement puzzled Jake, as he thought she was referring to draft beer. Businesses used banks at the time as agents to facilitate transactions between retail buyers, wholesalers and manufacturers, by issuing financial instruments called *sight* and *acceptance* drafts. In Jake's case, he would be delivering only acceptance drafts.

These documents specified agreed-upon prices, along with delivery and payment dates for specific products. Branches of the BNB across Canada that financed the makers of products being sold to the town's merchants, sent copies of drafts to the local branch where the retail outlets for these goods were located.

A bank officer usually delivered these drafts to their local merchants for acceptance. Once the retailer was able to verify valid delivery and good condition of his wares related to the draft, he could 'accept' it, thereby authorizing the local bank to pay for the goods out of his account with them, and remit funds to the manufacturer on his behalf.

In some cases, it was an opportunity for the bank to issue 'Letters of Acceptance', or 'Letters of Credit' to the merchants. Essentially, these were lines of credit for the financing of their inventory. For Jake, it was an opportunity to step out of the office, get some fresh air, and meet the townsfolk.

Sharon took Jake with her to a trial run demonstration and introduced him to the local merchants, some of which he already knew. It was lunch time when they finished the morning routine. Jake was enjoying his new job, at least this part of it. He went home for his lunch that second day and he was happy to describe to his mother what he had done that morning. He finished his soup and sandwich and left the house, his mother proudly watching him as he strolled out of their lane, walking with a purpose in his stride.

Two months quickly passed, and Jake's probationary period was now only a month away. Today he had decided to take a shortcut back to work after delivering his last draft for the morning to a business in the east end of town. He was wearing a new three-piece grey, pin-striped suit he had just purchased from his last month's pay, and he moved with a jaunt to his stride. He was looking forward to having lunch with Sharon.

Halfway back to the bank, he ran into a couple of close buddies who were hanging outside Joe's, the local pool hall where he had spent many Saturdays fleecing any newcomers that he and his pals could lure into a game or two.

Lennie Hachey and Donnie Mitchell were two of the best eight-ball players in town and they lazily rolled toward him when they saw him coming. They both had the jive and stroll of several teen movie stars of the day nailed down perfectly, thumbs in the front pockets of their denim jeans, shoulders moving in rhythm to their strides.

"Whoa, Jake, who died, man?" said Donnie, rubbing his hands on the front of his old leather bomber jacket as if to make some kind of mocking gesture regarding the poshness of Jake's attire. Then Lennie Hachey also cut in. "Nah, Jake's on his way to a wedding, right Jake?"

"Hey, get lost, you losers," retorted Jacob. He gave them a saucy smile and continued on his way. In a matter of seconds, both Donnie and Lennie had caught up with him, and Lennie took hold of his arm, stopping his progress.

"Wait up, Jake," Lennie said. "Do you know a guy at your bank, name of Doyle? Kind of a nerd, full of himself?"

Jake had taken the initial casual affront all in good stride, but now, seeing the serious look that Lennie and Donnie were throwing his way, he felt a chill come over him.

"Yeah, sure I do. Why?"

"Well. You better watch your back, man." Lennie made a gesture behind them toward the poolroom. "I over-heard some people at Joe's yesterday, saying that your banker buddy is getting a little over his head with the wrong boys. This involves some serious money and gambling debts, just so you know, okay? I don't think he's the type you would want to start hangin' with…"

Both Donnie and Lennie took a good look around the area where they were standing, then they slowly turned around and walked away from Jake, leaving him in a perplexed state.

As he walked along Main Street nearing the bank, Lennie's words about Ron Doyle stuck with him, and he began thinking about the sort of people he'd be working for and with. He had never met any of the young men or women who had started their banking careers in Chatham's banks. No doubt it was because he thought they were typically nerdy sorts who seldom hung out with the local jocks or the cool set. Not that Jake was the coolest guy in town. Far from it. But since The Esquires had become popular, he had developed a larger circle of friends, and now he wondered what impact this new job may have on his existing friendships.

Invariably, the guy's Jake hung around with were laborers at the local pulp and paper mill or construction workers. Also, many of them only worked seasonally, if at all. Yet, it seemed to Jake that all of them made decent money, and they all drove newer model vehicles. Now Jake wondered if he could stay on friendly terms with that crowd. Or, worse yet, maybe these friends would start the separation and avoid him. Suddenly, once again he was second-guessing his decision to work at the bank as he walked into the intimidating building and the strangers that worked there.

Last week Jake had 'graduated' to the position of first Teller. At this point he learned how to manage his cash, balance his daily journal, and perform 'sundry duties as assigned'. Much to his anger, the 'sundry duties' involved mowing the manager's lawn, which would soon include shoveling the snow from his driveway.

Also, being the only trainee at the bank, he was subject to a form of 'hazing', which at the time was practiced by all of the four major banks in the town. It usually involved in-house pranks, like having the trainee deliver a 'bag of Foreign Exchange' across the street to a competitor bank. In this practice a canvas money bag was filled with wads of newspaper and then it was 'officially' wax-sealed and given to the trainee with the explicit instructions to deliver it to a certain employee at the competitor bank. That employee, of course, was already aware of the hoax in play.

On Friday just past, Ron Doyle initiated a prank on Jake which, as it turned out, was extremely embarrassing to everybody. In this incident, he had personally instructed Jake to go across to the Bank of Toronto and ask to borrow their 'GL', which was their General Ledger. For bank branch offices, the GL is one of their most 'sacred' documents. It contains a complete list of all their financial data . . . assets and liabilities, earnings and expenses, commercial and personal sub-categories of loans and deposits, mortgages and investments. Everything.

When Jake entered the Bank of Toronto building on his 'errand', he was surprised to see a pal of his from high school, David Marsh was sitting behind the front counter at a desk, writing on a form. Jake caught his friend's eye and spoke to him. "Hey, Dave, what's happening?"

"Oh hi, Jake. Can I help you?"

"I didn't know you were working here, man. When did you start?"

"Just last week. What are you doing yourself?"

"I'm training next door at the BNB. Actually, I'm here to pick up your GL. We're just going to borrow it, I guess. Can you get it for me?"

At that point Dave Marsh, not any more the wiser than Jake, took off with a smile, saying "Sure thing, Jake. Anything for the competition. Have a seat, I'll be right back."

In a matter of minutes, young Marsh came out from behind the counter through a small swinging door and offered a file folder to Jake. "Here you go. Jane gave it to me and told me to make sure I placed it back in the tray where she got it. So just bring it back to me. Okay, buddy?"

Jack returned to his branch and personally handed the folder to Doyle.

That's when all hell broke loose, ending in a major meeting with Jake, Ralph Crawford, Ron Doyle, and Sharon Johnson. It lasted for the rest of the afternoon, though Jake was not part of the full meeting. He was there only to testify that yes, he had been given the GL document by his friend, another trainee, at the Bank of Toronto. After his statement, Jake left the office.

Crawford had to call his colleague, John Hancock, manager at the Bank of Toronto; Doyle had to contact his counterpart there, Ray Moar; and Sharon was left to deal with Jake. But really, what could any of them do? Certainly, they could not reprimand Jake. It was just something that the management teams at both bank branches had to accept. And most definitely keep under wraps. Something like this getting out to their auditors would be a nightmare for management.

As the weeks moved along, another sore point about his new employment was the business of balancing his cash journal when he was placed in his new position as a teller. Not often, but on three previous occasions, Jake had experienced 'shortages' in his day-end cash reconciliations. They were all close to the amount of $100, and it bothered him to no end. He knew this was a serious problem. It indicated he was being inattentive to his work, or even worse, that he had stolen money from his own till. Either way, if it kept up, his probationary period would soon come to an abrupt end, and he would be out the door.

Because of the nature of the work, numerous bank policies were always in place to at least deter employees from getting involved in anything immoral, unethical, or God forbid, criminal in their day-to-day activities.

One of these was the practice of management conducting surprise cash counts of tellers' cash holdings. Conducted randomly, the exercise involved the three mid-management staff members being Sharon, Ron Doyle, and the Personal Loans Manager, John Traynor, who personally conducted surprise cash counts on the tellers. Jake was not unmindful of the fact that so far Doyle had made a point of delegating who was assigned to which teller, and that Doyle had been quick to assign himself to conduct the cash-count on Jake's post.

It was Wednesday and Jake was having lunch with Sharon. He noticed a change in her manner, and he was now replaying the last 'surprise' management cash count in his mind. It was only two days ago on Monday. His decision made; he now spoke to Sharon.

"So, how do you think I'm doing here, Sharon? Think you'll ever make a banker out of me?" Again, they were eating at the Mic Mac restaurant, but Jake had intentionally avoided selecting any music from the mini juke in their booth. They had each ordered club sandwiches, it was early November, unusually warm. Sharon set aside her purse and returned Jake's serious look.

"You'll be gone before your probationary period is up this month if you continue to experience cash shortages."

"Could you be a little more direct?" Jake said with sarcasm. Then he was serious. "I want to say something. Since the most recent surprise count, something has been bothering me. During the count, Doyle accidentally dropped a roll of quarters under my wicket. He asked me to 'be a good lad' and retrieve it for him, which I did. But when I rose back up, I'm sure I saw him putting his handkerchief in his pocket."

"So?'

"So, why did he have it out when he hadn't sneezed, nor had he even used it?"

Sharon just looked seriously at Jake.

"And you think he took money from your till while you were not looking?"

"After we ran a balance and it showed I was short $100, I immediately checked the number of one-hundred-dollar bills in my drawer. There were fourteen."

"And?"

"That was one less than the number recorded on my previous day's journal. Sharon, I know for a fact I did not take in, nor did I hand out any hundred dollar bills that day. It's just something I'd remember. Plus, we both checked my deposit slips. There were no hundreds in play, period. We also looked at the specs on all of my cheques. My 'backings' all indicated payouts with bills under 100-dollar denominations."

Jake was referring to how tellers were encouraged to specify on the reverse of cheques they cashed for clients, how payouts were made: if a cheque for, say $560 was cashed, one might record this as 2/100; 6/50; and 3/20. The specs sometimes helped when trying to locate a teller's difference.

Sharon knew instinctively that Jake was telling the truth. It all fit with what she knew about Ronald Doyle. He had a drinking problem, a gambling habit, and a wife who liked the good things in life that were beyond his salary. Plus, there were shopping trips to Boston, a new Cadillac every three years, membership in all the requisite local clubs, and their two young daughters enrolled in private schools. It only took Sharon two weeks to gain this knowledge, and she constantly berated herself that it took as long as it did.

Jake mentioned another fact that Sharon hadn't picked up: both of Jake's earlier shortages in similar amounts had also occurred on the days of the surprise cash counts. Also conducted by Doyle.

"And there's something else," Jake continued. "On the way back from my deliveries this morning, I ran across a couple of old friends. They sort of warned me about getting too friendly with Doyle. Not that my friends would harm me. They mentioned that street rumors had Doyle hanging out with some heavy gamblers in town, that he was quote, 'over his head' with some bad guys.

From the look Sharon gave him, Jake knew he had just told her something she already knew.

Chapter Three

The weeks and months quickly sped by, and Jake got through his probationary period without any further problems involving Doyle. He paid extremely close attention to handling his cash, and he made sure he did not give Doyle an opportunity to rip him off. The teller's position was, however, getting to be a boring exercise. In addition, in January it was humiliating for Jake to be frequently summoned by the manager to shovel out his home driveway. Another time that month it had been necessary for him to break huge icicles from the third story eave of the bank's front roof.

Jake frequently thought of quitting. These menial tasks that had nothing to do with his training were getting to him, as was the cat-and-mouse game he was playing with Doyle. Damn, he still hadn't received a word of praise or encouragement from anybody there.

By the end of January, his training had advanced to tutelage under Teller 1, Justin Phillips, who was in charge of foreign exchange transactions, including the control of all of the branch's foreign currency holdings. In that regard, compared to other branches, their US dollar volumes were quite low. There simply wasn't that much FX trading locally to warrant larger holdings. Nor were there any local businesses that would provide much in the way of incoming US cash. Perhaps in the middle of the summer when tourists were visiting, but not during the winter months in Chatham. It worked well for Jack, though, giving him plenty of time to become familiar with any US dollar transactions that did happen.

Also, he would quickly absorb the know-how of handling the branch's storage and shipment of its mutilated cash, money the bank took in which was torn or soiled. It was another primary function delegated to the Teller No.1 position.

Every six months, it would be necessary to package and transport a shipment of such bills to the central Bank of Canada branch in Saint John, N.B. Two employees of Jake's branch, one of whom was Teller 1, usually accompanied one of the Management team. Certainly not Crawford, but usually Ron Doyle, John Traynor, or Sharon Donovan.

Today, February 12th, Sharon advised Jake he would be going with her in the morning to the province's oldest and largest city to deliver a parcel of mutilated cash to the Bank of Canada, and Jake was instructed to get his shipment in order.

Jake was excited.

To prepare for the trip, late yesterday the other two tellers had transferred several bundles of old worn notes to him. Notes that over time were soiled or torn. He recounted them, confirmed the dollar value was correct, then made up balancing entries to give to the tellers. He placed his teller's stamp on new wrappers around the packs of the notes and initialed the stamps, thereby officially taking ownership of them. At the end of the day, he then took this currency along with his own tray that was filled with regular cash, to his compartment in the vault. When he had turned off his combinations and opened his compartment, he was about to place his cash box in his compartment when he sensed something, and he turned around. He was startled to find Ron Doyle standing directly behind him. He hadn't heard him approaching.

"Hey Jacob," said Doyle. "Sharon's busy, so I'll lock you away for the night. Have you got your mutilated cash all bagged up and sealed, ready for tomorrow?"

"Ah, not yet. I thought Sharon and I would do that in the morning." The assistant manager's silent approach was still bothering him.

"It's a long drive, Jacob. Best to get on the road as soon as possible. I think we may as well do it now." But just then, Ron's steno, Ms. McLeod, came into the vault and told Ron there was a call waiting for him. "Okay, I better take that call, Jacob, so you can put your cash away now, and remember to close both combinations."

Jake could sense by the tone of Doyle's voice and the angry look on his face that he was ticked he had been interrupted.

As previously agreed, the next morning he and Sharon were the first employees in the branch. They opened Jake's compartment and retrieved the mutilated notes he had earlier wrapped in bundles of various denominations. Then they placed the money, $157,000, in a sealed canvas bag and carried it out to Sharon's car, where they put it in her trunk and headed out of town.

The drive to Saint John was a pleasant break from the office. Jack's keen eye for sporty cars feasted on Sharon's '62 Chevy Nova, which was in perfect condition and ran like a top. The vehicle was a powder blue, two-door hardtop, and although it only carried a 194 cubic inch six-cylinder engine, it had a lot of power when needed. Also, she had installed an outstanding stereo system, and Jake was pleasantly surprised when he spotted a couple of 8-track cassette tapes by The Beatles lying in the console between the twin bucket seats. When he considered her car, its contents, and Sharon's choice in music, his feelings for her edged up several notches.

"Would you mind if we listen to this?" he asked her as they got underway, and he held up The Beatles' new major hit, *I Want to Hold Your Hand*. They enjoyed the music as they drove through the village of Rogersville and southward for the ensuing forty-five minutes. This took them to the connection for the Trans-Canada Highway at the Moncton exit. From here it would be another two hours to their destination, and their timing was good. Jake was looking forward to delivering the mutilated cash to the Central Bank, then maybe having a pleasant lunch at an upscale restaurant somewhere in the city before heading back home.

Up to this point in their trip, they had both been quiet. Jake made the odd comment about the weather and how fortunate it was to have such good driving conditions, considering the time of year. Sharon gave him the odd smile, otherwise, keeping her thoughts to herself.

"There are more tapes in the consul there," Sharon said after the Beatles track had ended. Jake snapped another cassette by the Beatles into the player and leaned back to listen to his favorite rock group. Now and then he would take a quick peek at Sharon, smiling as she confidently drove the Chevy around the frequent slow turns on the TCH.

Sharon was an attractive lady. She wore her soft brown hair just above her shoulders and it glistened in the morning sun that filtered through pockets of hardwood trees growing only feet from both sides of the highway. Branches bare of foliage shone with films of ice from the previous night's storm. Again, they gave thanks to the good work completed by the Provincial government for clearing the highway so quickly.

The last Beatle tune had just ended, and Jake began rooting around in the car's consul when he came up with The Dave Clark Five's new release of their song *'Because'*, a slow love song.

"I like this tune," he said. "It has some nice bass work."

Sharon looked over at him, gave him a smile that caused his heart rate to accelerate. The light danced now in her eyes that were flecked with tiny points of green. He noticed a small spray of freckles over the bridge of her nose, affording her a look that was a lot younger than her years. Also, a light sheen of sweat had developed on her upper lip.

"So, you've been playing in your band for a while, Jacob. You must find it quite boring to be working in the bank compared to being a rock and roller on the weekends." He sensed she was flirting with him, and he loved it. Jake also had the impression she was now inviting him to open up and tell her a bit more about himself.

"Not boring at all, Sharon. It's a challenge. I'm pretty naïve with all this stuff, as you can see. But, hey, I like challenges and I think things are coming together."

"You're going to do well, Jacob, I can tell. But just a small bit of advice. You won't be on cash forever, but until you get promoted to either Credit or Administration, make sure you treat the currency you handle as if it belongs to *you*. Do not trust *anybody*, okay?" She looked seriously at him as she made this statement, which now confirmed his suspicions about Doyle.

"Good advice."

The Dave Clark Five tunes had finished, and now they were driving by the village of Petitcodiac. He played things close to his chest for the moment and asked her what types of music she was into.

"Oh, I like all kinds," Sharon said. "My mom sings in a choir, and she got me into piano lessons when I was just a kid. But I think I've disappointed her by not following her wishes for me to volunteer as the organist at the church. Instead, I've taken a liking to your kind of music, you know, the Devil's work," she said jokingly, giving him a naughty wink.

"Cool," Jake said.

By the time they entered Sussex, their conversations had revealed she was not that much older than him. According to her school background, he could put her age at around twenty-four or twenty-five. And like him, she had entered the bank as a trainee and had gone through the program, then had continued her career in the administration side of the bank.

She had also told him about the Employee Education Plan that was available to all employees of Canada's Chartered Banks, and that she had enrolled in it two years ago. It all sounded very good. Employees could take courses at home or at any university close to where they were working. In order to graduate from any of their courses, students needed to complete a series of exams that were issued by Queen's University in Toronto annually. Usually, after four or five years, successful participants could come out of the program with an accredited University degree. And the best part of all was that these studies were free.

It was close to noon when they had entered the Loyalist City via Rothesay Avenue, which would eventually take them straight downtown to Prince William Street where the Bank of Canada was located. As they drove through the old city, Jake noticed the many taverns, pubs, and bars that populated the drive downtown. He decided that, as far as New Brunswick was concerned, Saint John was the center of the province's entertainment action. This was where he would like to be transferred. And from what he had seen so far from his own branch, he thought it might be more exciting if he could steer his focus toward the bank's Credit group rather than get involved in Administration where Ron Doyle had elected to hang his hat.

They pulled into a parking bay and Sharon reached over Jake into the glove compartment and retrieved something. Before Jake knew what it was, she handed him a heavy object, and he realized it was a snub-nosed .38 Smith and Wesson revolver, the first one he had ever held. Most banks, Jake knew, carried revolvers to protect their holdings. The bank, after proper training, allowed their designated management staff to carry weapons in the normal performance of certain functions.

"Here you go, partner. The safety's here," and she showed Jake where it was located. "It's now in the 'off' position." Then they exited her car, popped the trunk, and she reached inside and pulled out the Bank of New Brunswick canvas bag. It held exactly $157,000 in Canadian dollars, notes of all different denominations in separate stacks of one hundred bills each, save for one half-bundle of fifty one-hundred-dollar bills. Sharon and Jake had sealed the bag earlier with melted red wax, and they used a vise-like instrument to impress the Bank's official seal into the wax, at the same time crimping a lead wire around the top of the bag.

"If someone tries to grab this from me, show your gun to the asshole! Let's go." And they left her Chevy Nova and walked out of the parkade across Prince William Street to the Bank of Canada. Man, she no longer sounded like a mild-mannered banker. He liked this lady.

The Bank of Canada was a five-story, gray brick Victorian building of commerce that had seen better days. They took an antiquated elevator that had accordion-style, folding wrought iron doors. Jake doubted it had ever been changed since Confederation. This took them to their destination at the third-floor level where a hive of activity immediately surrounded them as the doors unfolded. Probably thirty or more people, mostly men, were darting here and there, oblivious of each other.

Jake could tell Sharon was familiar with the area as she deftly made her way towards the rear of the room where they reached a closed door, labeled *Mutilated Currency*. A reception desk was placed in front of the closed door and a young blonde lady rose to greet them.

"Hi," said Sharon. "We're here from the BNB in Chatham to transfer some old cash to you guys."

"Follow me," said the lady and they walked through the door into a separate room which was actually a huge vault. Two armed guards sat at one side of the steel-walled room playing cribbage. When they saw Sharon and Jake enter with the receptionist, they hopped up out of their chairs.

"You have clients, George," said the blonde and a tall thin guard came over to them, bearing an ID nameplate designating him as George Phillips. Sharon made the introductions as the second guard joined them, this guy was named Lester Jones, a large black man.

Sharon gave them the bag which they opened with special pliers designed for that purpose, and they sorted the packs of bills into separate denominations on a side table. Then they began opening the bundles individually and feeding the bills into an electric bill counter. Jake had heard of these machines back at their branch and he had been anxious to see them in action. The electronic counter they used here worked perfectly. That is until the last half-bundle of fifty one-hundred-dollar bills was loaded and damned if it didn't tally out one bill short at forty-nine!

The guards just looked at Sharon and Jake. Then Sharon looked at Jake, her eyes shifting to the bundle that had his Teller 1 stamp on it. *What the hell?* thought Jake.

"Feed them through again," he said, his voice now rising in volume. George put them in the electric counter a second time, with the same result. Frantically, Jake now manually counted the pack, but to no avail. He looked sadly at Sharon.

"We'll have to change the contra amount, Miss," said Lester, and the dollar figure was altered to $156,900. Each of the four people in the vault was required to place their initials by the change and Jake was devastated. When it was his turn to do so, he saw Sharon from the corner of his eye quickly leaving the vault. He ran after her with their copy of the receipt, not reaching her until they were on the sidewalk leading back to her vehicle.

"Sharon," he said to her, but she kept walking. When they reached her vehicle, he grabbed her arm and turned her around to face him. "I know what you're thinking, but you've got to believe me. I had nothing to do with that half-pack of hundreds being short a bill. And yes, I know that was my own teller's stamp that was on the bundle. But dammit, I can only tell you that I counted it before wrapping it as late as Monday. You can check the date on the stamp if you care to."

"Come on Jacob, that doesn't prove anything. Doyle or anybody will still say you simply pulled out one of the bills from the pack after you bundled it. He'll make the case that, being as naive as you are, you were probably thinking the cash wouldn't be recounted by the Bank of Canada and you saw this as a way of getting away with it."

She got in her vehicle and started the engine. "Let's go. There's nothing else we can do here." He knew Sharon was pissed off at him. Reluctantly, he climbed into the passenger seat of her Chevy Nova.

"Sharon, hear me out, please. What Doyle or Crawford might think about this means nothing compared to what *you* are thinking. I did *not* remove that bill, Sharon." Dejected, Jake slouched back in his seat, and they took off for the long three-hour drive back to Chatham.

As they made their way down Prince William Street, Jake was desperately trying to think how the $100 bill could have gone missing. He concentrated his thoughts on the scene when he had his cash locked away last night by Doyle, and in a minute, it came to him. He had turned off his combination waiting for Sharon to come into the vault and do the same. But then he remembered how that son of a bitch had been standing behind him all the time. Dammit! Doyle had obviously watched him, and he had memorized Jake's numbers. It would have been too easy. The three numbers Jake had stupidly chosen for his combination were ten, twenty, and thirty. Jake knew Doyle had the vault all to himself after they left. He remembered Doyle telling them when they were leaving that he was staying behind, that he had a few things to do. "No worries," he had said. "I'll lock up."

Yeah right, thought Jake. It was one thing to have figured it out, but now what could he do about it? Well, for one thing, he would remember to change his combinations, the first thing upon his return to work.

By the time they were about ten miles from Chatham, it was almost four. Because of all that had happened and the awkwardness of going into a restaurant and probably having to rehash everything, she hadn't even bothered to stop for anything to eat. Jake was starving.

"Aren't you hungry?" Jake asked.

"I am, but we're almost back at the branch now."

"Well, here's an idea. We would have normally taken time for lunch, which means we wouldn't have arrived home until it was quitting time anyway, right?"

"Well, yes, I guess so, but___", then Jake cut her off before she could continue.

"Then let's keep going straight to 'Johnny's' in Newcastle, my favorite fish and chips joint in the world. And I have some cash on me, so my treat, okay?"

When she pulled into the driveway at his home, it was past six and dusk was turning to darkness. Just ahead of her vehicle, Jake's younger brother was whacking a tennis ball on their paved driveway against the side of their porch with a hockey stick. Jake was hoping for a little privacy to make his move but unfortunately, that was not to be. Robby stopped his relentless slap-shot practice for a second and looked up to see who was in the cool car that had just arrived. Seeing it was only his older brother getting out of the vehicle, he resumed his play. Jake took advantage of the situation, and when he ducked back into the Chevy Nova, he gave Sharon a quick kiss.

"Despite all that's happened today, I enjoyed it, Sharon. Thanks, and I hope you believe in me. See you in the morning." He jumped out of her car and ran into his house.

Sharon had a lot on her mind as she drove home to her two-bedroom apartment.

Chapter Four

She lived in a rental townhouse on the Lower Shore Road. The property was on a cul-de-sac in a small development that contained another five townhouses, all overlooking the beautiful Miramichi River. Sharon had moved into the rental three years ago and she loved the place. As a way of demonstrating her appreciation for her surroundings, and maybe to show some pride in her independence, she had meticulously erected a small bird feeder in the early part of last September beside her front doorway which faced the driveway. For the following two months, a sole hummingbird had regularly frequented the feeder. It was amazing to watch this beautiful little creature as it made its approach to the glass tube that contained a gravity-fed, syrupy liquid.

It surprised her that the tiny bird had stayed around the feeder as long as it had, and it was not until late October that she noticed it had finally left the area for southern climes. The ruby-throated species she had so admired would return to Mexico, and it saddened her to realize she would probably never see it again. Well, at least she had the fortune of enjoying him for as long as she had, even if it had only been for a couple of months. These thoughts extended into an image of Jake innocently stealing a kiss from her only moments ago, bringing a smile to her face as she entered her townhouse.

She had just settled onto her new cream-colored sofa and was looking forward to a relaxing Thursday night watching television. Maybe she would catch *Doctor Kildare*. It would start in five minutes at eight o'clock, and she got up to make herself a cup of tea when her telephone rang. When she answered the phone, it annoyed her to hear Ronald Doyle's rasping voice at the other end. He was a very heavy smoker, another thing that turned her off about the man.

"Hi, Ronald. I was just going to watch some TV, have an early night. What do you want?" *Why should she bother trying to pretend to talk niceties with the guy?* They had already been through everything twice now, and she was going to have to get tougher with him, dammit!

"Nothing special Sharon. I just thought I'd give you a shout to see how it went today in Saint John with the trainee." Sharon was certain he added a hint of disdain to his use of Jacob's title. And right then she decided she would not get into the business of the missing one-hundred-dollar bill. She'd prefer to do this face-to-face with him, and with Jake present. Maybe see if she could tell anything different from his facial expression when they told him about the missing $100.

"I'll tell you all about it in the morning, Ron. Right now, I'm dying to see my idol, *Dr. James Kildare*, okay?"

Her abruptness put Doyle off, but he was not about to let her know how much their 'break-up' was hurting him, so he put on a stoic front and politely bade her goodnight. Of course, he knew without asking that there would have been an issue at the Bank of Canada with the missing $100 bill. Yet, as hard as it was to not find out from her just how it all came out, he would have to wait until the morning.

Sharon's thoughts turned back to Jacob when she hung up the phone. He was so different from Ron. God, why she had ever let herself fall for that guy, she'd never know. But then, the more she thought about it, she realized her brief relationship with Ron was simply the result of a lack of networking on her part.

After graduation from Chatham High, Sharon had been so intent on becoming successful in establishing a career with the bank that she had neglected her own social life. Ever since she had enrolled in her courses with the Institute of Canadian Bankers Association four years ago, her devotion to the bank's distance-study program left her with very little time to socialize. And, while the ICBA had rewarded her with very impressive marks (so far, she had been carrying a ninety plus percent average), she had not yet received any form of recognition from her employer for her hard work. Several times, she had let it be known to Doyle and anyone else who would listen that she was willing and able to take a transfer to another branch. She had often thought it would be great to work in Moncton, Fredericton, or Saint John. Any larger center, for that matter.

She found the bank was very much a male-dominated institution, at least for the management departments. Oh sure, she was on the management team at her branch, but it was becoming apparent that her position there as Assistant Branch Accountant was more or less a token of it. It was a dead-end function, and she was certain she would be at her desk until her retirement. *Just like her mother!*

She just realized something. Maybe she had subconsciously started dating Doyle as a way of getting into the bank's management circle? *Dammit, she'd quit her job there before it came to something like that!*

The scream from her boiling kettle in the kitchen broke into her thoughts and she made herself a cup of tea. She grabbed her phone book, looked up a local number and dialed it without giving it a second thought.

"Jacob, the phone is for you," his mother called.

"Hi, this is Jake," he said, speaking on their upstairs phone.

"Hi Jacob, it's Sharon calling."

"Oh, hi Sharon, nice to hear from you. Is everything okay?" Jake's heart immediately started racing when he heard her voice, and he didn't know why she would call him. And why did he ask her if everything was okay? Sometimes he could get so dorky talking with her.

"I mean, I'm glad you called, I've been thinking about you…", he tried to explain.

"Well, I was thinking about you too, Jacob, and about what you were telling me earlier today. You know, what you were saying about Doyle."

"Yeah, I think tomorrow is going to be a rough day," he said, now realizing this was more of a business call than otherwise. But again, his spirits were lifted when she outlined how they should handle the situation.

When Jake arrived at the office the next morning, Sharon told him she had requested a meeting with Doyle for 9:15. Since they had not even reached mid-month, they had already experienced their busy period, which had been the last week of December and the first week of January. Most people would have completed their month-end banking transactions by now, so Jake would not be missed on either the Teller 1 post, or if he skipped a day without delivering his drafts.

Sharon was glad that Jake was looking forward to the meeting she had set up with Doyle. Initially, she thought of including Crawford but decided against that. Ron might have sensed something, and no doubt would have talked to the manager before the meeting. Instead, she suggested they meet in the staff room to make things more informal.

A cloud of blue smoke greeted Sharon and Jake when they entered the small room at 9:15. Ron Doyle sat in a chair at the only table, puffing on the ever-present MacDonald's Export A cigarette that hung from his lips.

"So, what's up, you guys? Did everything go okay yesterday, or was there some problem that you wanted to tell me about?" He was giving Jake a snide look. Almost like a smirk. *There it is!* thought Sharon. She could tell right away Doyle knew Jacob was going to be light by a hundred bucks with his contra yesterday to the Bank of Canada. Of course, he knew, because he had taken the hundred-dollar bill, just as Jacob had suspected.

Sharon took the lead. "Well, just so you know, Ron. I forgot to bring any cash with me yesterday, so I had to take a hundred dollars off the top of Jacob's cash for dinner and gas." She showed Doyle the altered copy of the contra. "But I'm putting through an expense voucher right now which I can use to make up for the difference in his debit contra that we had to change, reducing it by $100 to $156,900. You okay with that?"

Both Sharon and Jake stared at Doyle while he sat at the table, taking another long draw on his Export A, trying to think of a comeback. Jake had to admire the way Sharon had turned this all around on the creep. Ron was now between a rock and a very hard place. Doyle knew they had now effectively covered the fact that there *was* a missing $100 bill.

And Jake also knew that Doyle was pissed off to find out that Sharon would give up her valid expense money to Jake in order to protect him. But there wasn't a damn thing he could do about it, since anything he said now would only be self-incriminating. Furthermore, the bank did not require a receipt for meals or gas expenses within normal requirements. It was a brilliant move on her part.

"Sure, why not?" Doyle finally replied, a sour look on his face and he abruptly stubbed out his cigarette in an overfull ashtray and rose from his chair.

"Great," Jake said. Before Doyle reached the staff room exit, Jake added, "Say, Ron, when do you think we might get one of those fancy automatic counting machines they use at the Bank of Canada? Man, they are *slick!*" he said, closely making full eye contact with Doyle, not allowing his big smile to reach his own eyes.

So there . . . Jake had sort of officially let Doyle know that *both he and Sharon* knew Doyle had ripped him off. And they had done it in such a way that there was nothing he could do about it. Now that Jake was aware the guy was bothering Sharon, the gloves were off as far as he was concerned. From the expression on Doyle's face, both Jake and Sharon could tell Doyle could not take the matter further. There would not be another shortage report going into Jake's personnel file, at least because of Doyle's latest rip-off. And for Sharon, she was confident that things between her and Doyle would now come to a quick end.

Doyle never even bothered to answer Jake. He just got up and left the staff room. Before starting his day, Jake said to her, "That was a nice move, Sharon. I think he got the picture. And listen, I'll pay you back for the shortage replacement you just handled."

"Don't worry about it Jacob. It was no big deal, and it was worth it."

"Right," said Jake. "So, I'm off with my drafts. I'll give you a shout later, okay?"

"Sure," she smiled, and they both got on with their day.

However, the large old BNB building had suddenly become unbearably small.

After balancing his journal at the end of the day, Jake hung around on the pretense of doing some odd work until Sharon had left the branch. The only people left to lock up were himself and Doyle. Since they met with him early that morning, the tension in the office between the three of them could be cut with a knife. Jake decided now was as good a time as any to break the ice.

"So, Ron, have you got a second?" he asked.

Doyle lit up another smoke and sat at his desk. "What's on your mind, England?"

"Well, I was talking with Sharon on the way down to Saint John yesterday. Nothing serious, you know, I was just fishing for some info from her about how you guys think I'm doing here, fitting in, you know. I also asked her about the possibility of getting a transfer to another branch, maybe Moncton or Saint John."

"So, what did Sharon say?"

"She said she was happy with the way things were going and as far as a transfer, well she said I should check with you?" Jake could see the wheels rolling inside the guy's mind. No doubt he was thinking this might be a way of getting rid of his problem.

Jake wasn't aware of it, but many bank transfers came about as the result of some problem with the individual being transferred. Maybe the employee was a womanizer, or maybe it was somebody who just couldn't get along with a certain manager, whatever. Such transfers were not always to unfavorable places.

Doyle then appeared to make a decision. "Right. Leave it with me, England. I'll mention it to Crawford on Monday." Doyle was weighing two approaches that were available to him: he *could* advise Crawford that the kid had screwed up again by being short another $100 on the transfer of his mutilated cash to the Bank of Canada. To do this, though, he'd also then have to bring Sharon into the game since it was apparent she had befriended him. And he was not willing to risk having Sharon turn on him.

The only other way of getting rid of this upstart would be to try and arrange a transfer, as much as it irked him to do so.

Jake was home in time for supper, and he mentioned to his folks that he had talked to Ron about his desire to be transferred, preferably to Moncton. "So, you can finally stop worrying about me and the entire music thing, Dad. If a transfer comes through, I'll have to leave The Esquires." He placed a large piece of baked salmon that his mother had taken from the oven onto his plate then went after the bowl of peas, followed by a baked potato.

Only last week, Jake had received a call from Danny Thompson, the lead singer with the Centurions, formerly from Newcastle who had left to go to Toronto, leaving their colleagues, The Esquires to fill their place at the Exhibition dance hall. Danny had called to tell him their bass player Gerry Reynolds was no longer with them, and would he be interested in taking his spot? At the time, Jake was more than ready to take Danny up on the deal, but after discussing it with his dad, he had reluctantly decided to decline the offer.

"You're doing the right thing, Jacob, trust me," said his mother as they were eating supper, now getting into the conversation. "Besides, you can always have your music as a hobby." Jake let that go. He could not think of the day when his music would just be a 'hobby', and the band was constantly on his mind.

He was looking forward to their dance tomorrow night at The Ex. The winter months usually resulted in smaller crowds, but they were still close to being sold out. It was going to be a good night. Last Sunday they had nailed down the new tune by The Beatles' cover of the old Chuck Berry song, *Rock and Roll Music,* done with Lennon's raspier-than-normal vocals. Jake was anxious to hear how it would be received. After supper, he was about to retire to his bedroom and listen to a few of the new songs they were learning. Then he had an idea and called Sharon.

"Hey, Sharon," he said after some introductory small talk, "I know this is late notice and everything, but I was wondering if you might like to take in our dance at the Exhibition Hall tomorrow night?"

"Well, perhaps, but won't it be a little hard for you to dance and play at the same time?" she posed.

"No, no Sharon, I'm sorry, but yes, you're right, I can't dance and play. I don't even think I can dance." *Jesus! He was running off at the mouth again.* Then he heard her laughing and he realized she had just been teasing him.

"Sorry," he said. "See how you get me all mixed up."

"I would never want to mix you up, Jacob. But about the offer. Is this, like, a *date?"*

"See, there you go, teasing me again. Not a real date." *This time,* he thought. "Actually, the other guys usually bring their girlfriends with them, and, you know, the girls sit at the same table and dance with each other, and maybe you could, ah, join them?"

"I see. So, I'd be, like, your girlfriend?" When there was silence on the other end after she said that, she thought maybe she had gone too far with joking around. "Jacob, hello? Are you there?"

Then he broke out laughing. "Aha," he said. "Gotcha."

"You brat! Okay, I'll be, what do you call them, one of your group people?"

This increased his laughing fit, and he managed between guffaws to say "*Groupies,* they're called groupies. Listen, we'll pick you up around 7:30 tomorrow night. Dance starts at 9:00 but we need time to set up, run through a sound check, you know."

"Sounds good, but did you say *we'll* pick you up?

"Ah, yep. I still don't have my vehicle but Rick, our drummer, will take us there. Is that okay?"

"Um, of course. See you tomorrow night, Jacob!"

Jake was in heaven. Wow! He didn't think she'd go along with the suggestion, but she did. One thing he knew for sure, though. Tomorrow morning, he would definitely be going to Lounsbury Motors to look at a few vehicles!

Chapter Five

Sharon hung up her phone, went to the fridge and took out the bottle of *Pinot Gris* she had been saving for a while now. Carefully she poured herself a glass and laid back on her sofa, giving thought to the conversation she had just finished with Jacob England.

God, he *was* quite young. Was he too young for her? Probably. But wasn't he just so nice and refreshing after her relationship with Ronald Doyle? Definitely! A little voice inside was telling her she was 'robbing the cradle' and she should just drop this silliness. But another louder voice seemed to encourage the continuance of the new friendship that seemed to be blooming with Jacob. Well, she deserved to have some fun for a change, she decided. She climbed into bed, still holding a small amount of wine in her glass. She then made a mock toast to an imaginary figure.

"Here's to the future, Jacob. Let's hope we don't hurt each other too much," and she pulled the bed covers over herself and fell into a deep sleep.

Rick Thompson's 1959 Dodge sedan rolled into Sharon's driveway at 7:30 the following evening. Sharon went to the door and greeted Jake who was dressed in a brand-new corduroy gray and black, Nehru-style *Beatles'* jacket, a starched white shirt, a thin black tie, and black dress pants, finished by black Wellington boots, shined to the hilt.

"I like your outfit," she said.

"We just got these jackets last Wednesday. Pretty cool, eh?"

"They sure are. Listen, Jacob, I was thinking perhaps you and I could go in my car, then your friends won't have to go out of their way to drive us home after the dance. That is, assuming you have your driver's license?"

"Great idea, Sharon," Jake went over to Rick's vehicle and explained the proposition to Rick and his girlfriend Irene Miller. They both got out of Rick's car and came over to meet Sharon. Jake made the introductions, and they were soon on their way to the Ex. In truth, Jake had obtained a driving permit only last month. It required the presence of another driver with a valid license in any vehicle he happened to be driving until he obtained the real thing. Jake was embarrassed to have to admit this to Sharon, so this went unmentioned. In no time they arrived at the dance hall.

The Exhibition Building in Chatham was situated at the top of an elevated site overlooking the northwest section of the town. In addition to a large dance facility, it contained a curling club and another vast empty area that was currently being used as a storage facility. This space was transferred to a craft exhibition site during the summer. It housed numerous booths, tables, a flea market, and kiosks of all types. During that time, people accessed the 'Bill Lynch' fair grounds by going through that area of the building. On the other side there were various rides, games of chance, vendors of all sorts, and a racetrack that hosted sulky races, again a summer event.

When they entered the building, Irene and Sharon staked out a table on the right corner of the room near the bandstand, and Jake brought a couple of glasses of wine over to them. He went back on stage and began setting up his gear beside Rick. Within five minutes, the three other band members strolled in with their female partners: Johnny Peterson, their lead singer, with his wife Joanne; Hank Jamieson, lead guitar, and his girlfriend Mattie; and Billy Bragdon, their keyboard man with his date, Melody.

The outfits worn by the group impressed Sharon, and they even *resembled* the British stars. She hadn't yet heard the Esquires play, and that brought about other thoughts regarding her new friendship with Jacob. Such as, what were his friends like? Would they accept her into their circle?

As she looked around the table where the 'ladies of the band' (as she had now considered them) were seated, she realized she wasn't that much older than them. Joanne, the singer's wife, looked to be about the same age as herself. And the other girls were maybe only two or three years younger. So, Jacob was probably the youngest in the band, and he had no problems relating to these people who were older than him. This gave her some measure of rationale or sense of belonging to this different group of people.

She was entering a new chapter in her life, and so far, she was thoroughly enjoying herself.

"Good evening, folks. Glad you all could make it out tonight. Looks like we have another good crowd on hand, so let's ROCK 'N ROLL!" And just like that, Johnny Peterson had finished his quick intro, and The Esquires broke into their cover of the *Beatles'* tune 'Rock 'N Roll Music' that they had only added to their repertoire during their last practice. Sharon was now into her second glass of wine, and she couldn't believe how good they sounded. She was soon up on the floor dancing with Joanne, immediately followed by the other three girls, and they were having a ball.

The evening went well, and towards the end of the last set, Joanne told her how pleased she was that Jake had found somebody as nice as her. Sharon was at a loss for how to respond to that, not wanting to let the girls conclude that Jake and she were a steady item. God, this was only their first date, if one could consider it so. Yet, try as she might, she could not deny the feelings she had toward Jake, which continued to grow.

It was just as well Sharon had suggested they both go to the dance in her car. Whether it was because she was nervous at meeting the other girls, or simply because she broke out of her shell and enjoyed the evening, she was unsure. What she *was* certain about now, though, was her inability to drive home by herself, no doubt the result of having consumed at least four too many glasses of wine throughout the evening.

Jake smiled at her sleeping figure on the passenger seat, softly snoring, as he drove her Chevy Nova along the Lower Shore Road. Since the start of September, the band had arranged with the management people at the Ex to leave their gear there, and they could use the empty hall on Sundays for practice. Thus, Jake got Sharon back home at a reasonable hour after their gig. When he pulled into her driveway, she woke up and stretched her arms, yawning.

"Oh, man . . . are we home? Jacob, I feel so embarrassed."

"Not to worry. You were okay..." he said, getting a kick out of teasing her a little.

"If you say so. Would you like a coffee?"

"I'd love one," and they entered her townhouse.

Jake admired her setup as she put on a pot of coffee. She turned around to him and gave him a big smile. "I had a great time tonight. Sorry I went over my limit. And by the way, you guys sounded fantastic."

"I'm glad you had fun. The other girls think you're great, by the way."

"And I like them as well. Jake, would you mind if I grab a shower while the coffee's on? I can use one…"

"Sure, go for it," he said.

He could hear the shower running and he took the opportunity to look around the kitchen and her living room. Jake was impressed with all the latest modern appliances. Her living room even had a working fireplace, two logs sat on a wrought-iron grate all set to go. *Why not?* he thought.

After the fire was blazing and he had dimmed the lights, he spotted a cool Technica turntable and went all the way. A quick look through two shelves of LP's and he was listening to 'It's Over', the first song on *Roy Orbison's Greatest Hits* LP.

"Nice choice."

He didn't realize the shower had stopped running and Sharon had come up behind him. He turned to face her, and her beauty floored him. She was standing in front of him, a coffee in hand, wearing only a thinly veiled violet negligee. As she stood with her back to the fire, it was obvious she had nothing else on. "You are gorgeous," he said hoarsely.

He approached her slowly. "I know you've been doing a lot of dancing tonight, but would you mind?" He opened his arms toward her. She laid her coffee on an end table and went to him.

"I love this song," he said. It was Orbison's simple tune in E Major which was building to a crescendo finale as they held each other tightly. Then he kissed her gently.

"Come," she whispered as she took his hand and led him into her bedroom.

In the morning, Sharon drove Jake home and dropped him off early enough so as not to wake the other members of his household, namely his parents, Martin and Meg, his brothers Robby and Gerald, and his sister Grace. Before leaving the Lower Shore Road, Jake and Sharon had shared a couple of coffees over a long talk.

After last night's intimacy with Sharon, he was captivated by her. The fact was, Jake had never before been with another girl to that extent. Initially, it had been an awkward experience for them, but Sharon had gracefully (and eagerly) taken him through it all with dignity and consideration. He would be eternally grateful to her for the way she handled the whole matter. He believed he was truly in love with her. He couldn't wait to see her again, to tell her that basic fact . . .

As Sharon drove back to her townhouse, she too reflected on last night's activities. From her perspective, ever since their trip to Saint John she had seen Jacob as the antithesis of her last lover. She found herself easily attracted to him, and as soon as she had taken him into her bedroom, she knew it was his first time. It had compelled her to make the night with Jacob a beautiful thing, and it was.

However, she now realized it was going to be extremely difficult for the two of them to work near each other, while she would be constantly recalling every ecstatic act of last night, every intimate detail of each other's bodies. Well, she'd just have to have a serious talk with Jacob. She couldn't allow this to develop into something more serious. *Could she?*

Sunday morning Jake told his parents he had stayed at Rick's place last night after the two of them had gone to the local late-night hangout, *Ben's Lunch,* for something to eat. He wasn't quite ready to discuss his new relationship with his parents.

Yesterday morning he had planned to meet at noon that day with Charlie Guider, a car sales agent at Lounsbury's Chev-Olds, in Chatham. The rotund man met him as agreed and had taken Jake out for a spin in a brand-new Envoy Epic. It was as cheap a new car as he could afford, and it came with a full warranty, was great on gas, and even had a cool stick shift. Guider had told him he'd have it ready for him on Sunday afternoon, a rare feat of sales technique, and now Jake was in Guider's office with his father. Since Jake was not of legal age, his father had agreed to cosign a loan for him through GMAC, the dealer plan available to Lounsbury's, and they completed the deal.

He had even driven home with his father in the front seat beside him, proud as could be, even if Martin England, who had never in his life owned a vehicle, was unaware that his son was already breaking the law by driving without a valid license. No matter, Jake would write his test the following week and look after that detail. Right now, the only thing on his mind was calling Sharon and picking her up in his new car.

Sharon awoke to her front doorbell ringing at 11:15 am on Sunday. After dropping Jake off at his parents, she had fallen quickly asleep upon her return, and she was still slightly hung over from the excesses of the previous night. She slipped into an old pair of pajamas before going to the door and wondered if Jake was making good on his promise to get in touch with her today. *No, it was too early,* she chided herself, then began chuckling silently, remembering some of last night's antics. She threw open the door, now hoping to welcome Jake back into her townhouse. But it wasn't Jake.

"Ronald, what do you want? It's Sunday morning, for God's sake!"

"Well, good morning to you too, Sharon," Doyle said sarcastically. "Mind if I come in? I bring gifts," and he strolled by her with two cups of coffee and a box of donuts that he had picked up at the Five and Dime Store downtown on the way here. He noted the two ceramic cups sitting on an end table. One of them was full, the other half consumed. "Late night company?" he asked.

"Ron, if you must know, Jane Henderson came over last night. Not that it's any of your business. Why are you here?" *And she immediately berated herself for not coming right out and telling Doyle that she had been with Jacob.*

"Hey, it's a beautiful, bright winter morning. I just thought it would be great to take a drive somewhere, maybe go upriver and check out the toboggan slide at Red Bank?" Doyle said this with his smirk that she now hated. He was referring to a trip they made there in the summer. It had started innocently enough, but then it had turned out to be something she had regretted immediately after she had allowed him to take advantage of her in the middle of nowhere. How could she have been so gullible!

Doyle continued to woo her.

"C'mon, Sharon. Listen, let's start over again. I think old Crawford will retire soon and I can probably make an excellent case to take over his post. This could work out very good for you."

Sharon couldn't believe what Doyle was suggesting. "Ron, tell me I'm not hearing you correctly. Are you trying to suggest they might promote me to your position, work under you as your assistant, and presumably continue to have some kind of intimate relationship with you?"

"Well, it's not entirely impossible, Sharon," he said, but she quickly cut him off.

"No! I don't want to hear any more of this, Ron. It's ridiculous. The bank would never go along with that. Besides, it would be a breach of ethics, and I will not be any part of it."

"But no one needs to know of our relationship. Sharon, I love you. It would be so nice. We could have our jobs, stay in the area, and be together . . ."

She now doubted Ron's sanity. "Ron, no. You're married with children. It just wouldn't work. Besides, I am not in love with you, and I should never have allowed things to get to this point." She said no more, waiting for his response, thinking he was about to sob. After several beats, he regained his composure.

"You have feelings for the new trainee, don't you Sharon." It was an accusation, not a question.

"Okay Ron, that's enough." Sharon raised her voice and went to open the front door. "You'll have to leave now. This has gone too far! I'll be speaking with Mr. Crawford tomorrow morning. After all this, there's no way we can continue working together. And if I have to resign from my position, then so be it; but when he hears everything, maybe you'll be the one who is looking at a new posting!"

When she reached the front door and opened it, she turned around, intending to usher him out. As she made to pivot, he violently slammed the door shut and grabbed her with his free hand.

"Listen to me! Your young friend is on very thin ice. I got him that job there in the first place," he stated, pointing at his chest as he said this. He continued in his rant, "*I* will be equally responsible for his dismissal! Now I want *you* to get over this silly 'puppy love' thing you have going on with him, or I'll make it a point to talk with Crawford myself. Then we'll see in fact who should or *should not* worry about breaching ethics! Do you understand?"

Doyle then opened the door and stepped out into the bright sunshine. "By the way Sharon, you should check with your neighbors before bringing home stray cats!"

He left her standing in her doorway, too stunned to say anything. However, as Doyle drove away in his one-year-old Volvo, she made a quick gaze across her lawn to the townhouse next to hers, just in time to see a curtain close to what she assumed was her neighbor's bedroom window.

Chapter Six

John Dorsey was in bad shape. The tune by Johnny Cash, 'Sunday Morning Coming Down' kept repeating itself in his mind as he stumbled into the alleyway behind Jacobson's Men's Clothing off Main Street in downtown Chatham.

The small bag of cocaine he had purchased last night from Jimmy Whalen had maybe enough for one good hit left in it, and the druggie quickly hid behind a garbage bin and opened his kit. With shaking hands, he managed to roll up the worn coat sleeve of the thin jacket he was wearing. When he found a vein suitable for his purpose, he completed the task.

Mid-February in the Maritimes can be extremely cold and today was no exception. Despite the freezing temperature, in a matter of a minute John Dorsey had nodded off, the sorrowful song by Johnny Cash no longer on his mind. For that matter, nothing was on his mind, nor would there ever be.

Jake drove to the Lower Shore Road at a leisurely pace, a little past noon on Sunday, anticipating a nice brunch with Sharon. It was a beautiful winter day; he was in his brand-new Envoy Epic that still had that new car smell, and he was excited to be showing it off to her.

He rang her doorbell and waited anxiously for her to appear. However, when she came to the door, he was not prepared for the type of response he received. From the look of her red and swollen eyes, he could tell she had been crying recently He also noticed how she glanced suspiciously over his shoulder at the building next door.

"Sharon, why are you upset? What's happened?"

"Oh, Jacob! Come inside, we've got to talk."

Jake took off his light bomber jacket and followed her into the kitchen. Sharon put on a fresh pot of coffee and described the visit she had just experienced with Doyle. When she finished and they had both settled in their chairs with coffees poured, Jake had to hold his temper.

"If Doyle thinks he can threaten you, he should know it's a double-edged sword," he said.

"Exactly, but the same thing holds for you and me, Jacob. Don't you see? It's not a question of who *they* would believe," and she made air quotes to emphasize the all-inclusive bureaucratic word. "The fact is, this is a male world, Jake. Like other women in this business, this position is as far as I'll probably go. If push comes to shove, I think they'll find a way to fire me. At the very least, life will be very unpleasant there unless I do as he says."

Jake knew deep down in his heart she was telling the truth.

"You know, for a while now, I've been planning on getting away from Chatham myself. Remember the other day you mentioned I should talk to Doyle about a transfer? Well, I did, and he said he'd check into it. I think with what has happened, perhaps my chances of obtaining a transfer have just grown. I have a feeling Regional Office will advise me of something this week coming. If so, and if I get any say in the destination, I'm going to request a branch in Moncton or Saint John, Sharon. What do you think?"

"Well, Saint John is our largest city. A lot more is going on there, Jacob. And Moncton is closer to home. You should do well away from here. Anywhere, away from *him*."

"But I mean, what about *you*? Will you come with me?"

"That would be a pretty big step in our relationship, don't you think?"

Jake realized he had overstepped an unspoken line, and he eased back. "Okay, you're right. You don't have to make that decision right now, but I'd like you to think about it. With your experience, along with the progress you've made with your courses, you'd have no problem getting on with another branch in the city, Sharon. Or even a different bank."

"We'll see Jacob. I'm tired of all this. Let's talk about something else."

On Monday morning, Jake entered the branch to find Doyle waiting for him outside the manager's office and he quickly called him over to his desk.

"Good morning, Jacob. Mr. Crawford and I would like to meet with you if you have a minute?" he said, gesturing to Crawford's office, where the manager sat behind his desk. Jake took note of a different attitude now being shown by Doyle. Something was up. As they entered the manager's office, Crawford reached into a drawer on his right-hand side and pulled out a large empty coffee cup.

"Good morning, England. Before we start, would you get me a cup of water from the staff room?" he asked, handing Jake the mug. "Oh, and let the tap run for a while. Make sure it's cold, okay?" Dismissing his feelings of humiliation, Jake left the office as requested.

When he returned with the cup of cold water, he handed it to Crawford who turned his back to both Doyle and Jake. He then bent over and held the cup just outside the bottom drawer of his desk. After a minute he turned back to face his two employees who were sitting in the two wooden chairs facing the desk. Then he reached down to his right, picked up his 'coffee' mug, took a sip, made a small grimace, then said to Doyle, "Okay, what've you got, Ronald?"

"Well sir, last week Jacob here was asking me about the possibilities of getting a transfer. I told him at the time that I'd look into it, and you will recall I received your authorization to bring this under correspondence with our HR Department in Regional Office."

"That is correct," said Crawford.

"Well, today sir, we received this," Doyle said, passing an open envelope to Crawford. The manager took the envelope and retracted a letter typed on soft beige stock. He read the letter to himself, then simply tossed it in front of Jake.

"Christ, I hope they know what they're doing," Crawford said to himself. Jake then picked up the correspondence and read it. It was indeed a letter from the Regional Office of the BNB in Saint John, addressed to the branch manager dated Tuesday, February 15th.

Dear Mr. Crawford,

This writing refers to our discussions with Mr. Doyle at your office in the matter of Mr. Jacob England, currently a Teller Third Grade at your branch. We are pleased to advise we have arranged the transfer of this individual to our office at 14 St George Street, Moncton, N.B. where he is to take up duties as a Class 209 Assistant Loans Officer beginning February 27th. In the meantime, we would suggest you place Mr. England under the tutelage of Mr. Traynor, your Personal Loans Manager, to acquaint Mr. England with his new role in Moncton.

Please have Mr. England report to his new supervising officer, Mr. Donald Gray, Personal Loans Manager, upon arrival at that branch on the above date.

Details regarding Mr. England's remuneration and a brief memo outlining his allowable expenses regarding this matter will follow by separate mail.

Yours truly,
John D Jackson,
Manager,
Human Resources,
The Bank of New Brunswick,
Regional Office, Saint John, N.B.

Jake couldn't believe what he was reading. This was exactly what he was looking for.

"Well, sir," Jake said to Crawford. "I am thrilled with this transfer. I was hoping to get into our Credit Department, and I know this is probably one of the bigger Personal Loan operations in our Region. I am looking forward to working with Mr. Gray down there. And thanks, Ron, I appreciate your help." Jake offered his hand to Doyle who simply rose from his chair, ignoring Jake's hand. In fact, he hadn't even looked at Jake, but said to Crawford, "If there's nothing else, sir?"

Crawford raised his mug and took another drink. This one was a longer pull than his last, then with his familiar sour look, said, "No, Ron. I think that looks after everything here." He reached across his desk, pulled a file folder toward himself and began reading it as if his two employees were no longer there. Taking the hint, Jake went into the vault without any further discussion between himself and Doyle and retrieved his sack of pending drafts and sorted out those with today's presentation dates.

On the way past Sharon's desk, he quickly stooped down, smiled at her, and told her he'd call her after work. He then left to deliver his drafts, a large smile on his face.

One of Sharon's duties as Branch Accountant was to pick up the bank mail at the town Post Office each morning on her way into work, then sort it, and give it to either Doyle or Traynor. She had immediately recognized the Regional Office envelope with the Human Resources Department designation, and she was quite confident it had something to do with Jacob, since he had been in the meeting with both Doyle and Crawford for the past half hour. When their session had ended, the smile on Jacob's face when he walked past her told her something was up and that it was probably good news for Jacob. She then realized that, conversely, it was probably bad news for her.

Later that night after supper, Jake had called Sharon, and he arranged to pick her up around eight. He'd like to take her for a drive, he said, give her some news. When she got into his Epic and they were moving out of her driveway, he noticed a light was on in the bedroom window of the next-door townhouse. Furthermore, he was certain he had just seen the curtain to that window being pulled open. He thought about it, then flicked his lights to bright, then back to normal, and just for good measure, gave his horn a small toot and drove away. Sharon looked at him questioningly.

"In case you don't know who that woman in the townhouse window next to yours is? That's Joan Benton, a receptionist at the Bank of Toronto. If she is passing on gossip about you to Doyle, we've just given her another little tidbit."

Sharon's face became an angry scowl, then gradually turned into a sort of introspective smile as they left her driveway. After a five-minute drive on the Shore Road leading back to town, Jake took a sharp right on a small causeway that took them over to Middle Island. He parked in a lot on the far side of the island that offered them a view across the Miramichi River to the communities of Millbank and Oak Point. To Jake, this was almost a sacred setting, close to his ancestry, and he began thinking of earlier times.

It was here that the province of New Brunswick had erected several buildings in 1873. They included a small hospital, a unique lighthouse, and a home for the light keeper, his great-grandfather, Thomas MacFarlane. The lighthouse utilized a pulley system to elevate a container of lamps which, when lit, could be seen by incoming ships in Miramichi Bay.

A lot of immigrants came from Ireland during the outbreak of the potato famine, forming the strong Irish element of the Town of Chatham. Over the years, the few buildings were moved or destroyed and now there were only several commemorative plaques on the island to provide visitors with a bit of its history.

Jake's mother had once told him that she and her sisters used to come here as kids. Indeed, a few years ago, one of her sisters had even found an iron ring embedded in an oak tree that her sister knew had been used to hold a swing they played on when they were children.

Tonight, the island was a quiet spot where Jake was able to tell Sharon of his news about his transfer to the bank's St. George St. branch in Moncton. While he talked to her about the move, he could tell she was not as happy as he was. He also sensed that she was harboring feelings of jealousy, saying it would be nice if *she* could get a transfer herself. He remembered her saying she had already talked to Doyle about that, but it had gone nowhere.

"Well, I think you should try again. And if you're still not successful, then hell, leave the place. They don't deserve you there, Sharon. Like I said earlier, you'd have no problem getting hired at another bank if you want."

They had been sitting on a park bench that had been placed just up from the shore. Jake rose off the bench, walked down over a slope of snow and ice to the edge of the river which was frozen. As he looked across at the lights twinkling from several buildings on the other shore, his earlier euphoric mood had evaporated, and it was now replaced by feelings of loss and anger. He sensed their relationship was coming to an end, and he was frustrated by his inability to do anything about it.

When he turned around, he saw Sharon had started to walk down to the shore to join him. He waited for her and took her hand.

"I think you should take me home, Jake." This time he took note of her use of his shortened nickname, and it further saddened him.

When they were back at the doorway to her townhouse, he held her close and gently kissed her goodnight. After Jake drove away, Sharon's eyes were drawn to the hummingbird feeder attached to the wall by her door sash.

I guess, I won't have any use for this now, she said to herself, and she thought of the beautiful creature that had earlier entered her life for a short while, frequenting her feeder over the past summer and early autumn. She wondered if the hummingbird had ever made it to Mexico this year and if she'd ever see it again.

Chapter Seven

Ron Doyle sat in disbelief, contemplating the cards Jimmy Whalen had just dealt him. For the fifth hand in a row, he threw them in anger across the green felt table where he and three other men sat in a makeshift poker room in Darrel Harte's garage.

"They are not happenin' tonight, eh Ron?" the host sneered as he reached for the pile of chips in the center of the table and began stacking them with others at his allotted place. Darrel was ahead tonight, although the other two players still had evidence of at least a few successful hands. Doyle was the only all-out loser, and it really pissed him off to be as far behind as he was.

"*Shit* happens, and *that's* what's happenin' tonight, Darrel. I'm out of here." He rose madly, grabbed his light jacket, and stormed out of the garage. Before getting in his vehicle, he threw the Export A butt that had been hanging from his lips on the ground and stamped it dead. So much for trying to win back losses he had experienced from the previous week. By his calculations, he was now running a deficit of somewhere north of $5000. He climbed into his one-year-old four-door Volvo sedan and tore away from Harte's garage.

Ronald Doyle had several problems. He and his wife Margaret of seven years liked the good things in life, but both of them refused to acknowledge their material holdings came at a high price to the family of four on only one income. A four-bedroom Tudor-style home in Riverside Heights, two separate memberships at the Chatham Golf & Country Club, a couple of late-model Volvos, private schools, music classes, and dental bills for their two young daughters were some of the major items that had created a debt load now threatening to bankrupt him.

Doyle had only recently refinanced the mortgage on his house to the max in order to pay off a slew of credit cards his wife had used to pay for several trips. She claimed they were necessary visits to allow her to see her ailing mother in Toronto. *Yeah, right.* Too bad she wouldn't just pack up and move there. Permanently!

And those were just his financial irritants. This past summer, Ron had decided his love life needed rejuvenating, but his wife Margaret was not on his radar to fulfill that need. On the rare occasions when they had sex, to Doyle it was like his wife was performing some type of mundane chore. He felt unappreciated and he could not figure out where the romance in their marriage had gone.

Enter one Sharon Donovan from work. Now here was a sexy, pretty, lady, and in early July he was certain she had given him reason to think she might be susceptible to his approaches. On a couple of trysts with her, he had broken the golden rule of office work: *Never dip your pen in Company ink!*

But then, as suddenly as it had started, Sharon had broken off their romance, and as hard as he tried to win her back, she was adamant that their relationship was over. She had even threatened to speak to the branch manager about it if he persisted in calling her.

Adding to that frustration, he determined that the young trainee they had recently hired was probably behind the loss of his hopes of any further dalliance with Miss Donovan. He was not blind to the way the two looked at each other. Hell, everyone at work could see what was going on. But at least he had managed to get rid of one of his problems. Young England would soon be on his way to Moncton.

As he was driving home, he thought of how best to win back Sharon now that his competition was going to be out of the way. Yes, he would change his approach. Perhaps he'd be more attentive to her needs, maybe mention her name to some people he knew in the Regional Office. Maybe even give her the impression that he would go to bat for her regarding her career.

But then on a lark, he had a different thought. Rather than continuing on his drive home, he took a right turn at the bottom of University Avenue, then a left onto Wellington Street. He knew he shouldn't be doing this, but he couldn't help himself. As Wellington turned onto the Lower Shore Road, he drove to the familiar townhouse and saw her bedroom light was on. He quietly tapped on the door and was pleased when she appeared in a loose bathrobe.

"Glad to see me?" he asked.

Joan Benton closed the door behind Doyle and directed him toward the living room. He made himself comfortable on her sofa and accepted the glass of red wine she offered him.

"Late night at the office?" she asked.

"No rest for the weary. I just thought I'd drop around and say 'hi', you know. Hope I'm not imposing on you like this?"

"Not at all Ron. Although I *was* planning on getting to bed early," she said as she raised her right eyebrow suggestively. Then she poured a half-glass from the bottle of claret for herself and sat cross-legged on the sofa beside him.

"Well, I certainly wouldn't want to interfere with your bed schedule, Joan," Doyle said, giving her his trademark smile that had always worked before.

Joan placed her glass on the coffee table, rose from the sofa and stretched in a languish manner, her robe falling apart to reveal her nakedness. She then walked down the hall to the bedroom that he knew all too well.

Just before Doyle was climbing into bed with his 'some time' girlfriend, next door to them Sharon Donovan had heard his vehicle arriving and the sweeping lights over her bedroom wall had made her curious. For a minute she thought it might be Jacob returning and, unlikely as that might be, it prompted her to get out of bed and take a peek out of her front window to see if it might be him.

Well, it wasn't Jacob. She was, however, quite surprised to see Ron's Volvo in her neighbor's driveway. She looked at her clock radio and made a mental note of the time: 1:34 am, and she checked her door to make sure it was locked. Earlier tonight she had heard on their local radio station that the body of yet another young man, the third in the last two months, had been found in a back alley in town, apparently the victim of a drug overdose.

The town was changing, she realized.

Drugs.

When Doyle drove into the circular driveway of his home in Riverside Heights, it made him angry when he saw the master bedroom lights were still on. He was not looking forward to a hassle with Margaret at two-thirty in the morning, and he was simply hoping to drop into bed and go to sleep. Before going upstairs, he used their downstairs bathroom to clean up, then arrogantly strode naked into their bedroom. It surprised him to notice Margaret had now turned off the lights and was lying curled up facing the far side of the room, her back to him as if she were sleeping. *Fine,* he thought. *This is better than I expected.*

Despite his earlier quick cleanup downstairs, his wife could still detect the smell of liquor coming off him as he lay snoring next to her. In addition, she could smell another woman's perfume, and she reacted by quickly throwing her sheet and covers aside, storming out of the bedroom and sobbing as she ran into their guest bedroom, slamming both doors.

This was not something new to Doyle. He expected it and indeed, it would have quite surprised him had Margaret not reacted this way. He made a mental note to pick up some flowers and a nice bottle of white wine on the way home from work tomorrow evening. That usually worked.

In five minutes, he had forgotten the incident and was enjoying the sleep of the dead.

Chapter Eight

From Jake's perspective, the last three weeks at the branch had gone quickly. As requested by Crawford, John Traynor had undertaken the responsibility of introducing Jake to the world of consumer credit. He had studied manuals on personal loans, credit cards, collections, and residential mortgages. He took a quick liking to this side of banking, believing it to be a way of helping 'regular' customers. Blue-collar folks needed help in obtaining everyday things like cars, furniture, homes, and the opportunity to establish a good credit rating. He would encourage such people to set up normal savings plans for themselves, but he preferred to let other people in the bank like Sharon and Doyle be the experts in advising clients on the various riskier methods of wealth accumulation, such as Mutual Funds, stocks and bonds, derivatives, and similar types of investments.

Unfortunately, he still had the responsibility of looking after his cash and in that regard, he was required to help at his wicket in times of heavy customer traffic. At least this allowed him to keep in contact with Sharon, since she usually performed the cash lockup procedures each night. Sharon continued her studies with the ICBA and was now preparing for the last week of February when she would write her final exam. Once she had that in hand, assuming she was going to have her full accreditation as a Personal Investment Advisor, Jake assumed she would make her move.

While she and Jacob had continued to date, they both knew that the day was fast approaching when he would be moving to Moncton. She had still not decided if she would be moving with him or maybe hitting out on her own, perhaps to Saint John. She would wait and see how they both felt about their relationship when the time came.

As far as Doyle was concerned, Friday, February 27th could not arrive soon enough. Only three more days and he would no longer have to put up with young England's smug smile as he made his way around the office. A small group had planned a bit of a get-together Friday night at a local pub, The Ambassador, to bid the trainee farewell. Doyle had passed on the offer to take part, claiming it was his regular card night.

And in that regard, Doyle had dug quite a hole for himself. In the past three weeks, he had only claimed one small pot, whereas his deficit had now reached an amazing ten grand. It had been necessary for him to make a kind of informal arrangement with the other players in his group. One of them, Darrel Harte, was holding his IOUs to the tune of eight thousand dollars, and Harte was not too happy with having to wait for Doyle to come up with full payment. Unknown to Doyle, Darrel had received a Letter of Demand from the loans officer at the Bank of Toronto last month, requesting payment in full of a personal note for $5,000 that had fallen due at the end of December. Darrel was looking forward to seeing his money tomorrow night.

Tonight, Doyle was sitting in his Lazy Boy recliner after getting through a gloomy supper of ham and scalloped potatoes. To his anger, he had found that Margaret added onions to the potatoes, despite his frequent complaints about that infraction. He had caught the six o'clock news when the oldest girl, Becky, started nagging him, asking him when he was going to take her skating as he had promised to do last week.

"It's family night tonight, Daddy, and you promised!" she shouted.

"Get your mother to take you!" he fired back.

"Mom doesn't know how to skate. Besides, she has to look after Wendy. Wendy has a cold, Daddy. Come on, it's getting late." Her whining was getting to him now.

"Stop it! Margaret, do something with this child. She's being a real pain," he yelled at his wife, who was cleaning up the dishes in the kitchen. He went up to watch the news in their bedroom on the smaller set. After ten or fifteen minutes, he heard the door downstairs closing, followed by the sound of a vehicle leaving the garage. Just then, the telephone rang, and Doyle picked it up in exasperation.

"Yes?"

"Doyle, this is Darrel Harte."

"What can I do for you, Darrel?" Ron asked, a little concerned that this guy would call him at his home yet knowing what he was going to hear.

"Listen, Doyle, I need that money tomorrow night, okay?"

"Well, shit, Darrel, I thought we had an arrange____", but Harte cut him off.

"Fuck off, Doyle!" Now Harte was all business. "Hear me good! I am sick of all you goddamned bankers running the show on things. Your IOU to me was due three weeks ago. Our *arrangement* ended then. So, unless I'm paid what you owe me by tomorrow night, you are going to be in a world of hurt! Do you understand?!"

"Are you threatening me, Harte?"

"No, Ron. I'm *promising* you something, you puke. And unlike you, I keep my promises. See you tomorrow night, asshole!", and the line went dead.

Doyle hung up the phone, and he began biting his nails. He lit an Export A cigarette and went downstairs. Margaret was gone, apparently having taken both of the kids with her. For ten straight minutes, he paced a circle around his kitchen floor. Finally, he decided what had to be done and he pulled on his winter jacket. He went into his garage, and minutes later he was driving downtown in his Volvo. He quickly arrived at the parking lot next to his bank.

He entered the deserted building and crept to his workstation. He was extremely careful, in case anybody should enter while he was there, such as another employee or the janitor. In that unlikely event, he was ready to tell them he was simply staying late, getting caught up on a couple of items.

He was, however, about to go over the line. He had reached a point in his overall financial situation where he felt he had to take the bizarre steps he was now undertaking.

First, he went to his desk and retrieved the Smith & Wesson .38 revolver that he kept locked in the top drawer. Only himself, John Traynor, and Donovan had a key to access the gun. He then made sure the weapon carried live rounds. Without hesitation, he opened his combination lock to the main vault. Hurrying now, he opened Jake's compartment, knowing the fool had not even bothered to change his numbers, even after he knew Doyle had taken a hundred from his mutilated money the other week.

He chuckled to himself as he opened Jake's surplus cash can and retrieved three bundles of twenties, $6000 in total. He then replaced these bundles with three similar-looking packs he had earlier doctored. An actual twenty-dollar bill appeared on the top and bottom of each of the fake bundles, but he had filled the insides with magazine paper he had cut to the size of actual bills. He left the original wraps over the doctored bundles, the same wraps that bore Jake's teller stamps, which Jake himself had previously initialed, thereby acknowledging the validity of the bundles. Lately, Jake had been spending his time under the mentorship of John Traynor, preparing for his new role in Personal Loans. It was unlikely he would require the cash and therefore it would not be necessary for him to go near his cash compartment.

Doyle knew it would not be until closing time tomorrow night that the new teller Michael King would be taking ownership of England's cash. Doyle would make sure he was personally there to supervise the transfer. He would suggest the new teller wait until Monday morning before doing an actual physical count. At that time, he and the new teller together would then 'discover' the padded bundles of the twenties. By then, England would be on his way to their St George Street, Moncton branch, giving Doyle plenty of time to build a case against him, if need be. He could envision the trainee's surprise when he landed at his new branch and the manager there told him he was under arrest.

He was comforted with the feel of the cash and the hefty revolver under his jacket. The six grand would have to appease Harte for now. In any case, he had the gun for protection tomorrow night, and he planned to let the idiot know he was jerking around with the wrong guy.

Pocketing both the gun and the cash, he left the branch and drove home. Seeing the door to the guest room was closed, he didn't even bother checking in on Margaret. *To hell with her,* he thought, and he went to bed alone. Sleep came easily.

On Friday, Jake was a cheerful guy. He had made it this far and would soon be on his way to a new branch, a new environment. Yet, while he was certainly happy to be starting a new chapter in his career, he did have mixed emotions as he drove to work.

Sharon was on his mind a lot. He was wondering if she might decide to leave Chatham, simply resign from her position with the BNB and maybe come to Moncton to be with him. He was smitten by her, and he would hate to leave without her.

Time would tell. He parked his Epic behind the branch and walked around toward the entrance. Just as he was waiting for some branch employee to unlock the door, another person came up behind him.

"Last day, eh England?"

Jake turned to face Doyle, who was looking quite drawn and hung over.

"Er, good morning, Ron. Yeah, last day in Chatham. To be truthful, though, I'm looking forward to leaving, you know?"

"Well, just make sure you keep your nose clean in Moncton." Then, rather than waiting for someone to open for him, he stepped past Jake, opened the doors with his key and walked ahead of him into the branch. Again, he reminded Jake of what a jerk this guy was. *One more day!*

At noon, he and John Traynor went next door to the tavern for lunch. Halfway through their fish and chips, Traynor said, "Hey Jake, make sure you say hello to Don Gray for me when you get to Moncton. Don's a great guy; you're going to like him."

"Sure John, and by the way, thanks for the time you've spent with me over the past few weeks. I appreciate it."

"No problem. And if you repeat this, I'll deny saying it, but I know you've been getting the sharp end of the stick from Doyle."

Jake looked closely at Traynor, now forming a different opinion of the Loans Manager.

"Well, you're right, John. I don't know what the guy's problem is, but I don't see him winning any Employee of the Month awards."

"I think he's got some issues, Jake. Like those of the marital sort. Also, I think he likes his cards, know what I mean? Oh well, his problem, I guess," and he finished his glass of draft beer. "Time to get back to work, Jake. But watch your back around Doyle from now on."

At the end of his last day at the Chatham branch of the BNB, Jake signed over his cash holdings to Mike King, the newly hired teller, this time under the supervision of Doyle. This surprised him somewhat, since Sharon had been conducting that exercise of late. He shrugged it off and was about to call it a day when he heard Sharon calling everybody together for a quick staff meeting. He felt rushed, and he neglected to insist on having his cash counted, *in detail*.

The three fake bundles of twenty-dollar bills went unnoticed.

"Come up here, Jacob. Hey, everybody, as you all know," she said to the gathered group, "Jacob has just finished his training program with us, and on Monday he will start his new position as the Assistant Personal Loans Officer at our St George Street, Moncton office. Congratulations, Jacob,", and she handed a small, wrapped package to him.

It embarrassed Jake to be the center of attraction. He took the offered package, read the attached card, smiled at everyone, and opened it. It was a Hardy brass salmon-fishing reel, beautiful in design and no doubt superb in operation. Occasionally, Jake had fished for the elusive Miramichi salmon, but he had never been lucky enough to hook one.

"Wow! This is truly an amazing gift," he said to the group. "I can't wait for the spring to arrive so I can try it out. Thank you all so much."

"Well, now you have a reason to come back and see us from time to time," Sharon said to him, looking deep into his eyes. Jake met her gaze. The double meaning of her comment did not go unnoticed by anyone, particularly Ronald Doyle, who had been hanging on the fringe of the gathered group of employees.

"I sure do," Jake said.

"Well, folks," shouted John Traynor, "let's get on over to the tavern. Cold drafts are waiting!"

Jake and Sharon sat side by side in the taxi's rear as it slowly made its way down Wellington Street on their way to Sharon's townhouse. They had both felt that they had consumed too many drinks throughout his send-off to allow either of them to risk driving home. When the taxi arrived at her place and after Jake paid the fare, Sharon invited Jake in for a coffee. It was 10:30 pm.

Chapter Nine

The foursome tonight was to be the same as last week-- Doyle, Darrel Harte, Jimmy Whalen, and Lou Gerard. Doyle knew Harte well, and he considered him to be the one to beat. The others were not so well known, but from what he remembered from last week, they were there to learn. They were Darrel's followers.

He had arrived at the designated address around 7:00 pm. This week the game was being hosted by Whalen in his small cracker-box bungalow over the edge of Loggieville's municipal limits. So technically, it was still within the Town of Chatham's municipal jurisdiction, not that there was a concern about any town by-laws that might be enforceable around their card game.

As he drove along the Lower Shore Road, he was almost tempted to take a quick detour and make a drop-in visit to Joan Benton, but he had to maintain his wits about him tonight. A lot was riding on the game, and he would need every mental edge he could manufacture if he was going to be successful. At the moment, the last thing he needed was an image of Joan's naked body floating around in his head.

Before leaving the vacant branch earlier, he had tried to convince himself that he would simply use the six grand that he had taken from Jake's cash can and give it to Darrel. He would have no problem deferring payment of the remaining $4000 to a later date. He could beg off and tell the players he had made a prior commitment. He would say it was a last-minute invitation at the Curling Club his wife forgot to mention.

But after arriving at Jimmy's, he saw the table had already been set up. The green felt emitted a soft glow under a canopy of light from a suspended ceiling lamp, and a new pack of unopened *Bicycle* playing cards were like some form of aphrodisiac to his psyche. Doyle was hooked, plain and simple, and there was no way he could leave the environment now beckoning to him.

Darrel and his two buddies were already sitting at the table when he arrived. He noted the look of disdain Darrel was giving him as he withdrew two bundles of the twenties from one pocket of his bomber jacket and casually slid into the remaining chair at the table. He carefully removed the jacket and hung it over the back of his seat, then tossed the bundles across the table to Harte.

"There's four grand, Darrel. Keep my IOUs for the remaining six and give me a chance to win back my losses, okay?" He withdrew the third bundle of twenties from the pocket of his jacket that hung behind him, conscious of the Colt. 38 there. Darrel slowly gave Doyle a nasty smile, then shrugged.

"Why not?" Darrel said. Looking at Whalen and Gerard, he placed the bundles of twenties in a drawer that was part of the tabletop and instructed Lou Gerard to break open the new pack of *Bicycles*.

"Let's play some cards, boys," he said.

Jake relaxed beside the fire that was giving off a pleasant warmth from the burning birch logs he had ignited twenty minutes earlier. They were enjoying a coffee, and he realized it was a wise move that neither of them had driven home in their vehicles. Sharon had offered him nothing stronger than the coffee, and Jake was fine with that. They were listening to a tune by Ruby and the Romantics, *Our Day Will Come*. Sharon was pensive, staring at the fire.

"You're quiet tonight," said Jake.

"I guess so. Are you all set for your move to Moncton?"

"I have little to do. Pack a few clothes, some books, LPs, stuff like that." He continued to gaze at her, admiring her beauty. "Have you given any more thought about joining me?"

"Yes Jacob, I have." She put her coffee on the table in front of them where they were sitting on her sofa.

"I think it would be premature for that," she said seriously, obviously sad. She continued, not looking at him. "I've got to say, the thought tempted me. But I'd prefer to wait and see how you, or the *both* of us, feel about each other after you're established in your new job, your new surroundings.

"And Jacob, I should tell you another thing. My mom has not been feeling very well lately. She is going to see a doctor next week and I'm anxious about her health. Jake, it just wouldn't feel right leaving her side. What do you think?" she asked tentatively.

Jake took both his hands in hers, and now they looked deeply into each other's eyes. "I think I love you," he said. "But I respect your decision. Moncton is not that far away, and I still haven't told the guys in the band about the transfer. So, I'll be returning every weekend to play with them. At least for the short term," he said with a shrug. "If you agree, can I see you on the weekends?"

"I'm glad you feel this way, Jacob. That would be wonderful," and she raised her head and kissed him.

"I'm sure everything will work out fine, Sharon. Look, why don't you call me a cab and I'll let you get some sleep," this said with a little wink. "Maybe I can see you tomorrow, or you might even want to take in the dance at the Ex? We've got another two new Beatles' tunes nailed down!" and he started playing his 'air' guitar as she went to the phone.

"We'll see," she said, and she called for a taxi.

In ten minutes, the cab arrived and as Jake was leaving Sharon's driveway, somebody pulled aside a curtain from the bedroom window of the townhouse next door. Joan Benton noted Jake as he left Sharon's at 11:35 pm.

It was roughly 11:30 and Ron Doyle was finally having a good night. He had won back his previous losses, mainly from Whalen the host, and Gerard the Frenchman. If he converted his chips right now, he could return the $6000 he'd taken from Jake's cash compartment with another $1000 to spare. The idea sorely tempted him. Gerard had pulled stakes and was on his way home, and Jimmy Whalen had excused himself, saying he was going upstairs to his kitchen to get a 'treat', whatever the hell that meant.

The two were waiting for Jimmy to return and Doyle, seeming to come to some decision, looked at Harte and said, "What do you say, Darrel? Wanna play some blackjack?"

"Oooooh, you're feeling them now, eh, Ron?"

"You bet, asshole. I'm on a roll, man."

"Why not," Darrel said and grabbed a new pack of Bicycles from another small drawer under the table and broke the plastic seal on them. Just then, Jimmie entered the room carrying a bowl of popcorn in one hand and a full plate of nachos covered in melted cheese and salsa. He laid the bowls on the table, then reached in his front shirt pocket and pulled out two joints that he had rolled while he had been in the kitchen.

"You in for some blackjack, Jimmy?" asked Darrel, shuffling the cards.

"Nope, I'm broke," he said.

"Cut this for us," and Darrel passed him the deck, then put a stack of chips in front of himself. Gerard cut the deck and passed it back to Doyle, who drew a ten off the top, then passed it to Darrel who drew a King. So, an advantage to Darrel as Doyle, with the lower valued card, would have to play first. Darrel dealt down cards for each of them. Doyle peeked at his down card, which was the Queen of Hearts, then he arranged a neat pile of chips and moved them into the pile Darrel had already created. He tapped his Queen once.

"Five hundred. Hit me." Darrel threw him a five of spades. *Fuck!* "Again," he said. This time he received the four of diamonds, and he crossed it horizontally at the top of his five to show that was enough. Darrel smirked, turned over his down card to reveal the ten of spades. Then he casually flipped his next card off the top of the deck, which was the Queen of spades. "I'll pay twenty, Ron," he said in confidence, since Doyle was showing nine and that he would need to have an ace in the hole to win. Doyle angrily threw his cards back at him.

"Deal, asshole,"

Jimmy lit up his joint and passed it over to Ron. *What the Hell,* Doyle thought, *I may as well get a little buzz going!* He took a good hit off the doobie, which was his first big mistake.

Jimmy Whalen was a single guy and not great with his spending and saving habits. Yet the guy owned his bungalow with some fairly nice furniture, including an impressive stereo system, albeit a bit on the tacky side, and a late model Dodge Ram. There was no way he had gained all this on his meager earnings as a janitor at the local mill.

Nope. Jimmy had an extra source of income. He looked after the needs of a growing group of young misfits in town who had taken a quick liking to his wares. In particular, they preferred his brand of weed, which he had recently flavored with crystal meth, an extremely strong man-made opiate, fifty to one hundred times the strength of morphine. When he mixed in a small amount of meth with his home-grown pot, he increased any effects of regular marijuana considerably. States of euphoria and paranoia, including hallucinogenic feelings, were not uncommon.

Ronald Doyle was not a terrible poker player, even after having had a few beers under his belt. Probably his thirteen years with the bank had trained his memory cells in their capacity for numbers. Hence, he usually had some success at cards, despite the run of bad luck now and then that certainly accompanied all players. But tonight, after having just one hit of the joint that Jimmy passed his way, all the good luck in the world probably wasn't going to help him one iota.

As for Darrel, this was not the first time he had played under the influence. But the other times didn't involve the money he was now looking at, and he did *not* want to lose to the jerk that was sitting across from him. When the blunt had been passed to Darrel, he faked it.

When he threw the first card to Doyle, he had drawn it off the bottom of the deck and had given it to him as a down card. Now, he gave him one of the two Jokers that they had discarded earlier, just as a test. He watched for a reaction as Doyle *hyper*-carefully looked at the card, bringing it up to his unfocused eyes.

Doyle began laughing hysterically. He was bent over, holding his gut, pointing at the card, trying to talk to Darrel.

"Wow! Nice play, Darrel, hit me again. No, wait. I'm only joking!

Get it? *Joking*?" He took a drink of the beer that Jimmy had brought around earlier and now he started choking, beer coming out of his nose. It went on for another five minutes, and both Harte and Whalen were getting concerned.

"Man, that Joker was a *choker*," Doyle said when he finally caught his breath. Then Jimmy fell into a fit of laughter.

"Okay, if you guys want to fuck around all night, that's it. I'm going home," said Darrel, pretending he was becoming exasperated with the other two.

"No, no! I'm good," Ron said. Where's the can, Jimmy? I've gotta have a leak."

"Upstairs, first door on your right," said Whelan.

"Wait until I'm back, Harte", and he left the table, the other two rolling their eyes as he left.

Five minutes later, Doyle returned, looking somewhat better. While in the washroom, he had thrown some cold water on his face in an effort to come around.

"Deal again," and he settled back into his chair. In a second, he was peeking at his down card, and it was an ace. The Ace of Spades. Darrel took a down card for himself. A quick peek at it told him it was the Jack of Hearts.

"Well, let's see," Doyle said, and he sorted out the rest of his chips and pushed them toward the center of the table. "What do you say, Darrel? Have you got ten grand?" Darrel ran through the ante on the table.

"I do, Ron, but you don't. All I count here is seven…" and let it hang there.

"Well, you know I'm good for my IOUs…"

"Yeah, right. You're sure you want to do this? If you don't make it, you're gonna be down another five big ones, *plus* the six you had to pay back just now," Doyle was getting pissed off with all of Darrel's pontificating. Then he committed his second big mistake.

"Cut the fucking preaching, Harte. Either you're in or out," Doyle yelled.

"Very well," Harte said, now dealing an 'up' card to Doyle. The nine of hearts. Darrel saw the tell on Ron's face. It was a look of anger, disappointment, disbelief, or fear? Take your pick! Harte thought to himself, *I've got him!* Ron only had two moves: either hold and hope Darrel was not sitting on a face-card or better. Or he *could* take another card and hope it was another ace. He made the only proper choice and held.

Darrel had been practicing a certain draw from the deck for the past three consecutive months and now was the perfect time to put the move in place. Then he made a point of sneering at Doyle to get his attention while he deftly pulled another card from the bottom that had been next to the Joker he had earlier placed there. With a smirk, he threw his next card on the table, face up. It was the Ace of Diamonds. Then he dramatically flipped over his down card, the Jack of Hearts.

Doyle simply stared at the cards lying on the table. He could have sworn he saw Darrel's Jack give him an evil wink with its one eye as it looked up at him. Jimmy Whalen started laughing and pointed at the Jack belonging to Darrel.

"Hey, it's the Jack of Harte's," He screamed. "Get it? The Jack of *Harte's?*"

Then, in a fit of anger, Doyle stood and upset the entire table. Cards, beer, nachos, popcorn, and tokes went flying all over the place. He moved backwards when he did and grabbed his bomber jacket.

"I don't know how you did it, but you're a damned cheat!" he shouted at Darrel.

"That's it! You're out of here!" Harte countered, now standing, facing Doyle. At that point, Jimmy seemed to come out of the fugue he had been in and supported Darrel. He walked over to face Ron, placed his hands on his shoulders. "Ronald, just go the fuck home," he pleaded.

Doyle, now sobbing and way beyond his normal self, reached into the right-hand pocket of his jacket and pulled out the bank revolver, all the while wondering how things had ever reached this point.

Chapter Ten

Early Saturday Jake rose to a clear, crisp February morning and he decided to call Sharon. "Hey, how are you this beautiful morning?" he asked. He noted she was quick to pick up her phone since it was only 7:45.

"Hi, Jacob. I feel fine, considering the volume of alcohol I had last night. What's going on today?"

"Well, we have practice this afternoon at the Ex, before setting up for tonight's gig. And I'm going to tell the guys about my transfer. A discussion I'm not looking forward to," he added. "So, it might be a rough afternoon," he said, letting his thoughts hang out there.

"I understand, Jacob. But you've given a lot of thought to where you see your life going, and in my opinion, you're doing the right thing. Your music will always be with you, whereas this transfer is a good opportunity and maybe a one-time thing. Believe me, once you get settled in at the St George Street office, your outlook toward this career choice will change for the better. I'm sure the Ron Doyles in the bank are the exception."

"Yeah, I guess so, Sharon. But, you know, besides leaving the band behind, there is you. And right now, you are the most important thing in my life." Sharon sensed his anguish and truthfully, she felt bad for him.

"Well, Jacob, like I said last night, let's take this one step at a time. I also have strong feelings for you, and I think we're playing this right. If our relationship was meant to be, then a few miles won't end it."

"Okay, Sharon." Jake's mood was now somewhat assuaged. "Look, I'm gonna run and start putting things together for my exit on Monday. I'll give you a shout before leaving for the Ex tonight. Maybe you'll be up for coming to the dance with me, okay?"

"We'll see, I'm going over to Mom's today to see how she's doing.

Take care, Jacob," and their call ended.

At 9:30, Darrel Harte was just stumbling out of bed with a severe hangover. With effort, he recalled his activities from last night and immediately left his house and went out to his car. Opening the driver's side door, he was relieved to see the .38 revolver laying on the floor under the front seat, and everything came crashing back in his mind like some replay of a horror movie in fast motion.

Joan Benton was not a morning person. Laying in a warm bed on a cold winter Saturday morning at 10:15 was fine with her. She had nothing better to do today other than a wash and hell, that could wait. As she was lying half asleep, she became pissed off by the annoyingly sharp sounds of some dog barking nearby. Probably one of those small poodles.

Ten minutes later, and still the barking continued.

Goddammit, somebody shut that animal up, she murmured to herself, now begrudgingly getting up from the bed and going to her front window, closer to the source of the sound. This vantage gave her a great view of Middle Island where she now spotted a young boy trying to put a leash on his dog. But wait, now she could see the boy running along the small causeway that gave access to the island from the Shore Road. And he was running *away* from something because he was certainly in a hurry as he carried the small pup in his arms.

Joan was now fully awake and decided she may as well start her day. She went to her coffee maker and then retrieved the morning paper off her front step. *What a boring, shitty life she led!* she again self-exclaimed as she busied herself with her coffee and her morning paper. Then the sounds of either a police car or a fire department truck siren assailed her ears, increasing in volume as it approached from downtown Chatham toward Middle Island.

Jimmy Whalen's telephone rudely woke him at some time around 10:30. It was his buddy Darrel calling him, obviously upset.

"Listen, Jimmy, get over to my garage ASAP. This is important, dude, and we need to get our shit together!"

"Yeah, yeah, but__", Jimmy started to say, but his response was abruptly cut off by Harte.

"Now, Whalen! I mean it!" Darrel roared, the sounds of the police sirens steadily increasing in the background. Jimmy sensed the fear in Darrel's voice, which along with the sirens prompted him to quickly get dressed after the call was finished.

Meanwhile, Freddy McLean and his poodle Muffie sat with his mom Edith in the living room of their three-bedroom bungalow. Freddy's small house was about three blocks from the town side of Middle Island on the Shore Road. The police officer, who had only minutes ago taken Edith's call informing them of Muffie's discovery, instructed them to stay at their home and he would be coming to speak with them immediately.

"So, tell me once again, son, and take your time. Why were you on Middle Island this morning, and how did you make this awful find?"

Freddy McLean looked first at his mom, then back to the big police officer who had just asked him the question. It was hard for Freddy not to be afraid. The man was enormous. He wore a big black mustache, and his face was all filled with pockmarks like he had been sick a long time ago. The guy was older than his dad, who he knew was forty-five, because he was complaining about that fact just yesterday. He sort of wished his dad was here now, instead of his mom, but he was at work at the Mill in Newcastle, doing a weekend shift. And this cop smelled like his dad did sometimes after he had been drinking some beer.

"Yes sir," Freddy began. "Muffie and I were just taking a walk on The Island like I do every Saturday morning and Muffie started barking. She had gone off the trail there, you know, that goes through the birch grove just after the causeway ends. Then she ran off into the bushes and I could tell she was, like, excited.

"She just wouldn't stop, so I ran after her to see what she'd found. Like maybe a dead rabbit, or somethin', you know? And that's when I saw it. I mean him, you know …" and Freddy's voice now trembled.

"Detective Faraday, the boy is upset. Can't you please just finish your interrogation," Mrs. McLean angrily interjected.

"Okay Freddy, one more thing. Did you take anything from the body or touch it at all?"

"No sir, and neither did Muffie," said Freddy, now openly sobbing. Faraday had to stifle a small smile.

"That will be all, Mrs. McLean. I'm sorry to have to disturb you. Say nothing to anybody about this, especially the press. You can bet they'll be hounding you folks for details once the news is out. So just refer them to us, right?" and he passed her one of his cards.

If this wasn't a shit storm, he didn't know what else would qualify as one, Ralph Crawford thought, and he set aside his noon brunch of pancakes, bacon, and scrambled eggs that the live-in maid/cook/laundress, Mindy, had just prepared for him. He had lost his appetite.

The Chatham police chief had just informed him somebody on Middle Island had found the body of one of his employees, Ronald Doyle. He was told Ronald's wife Margaret was aware of the discovery and the police were now speaking with her. They would, however, like to have a word as well with Ralph. It was more work-related, they said, and would he please drop around to the department this afternoon.

Crawford put on his three-piece, gray pinstripe suit, selected a dark blue paisley tie for the occasion, and yelled out to Mindy that he'd be back by four this afternoon at the very latest.

"And by the way," he added. "Also tell the Missus when she's back from shopping that I plan on going to my meeting with the boys later tonight as usual. I won't be staying for supper, okay dear?" With a scowl on his face, he left his estate next to the Chatham Golf and Country Club and headed back into town in his new Cadillac Deville for the Chatham police precinct.

So far, it had been quite a morning. Detective Jack Faraday had taken the boy and his mother in his cruiser for the short drive to Middle Island where young Freddie took him to the body his dog had discovered. After the scene had been handed over to two other officers from his precinct, he drove the boy and his mother home.

Faraday had then called the Police Chief William Young on his car phone after obtaining an ID from the victim's wallet. The man was Ronald

Doyle, and Chief Young knew the name of the victim and his wife, both being members of the Golf and Country Club in town. He told Faraday he would contact Mrs. Doyle along with his boss, the bank manager, Ralph Crawford.

Detective Jack Faraday climbed into his cruiser and drove back to the precinct where he was about to conduct an interview the Chief had arranged with Ron Doyle's boss, Mr. Ralph Crawford. Jack only knew the manager to say hello to him on the street.

The word in town was that Crawford liked to party with the elite of Chatham. Faraday was not in his social network, and he did not expect the interview to yield much regarding the death of his employee. Yet he couldn't leave any stone unturned. At least maybe Crawford could provide a bit of information into Doyle's lifestyle. Or what he was doing in the last week or so leading up to his unfortunate demise.

As he drove, he thought of the body of the victim as it lay *in situ* when he had viewed the crime scene. Doyle was fully clothed, and there was nothing to indicate a struggle of any kind had occurred. His wallet was in his jacket and there was approximately three hundred dollars in it, thereby ruling out robbery as a motive. They were still awaiting word from the medical examiner to give them a cause of death and an approximate time that it had occurred. No weapon of any kind was found.

Yet notwithstanding all that, to Faraday there were still indications of foul play. For one thing, the site where Doyle was found was in a thicket of high ragweed. Add to that there was the position of the body, like he was dumped there. Both seemed highly irregular as signs of suicide. If the guy was going to commit suicide, how was it accomplished, and why would it be at that spot, lying in that manner? Still, stranger things had been known to happen when it came to somebody wanting to take their own life, so Faraday was keeping an open mind.

Chapter Eleven

The Chatham Police precinct was a brownstone three-story building located on the east end of town. According to the plaque on the cornerstone that proudly displayed the date of its establishment, it had been around for the past one hundred and fifty years. Probably because of its stone construction, it had withheld the massive Miramichi Fire of 1825, one of Canada's worst forest fires ever, that destroyed the town of Newcastle and several communities including Chatham Head, Douglastown, and Napan.

Jack Faraday had no interest in the history of the building. History was painful and something he avoided thinking about. He had been attached to the precinct since he first joined the Chatham Police department as a young rookie patrol officer when he was twenty-eight years old. Just back from overseas after the Liberation of Holland in WW11, he was full of piss and vinegar, newly married, with a bright future ahead of him. Unfortunately, his return from the horrors of the war brought with it an addiction to alcohol that Jack considered to be under control.

Under control was a matter of debate with his Chief. Not so, however, with his wife, and Jack found himself in a messy divorce after six years of arguments, no children, and the loss of his property, albeit mortgaged as it was to sixty-five percent of its value.

But give Jack his due, since over the years he had kept his job. Indeed, a break came his way through a murder case in Chatham back in 1959, when he helped to bring to justice a maniac that had taken the life of a young, well-to-do athlete and close relative of the Town Mayor. Jack was an overnight hero and suddenly he became John Faraday, Detective First Class.

However, not that Jack prayed for the odd murder in Chatham, but there had simply been no later opportunities for Jack to shine, and his addiction to the bottle did not care one wit about that. He struggled, and from time to time in the intervening years, he argued with his supervisors, became more of a loner, and was now hitting middle age, badly in need of something to help his sagging career. Hence, with the assignment of the 'Doyle' case this week, he was hoping to get back on track in the department and maybe he might even be able to look forward to retirement.

It was 12:45 pm when he strode down the hall to his office and he no sooner got seated behind his desk than he was informed by the front desk officer that Ralph Crawford was here to see him.

"Send him in, Frank," said Faraday and he leaned back in his chair.

Faraday rose and extended his hand to the bank manager as a welcome to his office. Once settled in, he began his interrogation.

"Mr. Crawford, you are aware you are here today in connection with the death of your employee, Ronald Doyle, which we believe occurred last evening or very early this morning, yes?"

"That is correct sir."

"Well, I simply want to get to know a little more about the victim. He worked with you, as I understand, for the last three years, give or take a few months. Tell me, what did you think of him?"

"What did I *think* of him?" Crawford parroted the question. "Well, sir, I found his work to be usually accurate. Very punctual, never late a day as far as I am aware. Doyle was quite knowledgeable in his position, and he passed this on to various subordinates and/or trainees in his time. Our specific branch has been a source of many very well-trained employees for the BNB over the years."

"Any faults you care to tell us about?"

Crawford thought about the recent hazing business with young England, and he felt he should bring this into the conversation. There were other similar cases in the past and the risk of him being found to be hiding something was too high. He decided in favor of full transparency.

"Ah, to be frank, I recently had to discuss the matter of 'hazing', as it is called, with Mr. Doyle. It seems he arranged one or two pranks on our new trainee, Jacob England. It is an old practice that we thought the bank had eliminated, but such was not the case. And so, we brought Mr. Doyle to task on that matter."

"I see. When did that occur?"

"When young England first started, sir." Faraday made a quick note on a legal pad he had placed in front of him, then continued. If the hazing thing turned out to be relative, he'd get full details later.

"What about his personal life? Are you aware of anybody that might have been holding a grudge against the victim?"

"No sir." In Faraday's experience, the answer came too quickly. However, he let it pass, for now.

"And during the past week, Mr. Crawford. Did he act strange or do anything different in his routine that sticks out in your mind?"

"Other than the hazing incident, no sir."

"Very well, then. I have no further questions. However, if you should think of anything that might help our case, please call me," and he gave the manager one of his cards.

As Crawford was leaving for the exit door, he stopped mid-stride and turned back to the detective. "Detective Faraday, I assume then, that this case is being looked at as a homicide?"

"Everything is still on the table, Mr. Crawford, including death by homicide, suicide, accidental, or by natural means. Good day sir," and he escorted Crawford out of his office.

Faraday stood looking at his feet, shaking his head while he was deep in thought, then he went back to his desk and pulled a large blue book, or *Murder* Book, as it was called, from the top drawer. Although they had yet to make a formal decision to treat the Doyle case as a homicide, Faraday had early on strongly suspected that this was how it was going to roll out.

He opened the binder to the section on witnesses, and he wrote a quick note on a page headed:

Bank Manager Ralph Crawford:

. Not much here, withholding something?

. Hazing re: trainee Jacob England?

He then moved on to the section tabbed 'Evidence' where there was simply a blank page. He picked up his phone and quickly dialed a local number.

"Yeah, hi Floyd. It's Faraday at the precinct. Just wondering if you might have anything for me?"

"Jack, are your ears burning? I was just gonna call ya'." *Yeah, right,* thought Faraday, not laughing. Picking up on the silence from the other end of the line, Floyd MacNutt continued. "Uh, we could not find any sign of trauma, Jack, but here's something you should know: your victim was a user. He OD'd, and that will be your COD. Crystal meth. We have the usual tracks on his arms to go with it," and MacNutt awaited the expected response from Faraday.

"Shit, then where's the needle, Floyd?"

"I didn't say it was an *accidental* OD, Jack. We'll be talking later, my friend," and he hung up.

Chapter Twelve

The Esquires had just finished running through their newest Beatle tune for what seemed to Jake like the 100th time. Johnny Peterson, the leader of the group who also carried the lead vocals for them, was becoming agitated. They had arrived at the Ex around 1:00 pm, ready to rehearse for tonight's gig, and now Peterson felt it necessary to say something.

"Are you okay, Jake? It sounds like something's bugging you?" and the rest of the band members were suddenly all staring at Jake expectantly.

"Yeah guys, I guess we should talk." Jake now unhooked the strap from his Fender Jazz bass and sat on a spare stool. "I've been transferred by my employer, the Bank of N.B., to one of our branches in Moncton."

"Oh, yeah?" said Johnny. "Congratulations." Deadpan in his response. "When?" The other guys stood stone-faced, waiting for Jake to continue.

"Well, John, that's the thing. I report there on Monday morning."

"I see. Kinda quick to drop this on us, isn't it?"

"You're right, John. Look guys, I'm sorry. They informed me of this on February 1st and I've been fighting with it for the past three and a half weeks. I know that this puts you in a bind, but I can commute until you're able to get someone to take my place. It's only a little more than an hour's drive from here, right?" Jake said, hoping he could diffuse the sour mood that had developed.

"Yeah, I guess so," said Johnny. "I think, though, that we may as well forget about learning any more new tunes for now. Not much point to it is there...", and he pulled on his winter jacket. "See you guys later tonight," he said and left the building.

Under the circumstances, there wasn't much else Jake could say or do. Facing the remaining three members, he raised both arms, palms outward, more or less in a sign of surrender.

"Sorry guys, really, I am," he said, then he put his guitar on its stand and strolled off the stage. This was the very worst day of his life. It was even worse than the day when he had found out in Saint John at the Bank of Canada, that Doyle had ripped him off. And just like that, his mind was once again in a confused state about whether he wanted to continue working with the bank.

Constable Don Flynn sat across the desk from Detective Jack Faraday in the Chatham police station. It was getting close to 4:00 pm and he had just arrived on his evening shift. They were discussing the results of the meeting Flynn earlier had with Mrs. Margaret Doyle. Faraday had already told Flynn about his talk with Floyd McNutt from their forensic department, and they wanted to compare notes.

It was some months ago, as Faraday vaguely recalled, during a late supper following Flynn's shift, when they had a beer together at one of the local taverns. After their third beer, Faraday suggested they refer to each other by their first names. At least when they were working together, or in informal situations.

"That works with me, John," Flynn had said.

"It's Jack, Don. Call me Jack," and since then he did.

"Well, Jack," he said to his supervisor, "I have the feeling that Margaret was not that broken up over the death of her husband. I mean, when she was relating their last few days and nights together, she was pretty void of any emotion. So, it prompted me to ask how their marriage was going, and she told me it was as good as she could expect it to be, considering she was trying to live with an addicted gambler for the past three years."

"Aha, zee plot, it thickens," Faraday said in a fair imitation of Peter Sellers as Detective Clouseau in The Pink Panther.

"Yeah, I want to look at the victim's finances. Also, it might be a good idea to talk with some of his fellow workers and even get a subpoena on his last few months' telephone records."

"Sounds like a plan, Don. I've already talked with the manager at the bank and a name came up, a young trainee, Jacob England. Seems that Doyle had recently got himself into a bit of hot water with his boss for pulling a couple of pranks on young England. You know, like hazing. It's some kind of in-house trial they like to put their new hires through.

"So, I'll speak to him, and you can see some others in the management group there, okay? I understand the bank has just transferred Mr. England, and he'll be leaving for one of their branches in Moncton on Monday morning. That means I want to see him tonight or tomorrow. Let's get together on Monday and see what we've got."

Sharon returned from her mother's apartment in the west end of town around 7:15 pm. She noted her telephone answering machine was flashing, and she called up the message. It was from Jacob, and he sounded somewhat gloomy. He mentioned the talk he had with the band concerning his transfer to Moncton, and that it did not go too well. He added that it would probably not be a great idea to come with him to the dance tonight and he'd call her first thing in the morning.

She put on the coffeemaker and took out a cold plate of leftover lasagna from the fridge, then stuck it in her new microwave oven. *Well, since I won't be going out tonight, I may as well enjoy a good movie*, she thought to herself, and she turned on her TV.

She had just finished her lasagna and there were no movies on until later, so she opted for the popular series called *Peyton Place.* She was just getting into the episode where somebody buried Gus. Allison, the spoiled blond in the wheelchair, gets pissed off at Russ when he forces her out of the chair, and then in a frenzy, she cuts off her hair!

Wow, that was drastic! thought Sharon, then the sound of the doorbell ringing interrupted her viewing. When she opened the front door, a stranger was standing in front of her. He was tall, wearing a black topcoat over a dark brown corduroy sports jacket that covered a blue button-down dress shirt, *sans* tie, and a pair of blue jeans.

"Miss Donovan?" the stranger asked. "My name is Don Flynn with the Chatham police department. May I have a word with you please?" He flashed his badge to her. The presence of a police officer took Sharon by surprise and looking behind him, she saw what she assumed must be his unmarked grey sedan in her driveway.

"Certainly, officer, please come in," she said and directed Flynn to a seat in her living room. She immediately turned off her TV and sat across from him on her sofa, question marks in her eyes.

"Sorry for any inconvenience, Miss Donovan, but we are looking into the death of one of your colleagues at work," and here Flynn took in the audible gasp with the startled look that came over the lady across from him.

"Who__," she asked when he politely cut her off.

"It was Mr. Ronald Doyle, Miss," and he immediately took note of the changes in her facial appearance. Had it gone from an initial one of concern/curiosity as to why a policeman was here, to one of relief, or disbelief perhaps? Maybe a combination of the two?

"A young boy discovered his body early this morning, and we are treating it as a homicide. We understand you worked closely with the deceased, ma'am. Is there anything you can tell us that might help our investigation?"

"Oh my God! I can't believe this! Ronald? How, uh, where did this happen? Good Lord!" She was distraught at this news, but she rose from her seat. "Forgive me, Constable. Would you like a coffee? It's fresh?"

"Yes, please," he said, and she went into her kitchen. Flynn looked around his immediate surroundings while she was busy getting two coffees together. There wasn't much to take note of. A few pictures of an older couple whom he assumed were her parents, and several framed certificates from the Institute of Canadian Bankers Association proclaiming her achievement in various financial exams over the past two years. The room, though, was void of any photos that could be of close or intimate friends. She soon returned with coffee on a silver tray and again settled onto the sofa.

Don said, "I'm afraid I can't get into any of the details surrounding his death, ma'am. This is true with any ongoing investigation," he explained. "But the more people we can eliminate from the list of known acquaintances, the easier it is for us…,"

"I understand, Constable. You want to know where and what I was doing at the time of Ronald's death."

"Yes ma'am." It was a small thing, but Flynn noted her reference to Doyle by his first name. Interesting. He awaited her response.

"Well, if his death occurred last night, I can tell you that myself and many other staff members from the bank where I work were all at a 'farewell' party for one of our employees. It was at the Ambassador Tavern next door to the bank. I was there until around 10:15 when we left and came back to my place."

"We?"

"Ah, yes. I came home with Jacob England, the guest of honor. Jacob is a trainee at the branch who just received a new posting to one of our Moncton offices." There it was again, Flynn noted. There was a small hesitation to give out this bit of information. And there was a different facial expression, one of somebody attempting to explain something else? Flynn tucked that away for later use.

"Are we able to verify this, ma'am?" Now Flynn realized Miss Donovan was becoming somewhat perturbed.

"Certainly, officer. Because both of us had been drinking, we called a taxi, Miramichi Cabs, if you must know, and we arrived here probably close to 10:30. Jacob and I had a coffee, talked for a while, and I ordered a cab for him, which I assume took him back to his vehicle sometime around 11:30. And you can check that as well." She stood, and it was now apparent that her cooperation was quickly coming to a close.

Flynn took the hint and rose to leave.

"You've been most helpful, Miss Donovan. I apologize for taking up your time and I am sorry for the loss of your colleague." There was no verbal response from Donovan. She simply looked at him sadly as he opened the door to leave.

"Good night, Miss Donovan, and thanks for the coffee," Flynn said. Before leaving, he gave her one of his call cards.

Sharon closed her door and went directly to her bedroom. She was still sobbing softly as, next door to her, Joan Benton closed her window curtain.

Chapter Thirteen

Faraday took a quick look through the main entrance door at the Ex. Inside, he saw a mass of bodies writhing in motion to the loud music being generated by the band known as The Esquires. He recognized the song as something he frequently heard on the local radio channel by a group the kids called The Beatles. According to what he had heard, they were a British band that was taking the country by storm.

Since it was almost midnight, he knew the dance would soon be over, so he waited for young England to leave, and then he would approach him. The ticket seller at the entrance had already pointed out the bass player to him, so he should be easy to pick out of the crowd. And now here they came, approximately three hundred young animals, sweaty, half of them over the legal alcohol limit, and several of them, given their glassy-eyed looks, were probably on pot or God knows what else. When the crowd thinned out, Faraday made his way through the horde and approached the stage at the front of the hall. The band members were all leaving the stage empty-handed, save for the bass player who had remained behind packing up his gear. Faraday waited for the others to walk by him, most giving him a second look, then he approached the stage.

The detective rested his tall, lean body against the railing that ran across the front of the stage, his long arms hanging over the top bar.

"Jake England?" he asked, and he watched the young man stop what he was doing to give him his attention. "My name is Detective Jack Faraday. I'm with the Chatham Police Department. You got a minute?"

Jake walked over to the police detective and took the card that Faraday extended to him, quickly scanned it, and put it in his wallet.

"What can I do for you, Detective?"

"We're investigating the death of one of your colleagues who was found early this morning by a young boy out walking his dog on Middle Island.

"Jesus!" exclaimed Jake. "A *colleague*, you say. Who?"

"Ronald Doyle," Faraday replied, closely studying the young man's reaction.

"Oh my God! How the hell did this happen?"

Faraday could see that the news of Doyle's death had taken England by surprise. "Look, maybe it would be best if we could go somewhere, perhaps get a coffee?" he asked. "Do you need a hand with something here?" Faraday was using the offer to help for a reason.

Jake could not help covering his face with his hands, and he spoke in an uneven voice. "Ah, sure, Detective. This is terrible news. I'm sorry if I am acting strange. Thank you, and you can access the stage through the small stairs to your left. If you want to give me a hand, we can lug my amp and guitar out to my car. It's in the parking lot."

By the time they had Jake's gear in his car, Jake had time to realize the seriousness of the moment. *Somehow, Doyle was dead, and the police were investigating his death. He would have to be cautious of what he said to this guy.*

"I know it's late, Mr. England. If you prefer, we could do this at the precinct tomorrow," Faraday said, waiting for Jake to give him the okay to enter his vehicle.

"No, that's okay, Detective. But please try to make it brief. It's been a long night that was tense. It started earlier during rehearsal when I had to tell the guys l was being transferred to Moncton. It means they are going to have to find a replacement for me." Faraday could easily tell that had been a tough decision for the young man to make. He sort of felt sorry for him as he watched Jake get into the driver's side of the Envoy Epic. He followed suit and opened the passenger door.

To break the formality of the moment, Faraday then stated, "I understand, son. By the way, is it okay to call you Jacob?"

"Jake, please call me Jake." *Weird as it was, but that small statement reminded him a lot of his younger partner Don Flynn.*

"Okay, Jake. I understand you started working at the Bank of New Brunswick this past September as a teller?"

"Yes sir. I finished my training and probationary period, and I have just received an appointment as an Assistant Personal Loans Officer at our St. George Street Moncton branch, starting Monday," Jake responded with a smile. It was the first smile Faraday had seen him make, and he sensed the young man was proud of his promotion.

"Congratulations, Jake. You must be eager to move forward to your new posting. But do I also sense that you have some mixed feelings about the move?"

"I guess it's obvious, especially to a detective, eh?" Again, that bright smile. "The Esquires band has been a terrific experience for me," he said. "There are other matters, as well." With his last vague statement, the smile on Jake's face disappeared, and there was an awkward pause.

When Faraday received nothing further, he proceeded with his questioning. "Jake, as part of our process, we must eliminate as many people from your colleague's circle of influence as we can, you understand?"

"I noted on your business card, Detective, that you are working in homicide. I gather then that you think somebody killed Doyle. So, am I considered a suspect in his death?"

"Jake, everyone who Doyle knew could fall into that category at the moment. That's why it's important if you can account for your actions last night and early this morning. We simply need to cut down the list of people, you see?"

"Okay, I guess." England seemed to accept the logic of having Faraday conduct the interview. He continued.

"There was a little 'going-away' get-together for me last night at the tavern, The Ambassador," Jake specified. "Most of the branch staff were there from six until around 10:30. I left my car behind the bank where I parked it and got a cab. Then my friend from work and I went to her home off the Shore Road. We talked for a while and had coffee, after which she called me a cab and I went back to the bank to get my car. From there I drove home, which is just off Princess Street here in town. By that time, it was probably close to midnight, and I went to bed. Is that all, Detective?" Faraday noted the change in Jake's attitude. Not that he had become rude or antagonistic, just that he was letting him know he was nobody's fool.

"Should I get a lawyer, Detective?" Jake added.

"I don't think that will be necessary, son. But that's entirely up to you. Well, that's all I need for now," Faraday said, opening the door to the Epic. He reached over the stick shift and offered his hand. "I apologize for the lateness of our meeting, and thanks for your help. If you think of anything further, please contact me, day or night." After the handshake, Faraday stopped when he was almost out of Jake's car and turned around to face him, holding the door open.

"One other thing, Jake." Faraday's manner reminded Jake of the similarity of his actions to the current TV celebrity, *Columbo.* "Are you familiar with the term 'hazing'?"

"Ah, sure, Detective. It's a practice used a lot in college these days, just a tradition of pranking newer folks in an institution. I guess you heard about my experience with it," Jake said as a statement. And the small smile had returned.

"Yeah, your manager at the bank, Mr. Crawford, mentioned it." The two just looked at each other for a bit. Then Faraday shrugged his shoulders.

"No big deal," he said and finally he exited the vehicle. Jake watched Faraday slowly walk over to his one-year-old, department-issued Ford Custom. Jake waited as the cop started the motor and raised his hand in a thumbs-up gesture to Jake as he drove away.

Chapter Fourteen

The town workers had cleared the streets of snow in time for most citizens, at least those so inclined, to attend the church of their choice. Besides the predominant Catholic cathedral sitting on its high overlook at the top of University Avenue, the other mainstream representatives were all there. The United, the Baptists, the Presbyterians, the Anglicans, and even the Mormons. No synagogues or mosques were in Chatham, non-diversified as the community was.

It was after 10:00 am. Jake lay in bed pondering the news the police had given him last night concerning Ronald Doyle. My God, it was all so unreal. Not to mention the fact that the detective had found it important enough to call in Jake and question him regarding his whereabouts at the time of the homicide. He got dressed and went downstairs to catch his folks before they left for Sunday service at Chatham United Church.

As expected, they were horrified to hear the news from Jake, and he knew they would be seeing Ron's parents at the service this morning. Jake was not a regular churchgoer, so he sent them on their way. Perhaps they could provide some solace for Ron's parents.

He then called Sharon.

"Oh my God, Jacob, I can't believe it!" Once they started talking, he told her how Doyle's death was now being considered a homicide.

"Constable Flynn visited here last night. I think it was around seven-thirty, and he was here for an hour or more. Jacob, he wanted to know where I was, you know, and what I was doing. Like he was almost asking me if I had an alibi or something? I'm sorry, Jacob, but I mentioned you were with me," she said. She sounded a little embarrassed, and he wondered if it was for him or herself.

"That's okay, Sharon. I told Faraday the same thing, just left out your name and address."

"Jacob, I'm not concerned with who knows about our relationship, just so you know," she said.

"Thanks for saying that. I feel the same way. God, about Ron, though. How could something like this happen, and who do you think might be responsible?"

"I simply don't know, and it's terrible, Jacob. I can't imagine. I mean, right here in Chatham, and somebody we know well, and even work with?"

"Look, I'm thinking of talking to Mr. Crawford first thing tomorrow morning and having my transfer delayed, at least until the police sort this out. The last thing I want is to have anybody in the bank carrying any suspicions at all about either of us. What do you think?"

"I agree, Jacob. Anyway, a staff meeting will probably be necessary, I'm sure."

They said their goodbyes, and Jake spent the rest of the day clearing the snow out of his driveway. Afterwards, he relaxed while reading a Stephen King novel on the den sofa, then listened to several of his favorite tunes as he played along with them in his upstairs room. He was at a loss regarding the entire business of Ron's homicide, but try as he might, he could not put it out of his mind.

That same evening, Darrel Harte, Jimmy Whalen, and Lou Gerard were all sitting around Darrel's card table in his heated garage. The last thing on their minds was a card game. Darrel took the lead in the discussion, and he was not happy.

"So, I guess you guys have heard about Doyle, eh?"

"Shit, yeah," Jimmy said. "Some young fella found him in a ditch down on The Island?"

"Holy crap!" said Lou the Frenchman. "Well, you know, when I left de poker game 'ere, 'e was pretty outta it, dat guy!" explained Lou in his broken English.

"I dunno boys. But I'll tell you one thing. I don't want either of you breathing a word about our card game on Friday night to anyone! Got it?"

Darrel barked, giving each of the other two a menacing look.

"If the cops find out Doyle was here, and that *you*, Jimmy, gave him some of your *special* weed, they will be all over you like a dirty shirt. Besides, that money Doyle paid me was from a debt he had with me. I won that money from him fair and square, right? I don't need the cops getting weird ideas and queering that up on me. So, keep your mugs shut and we'll be fine."

He didn't know about Gerard, but he was sure Whelan had an idea that some of his cards came off the bottom of the deck. Well, at least he could trust Jimmy to keep quiet about it.

Their meeting at Darrel's broke up not long after it had started. The figure in the new black Lincoln checked the clock on his dashboard and determined that they were only together for twenty minutes.

So, a short and sweet meeting, the driver assumed. *Harte must be very concerned by this time. Good, that means he must have gotten the message!*

The snow that had visited Chatham on Saturday overnight and early Sunday morning was only a minor prelude for things to come later that day. The next late winter storm started after 8:00 Sunday evening and forecasters said it was to last well into most of Monday. It was a Nor'easter, and that type of system was usually the most dreaded in the Maritime provinces. By ten-thirty, most residents knew the town was in for a serious battle with the elements.

When Jake went upstairs to go to bed, he saw the storm raging outside his bedroom window, and he wondered whether their branch would even be open for business in the morning.

On a whim, he called Sharon.

"Hi, it's just me."

"Hey Jacob, I was on my way to bed for the second time. I went earlier, then had problems getting to sleep, what with, you know…".

"Yeah, same here. Plus, it looks like we're going to be having a pretty severe storm. Do you think there's any point in me trying to drive to Moncton?"

"Good question," she said. "I'm supposed to contact our Regional

Office and advise them on our weather first thing in the morning. If they decide to close shop, then we have a preset call list put in place to advise staff accordingly. Maybe you'd like to help me out?"

"Count me in. What time are you going to be at the office?"

"Let's say 8:00 am. Meet me in the parking lot, okay?"

Their call was ended, and Jake was able to get a full night's rest.

Jake awoke with a loud, rumbling noise outside of his bedroom window. He glanced at his bedside clock radio and reluctantly climbed out of bed to face the day. It was only 7:00 am, but he recalled telling Sharon he would meet her in the bank's parking lot at eight this morning. He grimaced when he pushed aside a curtain to reveal an overnight snowfall had dumped another six inches. The sound that woke him up had been one of the town's snowplows that had just finished clearing the lane beside his house.

As evidenced by the driveway entrance which he had only ten hours ago shoveled clear, Duck Murphy had once again filled it in. Most residents in this part of town hated the snowplow driver. They claimed Duck made sure to refill any open driveways when he was on duty, and that he very much enjoyed doing it.

After dressing, he made a quick call to Sharon to advise her he would probably run a little late because of the driveway work he was now facing. Her system transferred his call to her voice mail, and he left her a message. She was no doubt having to clear out her place as well.

It was 9:00 am by the time Jake finished his shoveling, had a shower, a quick bite of breakfast, and drove to the bank. He noticed Sharon's Chevy Nova was in her designated parking spot, but it also concerned him to see a Ford Custom parked in the visitor slot beside her. It was the same vehicle Detective Faraday was driving Saturday evening.

Jake waited patiently at the front door for somebody to allow him entrance. It was Sharon who eventually came to the door, and upon opening it for him, she gave him an odd look. When she rolled her eyes in a gesture toward the interior of the building behind her, he realized she was giving him a warning they had company, and this was not just a friendly visit.

As they walked toward Crawford's office, Jake saw several people were in the small area, creating a crowded scene. Besides Crawford, there was Detective Faraday, John Traynor, and Jake's replacement teller, Michael King. There was also a fifth seat, now vacant, where Sharon had been sitting. All of those in the office stopped their discussion when they saw Sharon and Jake approaching.

Jake suddenly experienced a feeling of nausea when he saw what was sitting on the manager's desk, and what he now realized was the object of the meeting. It wasn't only the open teller's cash compartment, the three bundles of twenty-dollar bills, and Faraday's presence in the office that worried Jake; more so, it was young Mike King and Sharon's vacant seat that gave Jake reason to realize two things. First, that he was now in a world of trouble, and second, as he gave Sharon a forlorn look, it appeared he had lost his only ally.

At that moment, everybody in the office sitting now rose from their chairs. Crawford looked at Faraday and they reached some silent form of agreement. The manager then instructed Sharon and Mike King to take the teller's cash in its metal box into the vault, but to leave behind the three bundles of the twenties. He then offered the use of his office to Detective Faraday so that 'certain' matters could be discussed with mister England. He added he had several calls to make, including his Regional Office.

"Mr. England, I will leave you with Detective Faraday now. I should tell you we have put your transfer to Moncton on hold for the time being. Detective, I shall no doubt be speaking with you later." With that, Jake and Faraday were alone in the office.

"Jake, have a seat," said Faraday, moving to reoccupy his previous position. When Jake took his seat, he addressed Faraday.

"Detective, what the hell is going on here?" he asked, trying to remain calm. He could not stop staring at the cash bundles while his mind raced back to last Friday evening as he recalled quickly signing off his cash holdings to King.

"I received a call from your manager about a half-hour ago, Jake. When I arrived here, I joined Miss Donovan and the teller, Michael King." Then Faraday grabbed one bundle. "Here, have a look."

Jake took the pack of bills and even before flipping through them, he knew what he was going to find. When he finished flipping through one of them, he looked first at the ceiling, then at the floor, then at the other two packs. Finally, he turned to face the detective, and he gave Faraday a sarcastic smile.

"Do you believe this bullshit, Detective? Man, once again he has truly framed me!" and he brought his hands to cover his face in anguish. When he did so, he saw movement through the side glass partition of the office. Sharon was walking past the glass frame on the way to her desk, looking at him now with a mixture of sadness, then anger on her face.

"Jake, if you prefer, we could do this back at the precinct. Either way, I'm sure you can appreciate the predicament in which you now find yourself. You transfer your cash to a new teller just as you are about to leave for a new posting, and it looks like you altered three cash bundles, resulting in a shortfall of $5880. The one person who could otherwise shed any light on this theft was found murdered the morning after your last day at work here. The same person who we know you had reason to hold a grudge against."

"Detective, I know this doesn't look good for me. But I'm telling you, I had nothing to do with the death of Ronald Doyle. Nor did I take that money from the new teller."

"But Jake, your stamp and your initials are on the wrapping bands to the bundles. I believe that is the process your bank uses to acknowledge the formal transfer of money from one teller to another. Who else could have taken the cash?"

"Doyle. He did this. He must have switched the cash with magazine paper the night before. I just never picked up on the ruse. On Friday night, we were all in a big hurry to get out of here. Unfortunately, I never insisted on having Mr. King count my cash in detail when he took it over from me. Doyle supervised the transfer of cash. Had it been Sharon, the person who normally does this, she would have ensured that we followed bank policy.

"I know damn well Doyle set it all up this way on purpose. You've got to believe me, Faraday."

"What reason would Doyle have for doing this?"

"I am told Doyle was having personal problems, like with his marriage, and also with gambling."

"Oh yeah? By whom?"

"I'm sorry, but I can't tell you. I was told by the person at the time that they would deny it if I ever made that claim."

Faraday could only shake his head when he heard all this from Jake.

"Is there anybody else on the staff here who can corroborate any of what you are suggesting?"

Jake looked seriously at Faraday.

"Well, there is somebody here who knows about the ongoing feud I've been having with Doyle, practically since day one," he said. "This person has been my ally, and I have been reluctant to ask the individual to get involved in such petty schemes Doyle has been playing against me."

"Jacob, this is serious. You are going to have to set aside personal loyalties if we are to help you. Who is this person?"

Jake could only sit motionlessly and look helplessly at Faraday. "I'm sorry," he said.

With that, Faraday stood and took the three 'cash' packets with him and moved toward the office door. He stopped, turned back to Jake and said, "I would advise you to engage the services of a lawyer. You are not being officially charged with anything, but know this, young man. You are certainly being considered as a 'person of interest' in the death of Ronald Doyle."

The big detective was leaving when again he stopped and turned around to Jake. "One other thing," he said. Jake shuddered. This goddamn *Detective Colombo* routine was getting to him.

"I don't suppose you know anything about a bank-issued .38 revolver that's missing?"

"Jesus, no!" exclaimed Jake. "Check Doyle's home and car, Detective. That would be my guess." He abruptly stood and left.

Faraday followed Jake out of the office and went over to Sharon's desk where he signed a receipt for the three bundles he was taking with him as evidence. On the way out he caught Crawford's attention and told him he would be calling him within the next two days.

After Faraday left, Jake approached Sharon. He could tell she was thoroughly disappointed when they discovered the doctored bundles in Mike King's cash compartment.

"Sharon, please____," he attempted to explain. Sharon cut him off.

"Jacob, you may as well go home. We're closing the branch today because of last night's snow. Also, the weather forecasters are predicting another storm is coming our way, this one worse than the last. Besides, Jacob, there isn't much for us to talk about anymore." She pulled on her coat and left the bank.

The only other people in the bank now, Crawford and Michael King, stood in front of Crawford's office, glaring at him. Jake got his overcoat and left for home.

Chapter Fifteen

Jake was confused and worried as he drove home from the bank. As the result of the latest rip-off by Doyle, it looked like his new job was in serious jeopardy. On top of that, Sharon considered him guilty of taking the money and now it appeared she didn't even want to talk to him about it.

But worst of all was the seriousness of his situation. Christ, he could end up in prison! As Faraday had said, the police were seriously considering him responsible for Doyle's death. Somehow, he had to clear his name. He felt the best way to do that was to become more proactive. But what could he do to change Faraday's mind about him? How or where could he get information he could give to the police that would vindicate him, and redirect the focus of their investigation? Instead of going home, he drove to his old hangout.

Since working at the bank, he hadn't been into *Joe's Billiards,* and he approached the building with doubt; he was a little concerned that perhaps some of his old buddies, even if they were here, wouldn't feel much like talking to him. After all, hadn't he avoided them?

Several familiar senses assaulted him upon entering the pool hall. The soft clicking sound of the ceramic balls as they contacted each other and low curses coming from several people at a table on the far left were both music to his ears. His eyes took in the green felt of the pool tables, highlighted individually by the fluorescent tubes above them in the otherwise dark hall. He also welcomed the fragrance of the pine deodorant that the owner of the hall, Joey Cripps, always used on his floors.

He spotted two guys at the table to his right and walked over to them, grabbing a cue stick along the way from its cradle on the wall. The two young men halted their conversation and looked at him. "Well, well. Looks like the banker has left his uptown office and come down to play some pool with his old friends," said Donnie Mitchell.

"Yeah," Lennie Hachey chimed in. "Where ya been the past six months, England? I guess we're not good enough for ya, eh?" Jake could not dismiss the ugly sarcasm in Hachey's delivery. He laid his cue on the table and held up his hand, index finger raised. Then, saying nothing to them, he turned and walked back toward the entrance where a bar was open. The owner was behind the bar washing beer glasses.

"Hey, Joey! Can I have three *Mooseheads*?" The owner never questioned whether Jake was of legal age. The boys at table ten were okay. They never caused trouble, and that was the main thing. Jake returned to the table with his beers and said to his two pals, "Okay, boys. You got me. I've been a jerk, and I'm sorry. But right now, I'm in a jam. And I need somebody to talk to that I can trust." He waited; his eyebrows raised in question marks as he looked at them.

"Right! Then c'mon into our office," Lennie said, giving Donnie a wink, and the three of them moved to a small table in the bar area.

"I think I made a mistake working at the bank," Jake explained. "The people there are, well, not the type of, er, not the, ah, same as…" Donnie Mitchell noted the difficulty Jake was having and that it was embarrassing for his friend trying to explain things to them, so he cut him off.

"Forget that shit, Jake. We know what happened. They offered you a job. A good job. So, you took it. And Lennie and I both knew it was going to be hard for you to fit into that situation. So, we understand, and it's no big deal. Now, what's the problem you got yourself into?"

It amazed Jake how quickly and easily his friends listened to him. With relief, he explained the situation he had with Ronald Doyle, how he was murdered and had still managed to frame him, and why he had not wanted to bring Sharon Donovan into the mess, even if she could or for that matter *would* help him.

"I should mention that I heard Doyle had his issues and that he might have gotten himself in trouble," he looked hopefully at his friends.

"Yeah, Ron Doyle," Lennie said. "From what I hear, he was a real asshole. He was what you might call a *wannabe*," he added. "You know, acting like a hood around a few of the town's less-desirables, guys like Darrel Harte?" and he looked at Jake, waiting.

"I heard the name, but I can't say I ever met the dude," Jake answered.

"Good. Keep it that way," said Donnie. "The guy is a meth head, and he travels with some dangerous people."

Jake absorbed this information and slowly he began to realize why Doyle had recently made such a big increase in the amount of money he had taken from his cash. It had to be related somehow to Ron's relationship with this Darryl Harte guy that Donnie had just mentioned.

"Look, guys, you've given me something to work with. I'm going to approach Detective Faraday and see where this goes. And trust me, your names will not come up about any of this." He got up to leave. "And one other thing, whatever the outcome of all this shit, I promise to keep in touch. If you'll let me?" Jake opened his arms, and they hugged each other.

"Good luck, Jake. It sounds like you're gonna need it," said Donnie, and Jake left for the town precinct, deciding to first stop off for lunch at the Mic Mac Restaurant.

Faraday exhaled a long stream of smoke and stubbed out his cigarette. With a grimace, he passed the Medical Examiner's autopsy report of Ronald Doyle across the table to Constable Don Flynn.

"Anything new, Jack?" asked Flynn.

"Nah, not really. Like he told me upfront, Don. Doyle was using. You can see the tracks on both of his arms in the pics there," he said, pointing out the needle marks that were obvious on the arms of the deceased.

"It appears death occurred sometime between 11:30 Friday night and 12:30 Saturday morning. Check this photo of a smashed watch the deceased had been wearing. It stopped working at exactly 11:45 pm that Friday night," added Faraday.

"Right," said Flynn. "So, it could have gotten broken when he fell on the frozen ground on Middle Island?"

"Yep, or it could have happened somewhere else a bit earlier, and somebody then dumped him on the Island."

"Yeah, you're right. There are never any simple answers, are there?" Flynn said dejectedly.

"So, what did your friend at NB Tel dig up for us?" Faraday asked, changing the direction of their conversation.

"Oh yeah, Jenny Olson did us a big solid, Jack. You owe her lunch, by the way."

"*You* do, Don. And don't bullshit me. I know you've been hitting on her. Can't say as I can blame you," Faraday added, giving the younger cop a wink. "So, what do we have?"

Flynn opened an old briefcase and withdrew a file folder that contained various telephone records that the NB Telephone company had given him.

"We now have records dating back three months to November 18th, up to and including yesterday February 29th. We have been able to pull these for Ronald Doyle, Sharon Donovan, Jacob England's home telephone, and even that of the bank manager, Ralph Crawford."

"Good work, Don," Faraday said, and he spread the material in four groups, one for each of the four names, placed in order following their corresponding time frames. He then withdrew a few colored hi-lighter felt pens, and he began comparing the phone numbers on each sheet, looking for similarities of recurrences over one phone. He highlighted these in yellow.

He then sought numbers that appeared in higher frequency than others. These received a pink highlight. Finally, he used a red pen for numbers that were made to people from the four phones on the day of the homicide, that same night, and the following day.

"Okay, Don. Now we go to work. Call 411 and get a name and address for these yellow numbers. I'll do the same for the pink ones."

Fifteen minutes later, they determined they had made some interesting discoveries. The yellow highlighted numbers were the most popular, appearing on each of the phones belonging to Sharon, Ron, and Jacob (for their purposes, the two police had discounted Jacob England's parents and hereafter would assume the yellow-highlighted calls were made by Jake from his parents' house). The yellow numbers that were called from Jake's phone and Ron's phone were all to Sharon. Calls made to Sharon's phone in high frequency also came from Ron's number. Sharon made a few calls to Jake.

The bank manager Crawford had made several calls to two of his employees, Donovan and Doyle, and vice versa, from them to him. And finally, they determined the calls made by each of these parties on the day just before, during, and after the murder of Ron Doyle were to non-work-related numbers.

Doyle received a call from somebody by the name of Mr. Darryl Harte on the Thursday before the murder; Jacob called Sharon the day after Ron's death, and Crawford made a call to somebody by the name of Dexter Sharpe directly after Detective Faraday made the call to him.

After summarizing their results, Faraday dropped his ballpoint pen on his desk in a tired gesture and looked wearily at his assistant.

"Well, Don. I guess we have our work cut out for us." At that moment, the intercom on his phone rang.

"Sir, I have a young man here to see you, he says it is important. His name is Jacob England."

The intercom had been on open speaker. Faraday looked at Flynn and gave him his signature wink.

"Send the young man in," he said. He could not contain the grin that spread over his normal world-weary look.

Chapter Sixteen

Jake entered Faraday's small office to be confronted by the two large detectives. Unknown to him, Faraday had already talked to his assistant concerning his views on the young musician. Therefore, they considered his presence in their office somewhat of a godsend to them. Faraday may as well have said to Flynn, *"he's here to confess,"* from the look he gave to Flynn while awaiting Jake's entrance.

From previous experience working with Faraday during interrogations of suspected criminals, Flynn knew without even having had a prior discussion on the matter, how his superior would want to handle this one. He said nothing. He only listened to Faraday as he went to work.

"Good afternoon," said Faraday. "What is so important to bring you here on this stormy day?" He noted England's jacket was still half-covered with wet snow, and he pointed at a coat rack against the right wall of his office. "Hang your jacket over there and have a seat. Coffee?" he asked, getting up and going to the coffeemaker on the opposite side of his office.

"Sure. Thank you," Jake responded, then took a grateful hit of the hot liquid and extended his arm. "Jake England," he said to Flynn, offering his hand, which the younger police officer took as he simply looked seriously at Jake.

"I'm sorry. This is Constable Don Flynn," said Faraday, completing the introduction. "Again, what brings you here, Jacob?"

"Detective, I know things look bad for me right now, but you've got to believe me. I had nothing to do with the death of Ronald Doyle. I will take a lie detector test to prove this if you want."

"Have you seen a lawyer as I suggested?" asked Faraday.

"No, sir. I am innocent, dammit," Jake replied with confidence.

"You could have saved yourself a trip here, young man. Unless you have something new to offer, we will continue to follow what evidence we have at this point."

"Look," Jake replied. "I was speaking with some friends of mine earlier today, trying to find out more about Doyle. You know, his lifestyle, former contacts, people with whom he may have had outside dealings. I was told by some people that he had a gambling addiction, poker specifically. I was told one of his fellow poker pals was a local badass named Darryl Harte." Jake noticed the look that the two officers immediately gave each other and continued.

"I can see Harte's name rang a bell with you. Look, I'm pretty sure Doyle took that six grand from my cash box at work to pay off a debt to this Darryl Harte fellow. Leading up to that incident, there had been a couple of other smaller rip-offs that I didn't bother to bring to the attention of the bank manager: one for fifty bucks, another for a couple of hundred. I think he did that just to, well, to get rid of me."

"Why would he want to get rid of you? Didn't he just hire you?" asked Flynn.

"Sure, they hired me as part of their bank's annual addition to their trainee program, which is an incentive by their Regional Office, not something that was developed by Doyle, nor Mr. Crawford."

"So?" Flynn pressed.

"Well, see, this is where it gets a little dicey," Jake said. The officers could see Jake was struggling to keep something from them, maybe to protect somebody.

"Son, what are you holding back?" Faraday now demanded.

Jake thought hard before answering Faraday. *He knew somehow in the back of his mind that it was all going to come down to this*, thought Jake. He had thought of nothing else all last night and he had decided what to do. He hoped he was about to do the right thing.

"Okay, Detective. Doyle was jealous of me. I am in a relationship with an employee there. Doyle had been seeing her before me, but she told me she broke off with him last year."

"Who?" Faraday insisted.

"Detective, does it matter? I would not want to see her drawn into this whole mess. Besides, Doyle is now gone."

"Exactly. He's dead, son. So, he won't be able to bother her any longer, will he? Anyway, this will all come out in the open soon. We have phone records."

That last bit of information was too much for Jake. He suddenly realized that he was at their mercy, and it would benefit everybody to tell the truth. He nodded to the detective.

"Okay, you're right. It was Sharon Donovan. I have told her, and only her, what Doyle had done, how he had stolen from me. I was so goddamned naïve. But then I went to Doyle and told him I would take a transfer and get out of his hair, so to speak, if he could arrange one for me. It seems he did.

"So, this way, Sharon and I were thinking we could meet up in some other locale. Maybe she could also get a transfer to Moncton or Saint John, and she was looking forward to that. But now," he stopped mid-sentence. Faraday could see the kid was heartbroken.

"Now she thinks you took the six grand," Faraday said. And the senior detective had to acknowledge to himself that what England had just said all seemed to make sense. He believed him.

"Okay, Jacob. Let's say we believe you. You can account for *some* of your time the night somebody killed Doyle. We simply need to call the cab company. And we know you and Miss Donovan were speaking a lot to each other after hours, so that helps confirm your story regarding your relationship with her, whether that means anything. However, as for a lie detector test, they are not all they're cracked up to be. So, let's leave that for now." Faraday stood up from his desk, signaling their meeting had ended.

Jake stood as well. "So where do I go from here?" he asked. "I've got to clear my name. Remember, I have a job transfer still in the works, assuming the bank keeps me on its payroll."

"Look, we'll talk with Crawford. And also, Miss Donovan. There may be something we can do. Besides, there are some people we have yet to interview. We'll be in touch."

Jake left Faraday's office and drove home. He took notice that the storm which forecasters had promised earlier was now gathering momentum. Then, on impulse, he pointed his Epic toward the Shore Road.

Faraday and Flynn had just finished reviewing the summary they had made up from the telephone records they got from NB Tel.

Flynn lit his cigarette and took a long drag before speaking to Faraday.

"So, I gather you believe young England's story," he said.

"Don't you?"

"He sounds credible, alright. But man, he has surely put himself in a bad situation right now."

"Tell you what, Don. Let's check out Darryl Harte further. After all, he called Doyle at home the night before somebody murdered him. So why don't you do a run on his finances, and we'll see what comes up. In the meantime, I want to know a bit more about this guy that Crawford called, this Dexter Sharpe guy. He called him only a minute after my talk with him the other day. It just seems too odd."

Sharon Donovan opened her door to Jake and looked at him standing there, the snow swirling around his sad face. She simply did not have the heart to deny him entrance, so she turned and walked toward her living room, Jake following her after removing his boots and jacket.

"I've just been speaking with the police," he told her. "Sharon, they have our phone records. They know about us." In response, she simply held her arms listlessly in the air.

"Jacob, you know that's not why I didn't want to talk to you today." He didn't like the way the conversation was going.

"You think I stole that money." He said this as a statement of fact, not a question.

"C'mon, Jacob. You signed off your cash to Mike . . ."

"Yes, I did. But it was right before you called everyone together for your presentation of my gift. I plain screwed up. I should have insisted that Mike count my cash, but I felt rushed, and I neglected that *minor* matter," he said sarcastically, and he continued.

"I'll bet you ten bucks that Doyle had already doctored up those three bundles of the twenties, knowing I wouldn't need them the next day."

"Yes, but how would he have accessed your cash the previous night?"

Jake could only look sheepishly at Sharon, not giving her an answer.

"Jacob, no . . . tell me you didn't neglect to change the combinations for your cash compartment, especially after you suspected Doyle had already used them?"

"See, that's why I don't belong here, I'm too naïve! Too trusting of everyone. I'm going, Sharon, what's the use?" He hauled his boots and jacket back on and left, slamming the door.

Sharon couldn't believe what she had just witnessed. Then, just as she was about to lie on her sofa in exasperation, her front door flew open and she looked surprised at Jake, who was back standing on the threshold of her doorway, the snow blowing in as he scowled at her.

"And by the way?" he asked, before she could say anything. "Faraday wanted to know if I knew where the bank gun is. Only you, Doyle, and Traynor had a key to where you guys kept it. Do you have that gun, Sharon?"

She flew up at him. "How dare you!" she exclaimed. "How can you even think I could do such a thing?" She was irate, but that was fine. It was exactly the reaction that he wanted to hear.

"There you go," he said. His voice was suddenly soft, as were his eyes. "Of *course,* I know you didn't take the gun, Sharon. But the police might think otherwise. After all, your previous relationship with Doyle is a matter of record. Remember, they have logged your phone calls and those of Doyle. Your situation is not all that different from mine."

She looked at Jake and sobbed, suddenly realizing their predicament.

"Oh, Jacob, what are we going to do?" She came to him, and they held each other for a long while. Then Jake broke off and trudged back to the door. He turned back to face her.

"We'll work this out, Sharon. Trust me. The truth lies out there somewhere and I'm sure it will all come out soon. I've got to go home. My parents deserve to know what has happened today."

"I expect we'll be closed to the public tomorrow, so I'll call Crawford and advise him to stay home. Like before, we'll call our staff and the folks at Regional Office as per standing instructions. Jacob, come into the branch in the morning if you can drive the roads, and we'll do this together, okay?"

Those were the best words he had heard all day. He smiled and kissed her.

"You got it," he said, and he was on his way home.

Chapter Seventeen

While Jake fought his way home on roads that were quickly becoming difficult to drive on, Faraday and Flynn were sharing information they had uncovered in the last half-hour.

"Darrel Harte is the next guy on our list to interrogate," Flynn said. "The Credit Bureau report I got shows the guy has a bad credit rating, including a past due note for . . . are you sitting down?"

Faraday got a kick out of the young constable's delivery. It was good that he had a way of adding a bit of humor to the job.

Now Flynn continued with his report on Darryl Harte. "Would you believe, Chief, the Bank of Toronto has issued a Demand Letter to him on a short-term note that fell due last month, January 15th, for $5000?" Again, Flynn impressed Faraday. His assistant had just nailed a pretty good impression of Don Adams, the star in the brand-new TV show, *Get Smart!*

"Because of the storm, there is nobody at the local branch that I can talk to about this. But after getting this info, then hearing young England's story, we need to talk with Harte, wouldn't you say?"

"Okay, Don. I also have a bit of news. I had an interesting chat a few minutes ago with the man who Crawford spoke with immediately after the call that I made to him. His name, as I told you, is Dexter Sharpe. Sharpe is a principal shareholder and CEO of Chatham Pontiac Oldsmobile. He claims to be an *associate* of Ralph Crawford's, but he was very vague about their relationship. As for his chat with the bank manager the other day, he said he couldn't recall. He says he talks with many people, yadda, yadda. You know, there's something there though, Don. I can feel it. The guy was hiding something."

"There's nothing more we can do on this today, boss. What say we get home while we can, then take a fresh look at the file in the morning?" Flynn placed the phone records and his accompanying notes into the blue Murder Book. They turned off the office lights and went to their individual vehicles in the parking lot that had now grown to a depth of six inches in fresh snow.

From the time he arrived home, it had taken Jake the better part of two hours to explain to his parents the situation in which he now found himself. Martin England felt bad for his friend, considering the loss of his son, but when he took Jake's story into account, he understood why Jake had seemed so unsure of his decision to work at the bank. He told his son he would respect his decision to leave if it came to that, and Jake was grateful for his father's understanding. But before he came to any decision on the matter, he first needed to clear his name and Sharon's as well.

The morning sun was shining brightly over a pristine world of white powder that had grown overnight to a depth of one foot. The only things moving in Chatham were several snowplows, and the sound of one such vehicle broke into Jake's train of thought and awakened him. It was 7:30 when he finished showering and got dressed.

Darrel Harte had slept little the previous night, and the storm's result did nothing to uplift his spirits. He had received a phone call last night from the manager of the Bank of Toronto around 9:45, just after he had fallen into a drunken stupor. It was still fresh in his mind, filled with cobwebs as it was. John Hancock had sounded livid on the telephone. At first, Harte thought that the call was about his past-due note, and he was quite ready to tell the manager that there was no problem, that he would be in as soon as his bank was open, for Christ's sake. He had the money to pay off his note, and hey, the storm wasn't his fault.

Unfortunately, that wasn't why Hancock had called. It was worse than that. Hancock had been talking with his colleague Crawford at the BNB, who had been talking with the police. Hancock told him that Crawford had made veiled threats. So, Harte now called Jimmy Whalen and told him he wanted to see him, like yesterday.

When Whalen finally arrived, it was mid-afternoon. The town had plowed the main roads, but according to Whalen, it was still "tough goin'".

"So, what's the big problem, man?" asked Jimmy, a stupid grin on his face. Harte quickly noted his friend's telltale red eyes.

"Jesus, can't you try to stay straight for, oh, I don't know, maybe a few hours a day? Look at yourself! It's a wonder you made it over here. You're smoking too much of your product, you asshole." As expected, the only response Harte received from Jimmy Whalen was a slight grin, so he continued.

"Have you been talking with the cops over the past few days?"

"Shit, no way, man! Why would I?"

"Listen, they may call you about Ron Doyle. If they do, say nothing, understand? Nada!"

"Yeah, yeah, I got it."

"Good. Now, I have a little errand that I need you to do. Are you cool to help?"

"Sure Dee. . . what can I do?"

Harte reached into a cupboard drawer in his kitchen and pulled out a paper bag, which he handed to Jimmy. The bag was unexpectedly heavy when Jimmy took it from his friend's hand, and it dropped to the floor.

"Jesus!" Darrel shouted. "Be careful, man. It's a gun, and it's loaded. Look, Jimmy, I just want you to take this somewhere and get rid of it. Nobody must find it, nor can anybody see you with it. I'm thinking somewhere in the river might be a good idea, you know? Somewhere deep! Go on, get outta here." He gave Jimmy a twenty from his wallet. "Here, and I don't wanna know where you dump it."

Before completing his 'errand' for Darrel, Jimmy decided to make a quick run to a buddy of his in Loggieville, Dave Wishart, another meth head. Wishart had called him earlier, wanting to score another bag of his 'special' weed, so Jimmy had paid him a visit, which led to a delay of another hour to get rid of the gun.

Jimmy drove unsteadily back to town and down Water Street toward the Cunard Wharf. They had plowed the streets but only enough to allow one vehicle on the road at a time. It was now almost dark and there were no other vehicles ahead of him as he carefully maneuvered his Dodge Ram truck past empty storefronts.

He failed to note the new black Lincoln trailing behind him. Two figures sat in the Lincoln. The driver calmly smiled as he realized where his prey was heading. The snowstorm had now basically stopped but gusts of wind caused blowing snow to accumulate on the downtown streets, sometimes creating drifts, a foot or more in depth, and frequent whiteouts.

The driver now turned out the Lincoln's lights, but he could still make out Whalen's truck as it slowly navigated the drifts toward the end of the pier. Finally, it stopped, and the driver's door in the Dodge Ram opened. By this time, however, the Lincoln had reached a position parallel to Whalen, and when Jimmy was almost out of his car, the passenger in the Lincoln jumped out and tackled him. In a matter of seconds, the two men had wrestled Whalen back into the front seat of his truck, and he was now sitting between the two.

The smaller of them sat beside the passenger door and opened the bag that had contained the .38 Revolver, which he pointed at Whalen's face.

"Hey, Jimmy. What's happening? What's with the gun? Are you going to shoot some fish down there?" He pointed to the river. It terrified Whalen when he recognized the men who had just accosted him, and he knew he was in a dire situation.

"Guys, listen! I'm just doing what Darrel asked me to do! The gun has to disappear, you understand? C'mon, guys, you gotta help."

The larger figure who was sitting behind the steering wheel now jabbed a needle in Whalen's neck. Whalen's entire body went slack in a matter of seconds and the man climbed out of the door on the driver's side. Looking about, he was satisfied no town street workers were anywhere near them. The only sound to be heard was the wind that blew harshly off the river from the Northeast. He nodded to the man who had his arms wrapped around Whalen, holding him upright in his vehicle, then he went back inside the Lincoln.

Whalen knew what was about to happen, but there was not a thing he could do about it. Helplessly, he watched the man, now fully relaxed, pull a pack of *Old Port* cigarillos from his jacket and casually light one of them, immediately filling the truck with its rum-soaked aroma. Of all his body's motor senses, only three of them, those of hearing, smell, and sight, were working. All he could do was stare hysterically at the remaining assailant, who now removed both of Jimmy's gloves. He took another long drag on the *Old Port* and blew the smoke in Jimmy's face, smiling as he did. As he had been instructed, he waited for another three minutes for the drug to have its full impact on the victim.

When he was satisfied that sufficient time had passed, he wiped the revolver of any prints, then placed it in Jimmy's right hand, reached over his victim's immobile body and lowered the driver's side window. Then he pushed Whalen's arm outside while holding the weapon in Jimmy's fist.

"There now, Jimmy," he said. Next, he pressed Jimmy's index against the trigger and discharged a round. The wind and blowing snow muffled the sound of the gunshot. After this, the man brought Jimmy's fist, which was still holding the revolver, back into the vehicle. Then he rolled Jimmy's side window back up to its closed position, and he returned Whalen to a normal sitting situation behind the wheel.

"All right, Jimbo, here we go. Are you ready now?" He smiled at Whalen as he took Jimmy's arm with the weapon that still carried four live rounds and pointed it close to Whalen's right temple. Still smiling, he looked deeply into Jimmy's terrified eyes while he wiped down the door handles of the Ram.

"Bye, bye, now," and he pulled Jimmy's inert finger against the trigger of the .38 Smith & Wesson, making sure to avoid the inevitable back-spray. Jimmy's vocal cords weren't even able to create a last plea. He couldn't even scream. Unfortunately, the drug did not impair his sense of hearing, so for a nano-second he *did* hear one final thing: the report of the gun being fired.

The man left Whalen's Dodge Ram and walked over to the idling Lincoln and climbed in, his cigarillo jauntily pointing up from his clenched teeth. Then he gave a thumbs-up signal to the driver, and they took off.

The Lincoln drove away into the blowing snow, its lights off until it reached Water Street, then it turned south where the drifting snow and the empty streets swallowed it.

As of ten o'clock Monday evening, the snowstorm that had been raging in most of the province for the past two days had finally stopped. Because of a lot of overtime for the town's snowplow workers, most of the streets were passable enough for folks to go to work on Tuesday morning.

Jake was not one of these people. His manager, Ralph Crawford, had called him at home early enough to advise him that his transfer to Moncton was being held in abeyance, pending the results of the police investigation that loomed over everyone's head at the branch. In addition, Crawford instructed him to stay home for the time being. That was fine with Jake, since Crawford told him he would still receive his salary; and, more than anything, he wanted to clear his name and get on with his life. There were some things he could do in that regard.

Sharon Donovan worked aimlessly at her desk on Tuesday, counting the hours until she could go home herself. She had given a lot of thought to her discussion with Jacob, and she was convinced he had been telling the truth. Now all she wanted to do was work with him toward proving his innocence. Crawford had told her of his decision to have England remain at home.

She decided she would contact the police once she was home and convince them she was also innocent of any incrimination, including the theft of Jake's cash, not to mention the murder of Ronald Doyle.

Detectives Flynn and Faraday sat across from each other at the desk they shared in the homicide department of the Chatham Police precinct. Faraday was just reading the last of the report he had received from Floyd MacNutt, the Chief Medical Officer. It had outlined the cause of death for one James Whalen.

"Looks like suicide," he said to Flynn. "The guy shot himself in the head, for Christ's sake. Wait a sec', though, hold the phone. How do you pronounce this word and what the hell does it mean?"

Flynn looked at the word that Faraday was pointing to and casually said, "That's *Pancuronium*". He pronounced it like 'pan-cure-*OH*-nee-um'.

"It's a drug, Jack. A very potent muscle relaxant, used on animals by veterinarians, mostly. What's it doing in the Chief's COD report?"

Faraday wanted to ask Flynn how he knew what Pancuronium was, but that would have only taken the conversation down another one of Flynn's rabbit holes. Sometimes, the guy went weird on him with the odd bits of random esoteric knowledge he possessed. Although, like now, it was usually useful to him.

"Well, here's the thing. Besides a copious amount of cannabis and methamphetamine, we have this muscle relaxant. We know from your investigation of the victim that he was using crack and pot, but this other shit is way over the top if Whalen was using it as a recreational drug to get high. I think we need to look harder at this one, Don." Faraday called the number again that he knew by heart.

"MacNutt here," the familiar voice responded.

"Yeah, Floyd, it's me, Jack. Look, the autopsy on the young man that we found last night down on the wharf. Yeah, he was loaded with drugs. The cannabis and the Meth, I get that. But this Pancuronium, what effect would that have had on his body?"

"With the volume that I suspect he injected, he would have been essentially immobile, paralyzed. Looks like he obviously miscalculated the dosage, I'd say."

"What if somebody gave him the drug on purpose?"

"That's possible, I suppose. But I could see no sign of another fresh injection site."

"Well, look again, my friend. I'll bet you dinner that's what happened. Somebody murdered the guy, Floyd. I don't know why, but first things first, okay?" He hung up and looked at Flynn.

"Let's go visit a few people," and they left the building.

Chapter Eighteen

When Harte went to his front door, he was not totally surprised to see the two police officers standing on his doorstep. After briefly examining their badges, Harte allowed them into his bungalow. Faraday and Flynn each took a chair in the sparse living room and sat in front of a modest coffee table. Faraday, taking the lead, placed his briefcase on the table, opened it, and withdrew the Murder Book for James Whalen, which he had started only one hour previously.

"Well, detectives, how can I help you today?" asked Harte.

"Mr. Harte, do you know James or Jimmy Whalen?" Faraday continued in his lead role while Flynn took notes. After receiving the call from the manager at the bank, this visit was almost expected. He was wary, and he would be careful not to volunteer any unnecessary information.

"Yes, I do."

"In what way, or how did you know him?"

"We get together regularly, several of us, and play cards. I used to have Jimmy work from time to time in my construction projects as they came up, you know home renos, that kind of thing. That was when he was a little more reliable, you know, off the drugs. Is there a problem with that?"

"When did you last see Mr. Whalen?"

"That would have been last night, right here. We had a drink late in the afternoon, then he left. What's going on, Detective?"

Faraday decided it was time for a bit of shock therapy. He turned the Murder Book around so that it was now in front of Harte who was sitting across the coffee table from them on an old sofa. The photo was taken at the scene of Whalen's 'suicide', and it was over-the-top graphic. It hit Harte with all of its gory detail. The detectives watched him closely as his face turned ashen, and he immediately turned away from them.

Flynn went into the kitchen to pour a glass of water, which he brought back to the living room and gave to Harte. "Here," he said to Harte, "drink this." Harte took a large gulp of water and placed the glass back on the table. Flynn went back into the kitchen with the glass and came back into the living room with a glass of water for himself.

"Jesus!" Harte said. "Is that Jimmy?"

"It *was*," responded Faraday. "A town road worker found him last night at the Cunard Wharf. He was sitting in his car, which was still running. This was around seven p.m., possibly making you the last to see him alive."

"Holy Christ! Are you suggesting that I had something to do with this?"

Both Faraday and Flynn remained silent, simply staring at Harte. Harte then suddenly changed his tone and said, "I think this interview is now over, detectives. I intend to get myself a lawyer, considering the seriousness of the matter." He stood up and showed them to the door.

"So much for that source," said Flynn. He asked Faraday, "Jack, why didn't we simply cuff Harte and haul him down to the precinct?"

"Well, maybe we could've, but that would've ended up the same way. He said he was going to contact his lawyer and right now, we have nothing with which to hold him. Tell you what, Don. Before we speak with Miss Donovan, let's go back to the office for a minute. I'd like you to call your friend at NB Tel and see if she can get us phone records for Harte, find out who he's been talking with lately. I remember his name from the phone records we retrieved the other day. There was that call Doyle received a day or so before his death: it was from him."

When they arrived back at the precinct, Don immediately called Jenny at NB Tel. Faraday was not surprised when Flynn dialed the number without having to reference it from anywhere. He spoke quickly and hung up the phone on his boss's desk with a smile.

"Okay, boss. Let's go talk with Miss Donovan now." *Was that a smirk or another smile?* thought Faraday, and the two left the precinct and headed for the Shore Road. When they had driven a bit further, Don pulled something from his jacket pocket which he had wrapped in a cloth handkerchief. It was the water glass that Harte had used a short while ago, and it had Harte's prints on it. "Jack, I think this will come in handy," he said to his boss with a sly grin.

"You devil!" Flynn had again impressed Faraday.

It was 8:15 pm when Sharon admitted the two detectives into her townhouse on the Shore Road. She had finished a late supper and had just settled down with a glass of red wine in front of her television when they arrived.

"Detectives, please come in. I was about to call one of you, so this is a timely visit." The detectives looked at each other and followed her lead into her living room. Because he was the one to speak with her earlier, Flynn suggested he'd take the lead. And Faraday had agreed to take notes.

"Miss Donovan, we're here to clear up any relationship you may now have or have had at one time or another with any staff members at your office. Please be candid."

"Very well, Detective. Ronald Doyle and I had a brief affair last summer. It lasted only a couple of months, and I realized it was not going anywhere, so I broke it off. Ron was not happy about the way it ended, and frankly, he had been bothering me frequently, calling me here at all hours of the night. Finally, I had to threaten him. I told him if he didn't stop, I would bring all this to the attention of the branch manager, Mr. Crawford. Then, all this other business happened." She ended her story by placing her hands over her eyes, clearly upset.

"What about you and young Mr. England?" Flynn asked.

For a moment, Faraday detected a bit of surprise in Donovan's eyes.

"Ah, yes. I forgot he told you guys about us." She smiled when she said this, but strangely, Faraday now noted this was a statement she made with pride. "Jacob and I are more than friends," she began. "It is something that just happened over the past few months. We both know how it must look to everyone, including you. And we know our relationship certainly leads to a motive in the death of Doyle. But believe me, detectives, that was not the case. Jacob had recently received his advice of a transfer to Moncton. We have discussed the possibility of me resigning from my position here and moving there," her voice faltered, and she began sobbing, "to be with him. This is all too much for me to comprehend!"

This time, Faraday was the one to get a glass of water for the witness in duress. When he re-entered the living room, Flynn had offered her his handkerchief. When he gave her the water, Faraday asked her, "Miss Donovan, will we find your fingerprints on the bank gun that has been missing?"

"Undoubtedly, Detective. Have you found the gun?"

"Unfortunately, yes, Miss Donovan." Faraday decided that now was not the time to get into the death of James Whalen with this witness, but he *did* ask her, "Ma'am, where were you last night between 6:00 and 8:00?"

"I was here, at home. Jacob was here as well. He left to go home around 7:00. Why, Detective?"

"We'll be in touch, Miss Donovan. Thanks for your time and have a good evening."

The two detectives left Donovan's townhouse and drove back into town. At least the town workers had plowed the roads, and for a change it was a clear, calm night. The moonlight twinkled on the frozen river, lending an air of serenity to the evening.

"Let's check the telex at the office, Jack. Maybe my friend at NB Tel has sent us something interesting," said Flynn.

When they got back to the precinct, a roll from a telex report lay on his desk, placed there by the office secretary before she had left for the day. They both got settled across the lone desk from each other, and Faraday read the transcripts, passing each one over to his assistant as he was through with it.

"Okay," said Faraday when they had both finished reading. "Let's recap. First, we have these calls between Doyle and Donovan over the previous three months, many of which were made during late hours and/or on weekends. You can see that only two of these are going *to* him from her. Both of these were when she had first started in her relationship with him. This sort of backs up her story."

"Right," said Flynn. "The next series of calls that stand out are between Donovan and England. They start after her breakup with Doyle. Again, this tallies with her story. There are only three calls, two from him to her."

"Now, Don," said Faraday, referring to his stack, referencing calls made and received on Darrel Harte's phone. "Check this. Here's a call to Harte on the night Whalen was murdered. It's placed from a number belonging to the manager of the Bank of Toronto, John Hancock. And there's the call made by Crawford, the Bank of New Brunswick branch manager. Keep in mind he completed that call immediately after *my* call to him the day after the Doyle's murder. It was to the owner of Chatham Pontiac Oldsmobile, a Mr. Dexter Sharpe. So here we have three of the town's heavy hitters in the business community. Normally, not that unusual, but the timing and the involvement of Harte in one of these calls, to me at least, is too damned coincidental."

Before Faraday could say anything further, his telephone rang, and he answered it. After a brief discussion, mostly one-way from the caller, he hung up the phone.

"That was Floyd at the hospital morgue. He had a second look at Whalen's body and located a fresh needle puncture at the back of the deceased's neck. There's no doubt now, Don. Somebody murdered him."

Flynn was silent, heavy in thought. Then he said to Faraday, "Jack, how closely did *we* examine the vehicle that contained Whalen's body?"

Faraday now had another burst of respect for his junior assistant. He rose from the table and put on his overcoat. "Of course, Don, you're right. Since we were originally working on the presumption that Whalen's death was a suicide, we were not as diligent as we should have been. Let's go," and they were off to the pound where Jimmy Whalen's 1966 Dodge Ram had earlier been towed.

Chapter Nineteen

Four men sat at a circular table in the rear section of the Chatham Curling Club upper lounge floor, oblivious to the five ice sheets fully in play one floor below them, but visible from their side of the glass separation wall. The men wore serious-looking faces and two of them, the bankers, appeared scared shitless about something that one of the other two, the car dealership owner, had just said.

"It's like I told you the other day, Ralph. This is about money, plain and simple. We need more funds to keep some people happy. What happened to your assistant was not an accident. You understand that, right?"

"Jesus, Dexter, this is getting out of hand. You told both John and me that we would see a quick return on our investment and that would be it. You practically guaranteed it was only going to be a one-off transaction, and that from then on, your guys could manage things."

"Exactly," John Hancock now spoke up, seemingly with some bravado. "In fact, Dexter, your guy Harte was in to see me after the storm and paid off the Demand note of $5,000 that I advanced to him, against all bank guidelines, I might add. For a while, it did not look good, but he came through. So now I assume things are working out for him?"

"You idiot!" The nonchalant attitudes displayed by the two bankers enraged Dexter Sharpe. "If things were going well for him, why do you think they found Jimmy Whalen yesterday evening down at the wharf with a gunshot to his head?"

When Sharpe made this comment, none of the three men who had just spoken noticed a small smile forming on the face of the larger man who was sitting beside Sharpe. This was Harold Morin, a new member of the Chatham Golf and Country Club and the Chatham Curling Club. These associations were in addition to the Chatham Chamber of Commerce, the Miramichi Fish & Game Association, and the Newcastle Long Gun Club.

Morin was new to Chatham, having arrived in town only last year. As the only veterinarian in the immediate area, he had quickly established a healthy volume of clients. Until his arrival, most of his customers had been taking their pets to the vet in the nearby town of Newcastle. Yet, even with the decent cash flow that his new business was presumably generating, both the bankers at the table still had questions about the man's financial sources.

How, for example, was he able to afford the new four-bedroom house next to the Golf and Country Club? And how about the new Towne Lincoln he had recently purchased? Hell, neither Crawford nor Hancock knew where he did his business, only that he didn't bank with *them.*

"I heard that Whalen shot himself," Morin now entered the conversation.

"Whatever," replied Hancock. "*Something* terrible got to the guy. And I know he and Darryl Harte were close friends."

"Yes," added Crawford. "And when you add the fact that Ron Doyle was a regular player at card games hosted by Whalen and Harte, it gets too damned close for my liking. Besides, the police are starting to ask questions."

"You too, eh Ralph?" Sharpe asked this. "Well, I had a call yesterday from Detective Faraday regarding the call you made to me, for Christ's sake. Listen up, you two. We've got to be careful who we speak with. The authorities have nothing, believe me. But we want to keep it that way, so watch what you say to people. You two have done nothing criminal. You have simply entered into a personal business deal. And I am asking you now for one final cash investment of ten grand to ensure the project we have financed is successful."

"Well, I'm in," said Morin, a little too quickly. "My experience in this type of activity has been nothing but good. Mind you, Montreal was a much bigger market. But the product, production lines, margins, sales model, and client profiles are all the same. I see no reason we all shouldn't make a very large profit here."

The bankers looked at the vet with fresh interest. He was speaking their language, and their greed soon overtook the earlier sense of fear in their minds.

Each of the men now stood, shook hands, and headed to the exit of the curling center that led onto a back parking lot and their waiting vehicles.

Morin got into his Lincoln then drove to the west side of town toward Newcastle. Just outside of the town, some six miles from Chatham, he turned down a side street in the small community of Chatham Head. At the fourth bungalow on his left, he pulled into a small driveway behind a beat-up old Plymouth sedan.

At first, Morin thought nobody was home. He knocked louder on the side door, which finally opened to reveal a small man dressed skimpily in jeans and a dirty, white tee shirt. The figure opened the door, and Morin followed him through a small porch area, then through another door into the man's kitchen. Morin needed to stoop when he entered.

"What's happening, Harold?" The smaller man was probably in his late forties. He was balding, with sideburns that reached his mid-jaw line. Deep furrows in his forehead belied a life unlike that led by Morin. His eyes were black and shifty, not contacting Morin's, and he scratched the four-day growth on his face, looking behind Morin, checking things out.

"I'm here alone," said Morin. "And I'm cool. I just had a meeting with Dexter and his banker buddies. We're ready, my man."

A nasty smile appeared on the other man's face.

"Come on in, let's talk."

It was mid-afternoon on Tuesday. After speaking with Jake, Detective Faraday and Const. Flynn both approached the Chief of Police William Young with the information they had learned to date. Chief Young was the one to come up with the idea, and it made some sense to the detectives.

"Since you believe the testimony of the young bankers, why not take it a step further?" Chief Young asked. He was referring to Jake and Sharon. "England seems to have connections with the street people here in town. Miss Donovan and England are obviously serious about each other, so we may as well also have her in this to give him some support.

"I think England and his friends can help you get to Harte. For a while now, we've been trying to find the source of a meth supplier. You know what, boys? I think there's a tie-in with Jimmy Whalen's sudden demise and the drug problem in town."

And just like that, they received the Chief's concurrence to meet with England and Donovan as soon as possible. Also, Chief Young suggested they should continue to hold the impression of suspicion over the two bankers, at least for the short term. By doing so, he hoped the two would continue to be forthcoming with any information they uncovered. Flynn called Jake and Sharon, and he arranged a meeting at his office early that evening.

Their meeting with the two policemen lasted for over an hour on Tuesday evening. Sharon had met Jake at the town precinct right after work, and they had got down to business shortly after 5:00 pm. It soon became apparent to Jake that with Doyle gone, he was still the prime suspect in the theft of the $6000 from his cash compartment at the bank.

And if he could not defend himself from that crime, he knew it would not be a big leap for the police to also consider him as a suitable candidate for Doyle's death. Not only that, since the police were aware of his relationship with Sharon, it would also be reasonable for them to conclude she was part of some cockamamie scheme he had dreamt up.

"Okay, Jacob," said Faraday. "Just so I have this right, you are saying it was Doyle who took the six grand from your cash? And you, Miss Donovan, believe this story?" Faraday gave both of the witnesses a hard look. The two bank employees nodded their heads vigorously in agreement.

"Further to that, you have reason to believe Doyle could have owed money to Darryl Harte. You think Harte is some sort of partner-in-crime of Jimmy Whalen's, the guy we found the day of the storm?"

"Yes, sir," Jake said. Faraday sensed the fear in Jake's voice, and he pressed this factor to his advantage.

"Well, here's the bad news, folks. The gun we found has Whalen's prints on it, and the gun is registered to the Bank of New Brunswick. We also recovered a thumbprint belonging to you, Miss Donovan. And two latent prints from *your* right hand Jake. Care to comment, folks?" The detectives were confident now in their approach.

"Sure," said Jake, now responding with a bit of anger in his voice. "My prints are on it from the day Sharon and I took mutilated cash to the Bank of Canada two months ago. Sharon's prints would be on that gun for the same reason, Detective."

Faraday looked at the two bankers for a long time without responding to Jake. Then he gave them a small grin and shook his head.

"I gotta give it to you kid, you seem to have all the right answers," Faraday slapped both of his huge hands on the desk in front of Jake, then he stood up. He looked over at his partner and said, "See what I mean, Don? The guy's gotta be innocent. Same as you, Miss Donovan. Mind you, your alibis for Whalen's murder are a little on the weak side."

"Whalen was *murdered?*" Jake exclaimed.

"Uh, yeah. I guess we forgot to mention that," he said. "Look, you guys. This is very serious business, but you *are* involved to a certain extent. So, you are in jeopardy." Faraday stopped and appeared to reach a decision. "Listen, if you are telling the truth, I think we can keep you safe. However, we'll need your help."

The two detectives spent the next half-hour developing a plan that would let Jake get closer to the truth. If he had the nerve and if he could trust the police.

Sharon and Jake were sitting at her kitchen table, each with a fresh cup of coffee, and they were rehashing their meeting with the detectives. Jake was taking the lead, trying to calm Sharon, who was in a great deal of stress over the entire situation.

"Oh my God, Jacob. Ordinarily, I'd just suggest we go to the police about this, but that's exactly what we just did, and it sure hasn't helped us much." She was again on the verge of sobbing.

"I know this is freaking you out, Sharon. But trust me, we'll get through it. I think Faraday and Flynn know what they are doing. I don't know about you, but I sure can't afford a lawyer. Besides, what could a lawyer do? Hell, we're innocent, and the cops know that. I think they are just using this as an excuse to get us on their side, see?"

"Jacob, this is dangerous. People are being killed!"

"I know. And you're right, we'll have to be very careful. I want you to stay very much in the background of this. I know a few guys who I can talk to, maybe get a bit more info for the detectives. It's just as well the bank has temporarily suspended me. At least, now I have the time to look into some things that Faraday talked about." He finished his coffee and put on his jacket.

"I'm heading out, Sharon. Keep your doors locked, just to be on the safe side. I'll call you later tonight, I promise." He kissed her softly and went to his car, driving back to town.

Chapter Twenty

When Jake entered *Joe's Billiards,* it was eight-thirty. Only two of the eight tables in the local pool hall were active. Lennie Hachey and Donnie Mitchell, Jake's closest friends aside from his band mates, occupied the table farthest away from him, and they looked up when they heard him approach.

"Are you guys looking for a game or just practicing?" he asked them. "I know you both can use it."

"Not if we're playin' you," Lennie retorted.

Jake laughed. It was good to be with his buddies again. He had been feeling strained over the past week, and now he could almost feel the built-up tension running off his body.

"Who wants a beer?" Jake asked, and soon the three of them moved to the bar area and got down to business.

According to Faraday, Chief Young had for some time suspected a group of unpleasant characters from out of town had set up some type of drug ring in their community. He saw the recent deaths as being connected to such a group, and he dearly wanted to be the one to bring this to an end.

The Chief had agreed to go along with the plan to enlist the help of young England, but only on the strict condition that Faraday could guarantee the young man's safety.

Therefore, Faraday kept repeating to Jake throughout their meeting, the absolute necessity for Jake to keep everything about his involvement in the plan to himself. Jake understood the seriousness of what he and Faraday had discussed, so he had to be careful in his selection of words with Lennie and Donnie.

"So, how's the job at the bank going?" Lennie asked.

"That's the thing, guys. I guess you could say I'm on a kind of 'suspension'. There was a theft at work. It involved me and Ron Doyle. So, the police are involved and I'm off until they conclude the matter. The fact is, I am innocent."

"Man, that's gotta suck," Donnie Mitchell said.

"Doyle set me up, but dammit, I can't prove anything. And now that he's dead, it's just my word against a long-time former employee. You know how this is going to end, right?"

"Jeez, Jake, you're right," Lennie said. "And, hey, I don't wanna speak ill of the dead, you know, but like I mentioned the other day, that guy Doyle wasn't all that much of a model citizen."

"So you said, Lennie," replied Jake. "Something about his association with Darrel Harte and *his* crew. Maybe a gambling habit he had?" *There, he threw out a line to them. Let's see if he'd get a strike with it.*

Donnie Mitchell looked hard at his friend Lennie, then back at Jake. "Jake, you never heard this from me, but Doyle, whether or not he knew it, was in way over his head with Harte." Again, he looked at Lennie Hachey and continued.

*"*What do you know about Jimmy Whalen, Jake?"

"Uh, not a lot, Donnie. Isn't that the dude they found down on the wharf the evening of our last storm? Somebody said he shot himself?" Jake said nothing about the police finding the bank's .38 revolver with Whalen's body. Again, Jake saw his friends look fearfully at each other. Donnie picked up his *Moosehead* beer and took a long drink from it.

"Whalen and Darrel Harte were good friends. They took turns hosting their card parties. Now hear me good, Jake. Everybody in town knows Whalen. Strike that. Everybody *knew* Whalen for his *special* street product." Jake just looked blankly at Mitchell, who then continued. "He was growing his own pot, Jake, but hitting it with meth. The word around town was that he cooked that shit himself in some cabin back in the Napan woods."

"Guys! If true, then I see what you mean about Doyle being out of his league. That's bad-ass stuff, I guess. Never tried it. I hear it's very dangerous and highly addictive?"

"My friend, you do *not* want to try it. *Ever!*" Donnie emphasized.

"Well, with Whalen gone, that should put an end to at least that local problem, no?"

"No way," Lennie Hachey said with a certain amount of disgust and anger in the tone of his voice. "You watch. Give them a week, tops, and they'll be replacing Whalen at his *cookhouse* with some other loser.*"

Jake couldn't help noticing the change in Lennie's voice. He was now practically sobbing. "Sorry," he said, quickly wiping his eyes.

"No, *I'm* sorry, Lennie. Did I say something personal there?"

"Well, yeah. My older brother, Frank. I don't think you knew him, Jake. He, ah, committed suicide last year. Jumped off the bridge. He was a meth head, Jake. He was hooked on that shit that Jimmy was pushing. I know it, but like your situation with Doyle, I don't have any actual evidence to prove it. And you know, Frankie was just another town druggie, no huge loss," Lennie said. His statement left unfinished; Lennie began to peel the label off his empty beer bottle.

"Lennie, you said *'they'll'* be replacing Jimmy Whalen with a new loser. Do you know who *'they'* are?"

"No, I don't, Jake. And listen, I think you should just stay the hell out of this entire bunch of shit. Hopefully, you'll get back in with the bank and you can continue with your life. My advice would be to get the hell out of Chatham."

"Here's the thing, Lennie. I can't leave. At least not before I clear my name. If I leave now everyone in town will believe I took the bank's money, even if the cops can't prove it. I can't have that, dammit! Besides, Sharon Donovan and I, ah, she works at the bank, and you know …"

"Yeah, I get it, Jake," Lennie said. "You and she are in a 're-*lay*-shun-ship," he added, now teasing Jake. His somber mood had vanished.

Jake smiled. "Guess you're right. But yeah. And the thing is, she is kind of involved. We've got to clear our names, guys."

The three sat in the bar area, finishing their beers, and watched a game of eight-ball being played by two young men on the table next to the one where they had been playing.

"You guys want another beer?" Jake asked, knowing Lennie and

Donnie had never turned down a free beer in their lives.

They left their places at the bar and Joe handed them each a fresh pint bottle of *Moosehead,* which they brought with them to the table next to the young eight-ball players where they could check out the guys next to them. Neither Jake nor his two friends knew the two young men, and depending on the caliber of their pool skills, they might get a game going.

If it came to that, this was Jake's playbook. He couldn't remember the number of times he and his close pals went into their act. When they were sure they had a couple of strangers next to them who might want to take advantage of some 'easy marks', the three locals would fake being drunk, and pretend they were quite inept at the game. It might be an opportunity to make a few bucks, get his game back, and feel a little better about himself. In a matter of minutes, he had the two young guys pegged. He was quite certain they were young airmen, stationed at the airbase just outside of town. From their loud language, he could also tell they were boastful and somewhat rude. Perfect.

He turned to each of his friends and gave them a meaningful look. It was the look that told Lennie and Donnie, *hey boys, we got a couple of fish next to us here. Let's have some fun.*

Jake started laughing and stumbling around the table. Lennie and Donnie got into their roles, and they began their 'sting'. Jake struck the cue ball to break the group of fifteen colored balls that Donnie had just racked into a tight-knit triangular pack. Eight of them, the one-ball through to the eight, were all solid colors; the remaining balls, numbered nine through fifteen, were stripes. Each of them had a white stripe over similar colors as their related solids. The eight-ball was a solid black.

"Oops!" Jake loudly exclaimed, as his cue ball flew in the air over the racked balls, not hitting any of them, and landed close to where the two young airmen were playing.

"*Shcuze* me", Jake slurred, as he stumbled over to pick up the cue ball for their table from the floor by the airmen, overacting to set up his marks. They were playing a game called 'Five, ten, and'. This was Jake's favorite money game, where the object was to make as many 'money balls' as frequently as possible. Specifically, these were the five, eight, ten, and fifteen.

Before the game, the players would decide what the 'value' of these balls would be. When a player put one of these balls in a pocket, he would receive from each of the other players whatever value was in place. The rules called for the game to be played in a straight rotation format, whereby the one-ball had to be made first, then the two, the three, and so on through the remaining twelve balls.

The skill, however, lay in being able to make as many of the money balls in various ways, so long as the first ball struck was in its proper sequence. For example, say the three-ball was the next to be played. One could hit the three-ball first, which could then strike, say, the eight, and direct that money ball into an available pocket. This was called making the eight in a valid 'combination' shot. In that case, the other players would pay the shooter, who would then remove it from the pocket and place it on a fixed circular spot on the table, so designated by a small circular white decal. It would once again be in play, and any player could make it again, either through rotation or as a 'combination' shot.

Another way of making a money ball was by using the cue ball to hit a required *non-money* ball first, then carom the cue ball onto a money ball and direct the money ball into a pocket. Again, the money ball would be 'spotted' for future use.

Jake and his partners were quite adept at any of these types of shots. In their current game, however, for the sake of putting on a show, they certainly didn't exhibit any of these talents. Indeed, the players at the table next to them assumed they were three local drunks. The two young airmen had seen that Jake and his buddies were playing the popular game of eight-ball, paying five dollars to the winner.

The taller of the two was probably in his mid-twenties, wearing a blond brush cut and an acute case of acne. He ambled over to Jake.

"Hey, my name is Stuart. I don't suppose you'd care to allow us in a game or two, would you?"

"Sure, why not? Okay with you Lennie? Donnie?" and he burped loudly. "But just so ya know, Stuart, we're playin' for money, okay? Five bucks a game."

"Oh, that's okay. This is Howard." Stuart brought his friend over to Jake's table, a shorter guy, black mustache, coke-bottle glasses hanging off an oversized schnozzle. Jake made the introductions all around.

"But" continued Stuart. "Eight-ball is kind of lame. Want to make it a more friendly game of Five-ten, and? Say, five bucks a ball?" He gave Jake a huge grin that was not at all friendly. Jake studied the floor, pretended to look doubtful, then he turned back to the blond guy.

"It's your call, but go easy on us, boys." Unseen to the airmen, he gave a wink and a smile to Lennie and Donnie.

Game on.

Chapter Twenty-one

The first thing to strike Faraday's senses when they entered Jimmy Whalen's Dodge Ram was the powerful odor of stale cigar smoke. *At least,* thought Faraday, *the scent of cigars hid the other smell which he was expecting. The forensics people had correctly not yet cleaned the vehicle, and there was evidence of the horror that had taken place all about them.*

When he commented on the stale smoke smell to Flynn, it did not surprise him to be corrected by his assistant.

"Boss, what you smell is the aroma of a *cigarillo*. It has a milder scent, probably rum-soaked," he said, sniffing the air in the truck's front interior.

Before Faraday could debate the point with Flynn, it only took them two minutes to find evidence that confirmed Flynn's statement. On the floor of the truck, just under the driver's seat, Faraday saw a clear cylindrical cellophane wrapper. The gold-leaf ring in the middle of the plastic tube bore the brand name and ad that read *Old Port Colt Small Cigars, Wine & Rum Tipped.* Faraday, a bit pissed off, nevertheless shook his head in wonder at the seemingly endless store of trivia carried by his assistant as he carefully picked up the cellophane wrapper using his pen. He then deposited it into a glassine plastic evidence bag.

They continued their search for another half-hour but found nothing further of interest. Their next stop took them to the office of the Chief Medical Examiner, where they dropped off the wrapper in the vague hopes that they might find prints not belonging to the deceased. They both then went home for an early night's sleep.

While the detectives were busy searching Jimmy Whalen's truck, Jake and his townie friends had hustled the two airmen out of approximately $200 by the time their marks had both realized what was going on. The two young RCAF corporals left the pool hall dejected by their losses, and Jake ordered a final round of *Moosehead* beers for the three of them.

"That was fun, boys," said Jake. "I needed something like that to pick me up."

"So what now?" Lennie asked seriously, obviously regarding Jake's immediate problem.

"I don't know for sure, Len. I'll talk to the detectives, see what they have in mind. Lennie, we don't have to talk about your brother, but maybe there's something we can do, as a kind of tribute to him, you know? If you're interested?"

"Absolutely, man. What did you have in mind?"

Donnie Mitchell then got into the conversation. "Count me in as well, Jake. Frankie was a good friend. What happened was not right, and somebody should do something about it before other people face the same end as poor Frankie."

"Okay. I'm going to speak to Detective Faraday about this and see what he can do. Do either of you guys know where this cabin is located?"

"No," said Lennie. "But leave it with us, Jake. "I know a guy who knows a guy. Call me tomorrow, man."

It was only 9:15, so Jake made a call to Sharon, and she agreed to see him. On his way there, he stopped to pick up two coffees and a box of glazed donuts, his favorite treats. When he pulled into Sharon's driveway, once again he noticed the movement of a curtain in the next-door neighbor's picture window. *I'm tired of this,* Jake thought to himself. Then, on impulse, rather than going directly to Sharon's front door, he quickly strode to the neighbor's townhouse and knocked on the door.

"Come on Joan, let me in. It's Jake England, and I know you're there. I think we should talk. Please."

The last thing Sharon expected to see on her doorstep at this hour of the night was her neighbor Joan Benton. Jake, yes, she knew he was coming down to see her, but why was he with the Benton woman?

"Hey, Sharon. I don't believe you have formally met your neighbor yet. This is Joan Benton. Joan, my girlfriend, Sharon Donovan. Ladies, I think it's time we discussed a few matters." When Sharon saw Jake's car in her driveway, she was at least pleased that he had arrived at her place initially, then had gone over to her neighbor's residence.

"Please, Joan. Come in," Sharon said. When she directed Joan and Jake to her living room, she offered them something to drink.

"I bought a couple of coffees but under the circumstances, Sharon, maybe, you know . . ."

"Of course," Sharon said, taking the hint, and she went to her kitchen. When she returned, she had three wine glasses on a tray, along with a chilled bottle of *Pinot Gris*.

"I hope this is okay. It's all I have at the moment."

"Excellent, thanks, honey." Jake then filled their glasses, and they eased back in their seats. Sharon and Jake sat on the sofa, and Joan Benton in the easy chair.

"So, Joan," Jake started. "We've known for some time now that you are aware Sharon and I have been seeing each other. We also know that you had been having a relationship with our former workmate, Ron Doyle. We're sorry for what happened to him, Joan. We want you to know that, right Sharon?"

"Yes, Joan. And can I say something else, since I believe we're going to be having a candid conversation? For a brief period last year, Ronald and I were also more than 'fellow workers'," she said with irony in her voice.

Then, for the first time since coming into Sharon's home, Joan spoke. "Oh, please spare me. Yes, I was having an affair with Ron. I also knew he had dated you previously, Sharon. Frankly, I know he still wanted you. And Jacob, there was a lot of hatred toward you because of your relationship with Sharon. So, let's not pretend we are all in one big *kumbaya* unit here," Her anger took Jake and Sharon by surprise.

"Look, I am not mad at you guys. And, Jacob, I can't be mad at Ron, can I? After all, he's gone. I'm mad at myself, don't you see?" Joan started to sob, and Sharon got up and went to the bathroom for some Kleenex tissues. Joan had somewhat composed herself when Sharon returned. She took a tissue from Sharon, dabbed at her eyes, and took a healthy drink of her wine.

"Our relationship was not good," Joan said. "Ron simply wanted another woman, and despite what he told me, there was no way he was going to leave his wife. I should have broken up with him long ago," she added, and took another long drink.

Sharon nodded to her in consolation. "I understand, Joan. I was in the same boat," she said, giving Jake a meaningful look. Jake then took over the conversation.

"Joan, Sharon and I are trying to find out more about Ron's lifestyle. When he died, he left me in an unpleasant situation. There was a theft at the bank, and he made it appear as though I took the money. I'm certain he stole the money himself, but I can't prove this. Is there anything you can tell us about his outside connections, or what he may have gotten himself into during the last year?"

"You mean his gambling habit?" she asked.

"Well, exactly! I heard he was a regular at Darryl Harte's poker parties?" He phrased his answer as a question, hoping and thinking that Joan's response to his first question showed she may know more about Doyle than the police possibly did. He waited for her next response.

"Yes. I knew Ron was spending a lot of time at Darryl's. And sometimes Jimmy Whalen would host a game. God! I'm pretty sure Jimmy had more going on than his card games, though."

"What do you mean, Joan?"

"I mean, Jimmy was dealing pot, for Christ's sake! Everybody knows that, Jacob. And I'm no angel. Occasionally, Ron brought some down here with him."

"Did he ever have anything stronger than weed?"

"Nothing that I could swear to, but sometimes Ron was just, well, way over the top, know what I mean?"

"So, you think Whalen was also moving some hard drugs to the locals?" Jake suggested.

"Again, I have no proof, but yeah, I think he was."

"Listen, Joan, you may get a call from the police about this. You've done nothing wrong, so you have nothing to worry about. But I think there are some bad people around. Be very careful who you talk with until they sort this out, okay? But know this: we're all friends here. You can talk to us whenever you want. Come on, we'll walk you back over to your place."

It was late by the time Jake got home. He had the feeling that things were moving fast. At least he felt that he and Sharon had gained an ally tonight. They realized Joan Benton was just another trophy of Ron Doyle's and they felt sorry for her. Who knew? She may provide them with additional information at a later time. For now, Jake looked forward to meeting with Faraday in the morning.

Chapter Twenty-two

It was 10:15 the following morning and Faraday had just been speaking with Floyd MacNutt at their forensics department. His partner Flynn sat beside him at his desk. The news was ambiguous. Yeah, they could pull a print off the cellophane wrapper found in Whalen's vehicle. Plus, the good news was that it did not belong to Jimmy Whalen. The bad news was that it was not from somebody currently in their records. Their thoughts were interrupted by Faraday's secretary, who opened his door to announce the arrival of Jacob England. Faraday ushered the young man into his office, and they got down to business.

"Good morning, Jacob. I gather you have still not returned to your job at the bank?" asked Faraday. "I wish we had some positive news for you. I know you must be eager to get this entire business settled."

"Well, yes sir, I am," replied Jake. "But more so for clearing my name, not necessarily for the job at the BNB. More and more I'm having second thoughts about working there. Maybe I was meant to do something else."

"Oh yeah? And what might that be?"

"I don't know yet. Are you guys hiring?" Jack said this with a small grin. Faraday thought the young man was probably only half-joking; but it was hard to tell. The kid had a way about himself. Confidence, street smarts, something. Faraday couldn't say for sure, but whatever it was, he liked the guy. He reminded him so much of Flynn, his assistant.

"Put on a few pounds, son, and we'll talk."

Jake nodded at the senior detective and sat on the chair that Faraday had pushed over to him. "I guess I could do that," he said. "In the meantime, what about our case?"

Faraday looked at Flynn and chuckled. "*Our* case?"

"Sure," said Jake. "I've been talking with a few of my friends. Guys who have a pretty good ear to the ground, and they tell me they think some people have a meth cookhouse operating somewhere in the woods. I'd like to help you and Don locate it."

"Son, that's a job for the police."

"Not to be too critical, sir, but my friends think you guys could use some help locally. They're good people, detectives, and they want to see this shit taken off the streets before we lose more of our young people to what these bad guys are selling. I think I can get into some circles that you and Don couldn't. It's as simple as that, sir. But I'd like to have your backing."

There, he had put the offer out to them. He was offering himself to them to be used as a sort of amateur undercover agent. And so far, Faraday and Flynn just looked at each other. At least nobody had thrown him out of the office. Yet.

Don Flynn pulled another chair over to Faraday's table and sat down with them. "Tell us what you have in mind specifically, Jake."

Just then, another meeting was being held, and it was about as far from Jake's as you could get, ideologically speaking. Harold Morin sat across from the man who had just finished lighting up an Old Port Colt cigarillo, much to Morin's dislike.

"Jesus, Alain, do you have to smoke those things?" Morin fairly yelled at the smaller man.

"No, I don't have to, but I want to. Now, why did you call me here? I got somethin' happening back in my pad, you know what I mean?" The man gave Harold Morin a creepy smile. He shuddered when he thought of the violence this man was capable of committing. Morin had absolutely no desire to know any more about this creature than he already did. His associate in Montreal had sent Alain Benoit to 'assist' him last week after Morin had explained their current 'cook' was a meth-head and the operation was in jeopardy.

All he was told by the associate was that this Benoit guy would make

Harold's problem go away. So, the less he knew about Benoit, the better. A tattoo on Benoit's right arm indicated he was a member of a biker gang called Popeye MC. The tattoo was a flag of the notorious Quebec gang showing the iconic cartoon sailor smoking his pipe while astride a motorcycle.

Morin rose from the table where the two were sitting in the rear of Morin's veterinarian shop, and he crossed the room and went to a side window, which he raised in anger.

"We paid you good money for your last job with us," said Morin. "But I'd like you to stick around the area for another couple of weeks, just until we get this operation underway."

"I don't understand what the big deal is, Morin. You now have, thanks to me, a meth shop in need of a new cook. You have the recipe for the product. Hire a new cook. No problem."

"You don't get it, Benoit. This is a small town. Everybody knows everybody. That includes our deceased friend, Whalen. I believe the police are now looking into his death as a homicide. That means we need to set up somebody for the police to look at for his murder before they consider me, the new vet in town, you understand? We need to give them somebody that was close to Whalen who knew what he was up to. Somebody with a checkered background."

"Do you have somebody in mind?"

"Yeah, I do," said Morin. "But I can't do this myself. I'll need your help."

"Tell you what, Morin. You get in touch with the man in Montreal and have him get in touch with me. That's the way it's done. *Capische*?"

"Yeah, sure." Morin was afraid of this. But it had to be done. There was just too much at stake. The numbers he had seen in Laval, Quebec predicted that he would be a millionaire three times over in as many years. And the plan only required one more investment.

He could handle it. He'd have to. Otherwise, his Montreal associate would come to see him, and that would not be good.

Jake, along with his buddies Lennie and Donnie, drove the back roads of Napan looking for some sign of the meth cook house they had heard was somewhere in this area. They were now on East Napan Road, the third and last bit of info Lennie's buddy was able to suggest as to the elusive 'cookhouse'.

The problem was none of them had any idea what they should look for. How big would such a building be? What type of structure housed a crystal meth lab, for Christ' sake? How many people were normally involved in the production of meth? These thoughts and more raced through Jake's mind as he sat in the front passenger side of Lennie Hachey's four-wheel-drive 1967 Ford half ton.

Lennie and Donnie both knew this part of the province better than he did, so they had elected to take his vehicle. Besides, the back roads were still very much covered with snow and Lennie's 4X4 was far better equipped to handle them than Jake's little Epic.

The community of Napan lies on the south side of the Miramichi River. This was farm country, mostly small dairy operations, some mixed vegetable farms. The Napan River, a small tributary of the mighty Miramichi, flows northeast alongside its parent to empty into Napan Bay, an initial small version of Miramichi Bay, and ultimately into the Northumberland Strait and the Atlantic Ocean.

There were many ways of accessing this area by boat from larger centers such as Montreal from the north, or Halifax, from the south. Jake thought of this as he viewed the terrain passing by outside the passenger side window of the Ford. Hell, they could probably move product to even larger centers south if they wanted. Places like Boston, New York, or Philly.

"See any signs of fresh tracks, Lennie?" Jake asked.

"Well, there've been a few people out and about. Just the regulars, though. I was hoping we'd see a lone structure with a snow-filled driveway and only one set of tracks in it."

"You mean like that one?" asked Donnie, sitting in the back seat. He was pointing back to where they had just passed a large copse of mature balsam firs that the recent storm had completely covered with snow. The trees hid a long narrow driveway running for about three hundred yards toward a large gray barn. This had gone unnoticed by both Jake and Lennie sitting in the front seat. Lennie pulled his truck to the side of the road, and they looked closer at what Donnie had seen.

There was only one set of tracks on the snow-covered driveway, which a late model GMC half-ton pickup had made. The truck was sitting there, the only vehicle in the yard where the tracks ended. Someone had parked the truck in front of an old rectangular building that was probably used at one time or another as a storage barn. There were three windows on the front of the structure facing the road where Lennie parked, and they were all covered with black plastic. The only sign of anything happening in the building was the GMC sitting in the driveway.

"What do you think, Jake? You want to have a look?" Lennie ventured.

Jake inspected the pickup and spotted the empty rifle rack on the inside of the truck's rear window. "I don't think that would be wise, Lennie. I think whoever is there is probably armed. There's an empty rack in the truck." He tried to look around the interior of Lennie's Ford. "You got any binoculars in your vehicle?"

"Nah," Lennie said. "Look, we know where this place is. We can always come back later. Besides, maybe it's nothing."

"True," Jake said. "But why put black plastic over the front windows? It's like somebody is hiding something. Shit, I wish I could read the back plate on the truck."

Then Donnie once again surprised them. "Ah, I think I can read that," he said. "It is, ah, DEJ8, no wait. DEJ301. Shit, are you guys blind?"

Lennie and Jake just looked at each other. "Eagle-Eye Mitchell comes to the rescue," Lennie exclaimed. "Come on, let's go back to town. There's a pen or pencil in the glove box, Jake. Make a note of the tag number along with the general description of the surrounding area. I think this is good info for your detectives, Jake."

An hour after Jake had driven to the precinct and Faraday had made a call to the Motor Vehicle Registry Department at the Province of New Brunswick in Fredericton, a minor celebration was in process in Faraday's office.

"This is excellent, Jake," said Flynn, holding the telex report for Jake to read. The registered owner of the 1966 GMC 910 half ton was one Darryl Harte, 715 Shore Road, Chatham, N.B. Things were falling into place.

Chapter Twenty-three

Dexter Sharpe was a better car salesman than he was a curler. His skip on the regular Thursday night men's foursome had earlier requested him to make a simple takeout against the opposing team, and Sharpe had missed the wide-open rock by a good two feet. The flub had resulted in his skip only being able to count two with his rocks on their last end, but it was one point less than the amount needed to at least bring the game to a tie and take them into an extra end. The skip, Ralph Crawford, was livid, and he was still ugly about it after the game while they shared a drink.

"Jesus, Dexter, I can't believe you missed that shot," the banker said.

"Forget it, Ralph, it's only a game," Sharpe retorted. The guy was getting to him. At that point, the lead curler on their team, Constable Herb Cable, broke out laughing.

Herb was actually the only official senior on the team, having reached the age of sixty-five. He could retire and begin receiving his police pension along with his Canada Pension and Old Age Security allotments. Much to the chagrin of the Chief, however, Herb elected to stay on. Not that he needed the money; it was simply that he was a widower, set in his ways, and had no one in his life besides his fellow police officers for company. He was a born gossipmonger and lived for the day-to-day mishaps of his fellow citizens to keep him in stock of sufficient tales of woe to spread around the town if, and when, he had an audience. Such as this evening, as the four men sitting at the table continued to verbally replay their game.

"What are you laughing at, Cable? I didn't see *you* making any great shots out there tonight," said Sharpe.

"Nuthin', Dexter. I was just gonna say that you weren't too sharp out there tonight. Get it? *Sharp*? Ha-ha!"

Now their second stone, John Hancock, the fourth man on the team, spoke up. "Say, that's a good one, Herb. Come on, Dexter, lighten up. Herb's only kidding, right, Herb?"

"Yeah, right, John," said Herb. But he could tell the others had quickly lost interest in what he might have to say. After all, he was not in the same league as these financiers. Even though he was just as good, if not better than them at the sport, he knew he was only there as a result of the fact that they needed a fourth, and he happened to be the last curler available. Other teams had grabbed onto all available younger, and less obnoxious curlers at the start of the year. So, Herb considered himself lucky to play on the team.

Like other times when he felt unwanted, he drew on his knowledge at work and his practice of spreading gossip to keep him in everyone's favor. And therefore, with a sudden lull in the group's conversation, he recalled a conversation he had overheard the day before yesterday between the Chief and Detective Faraday.

"Say, Ralph, I guess that young fella you got workin' there at the bank is thinkin' of comin' to work for us, eh?"

Neither Ralph Crawford nor John Hancock took note of what Herb Cable had just said. They were more interested in another game that was being played on the ice below the player's lounge where they were sitting. Dexter Sharpe, however, heard Herb, and his curiosity kicked in.

"Herb, can you use another drink? Yes? Boys, Herb and I are going to the bar. Are your drinks okay?" The other two nodded absently. When they reached the bar and were waiting for their new round of drinks, Dexter said quietly to Herb, "So Herb, what's this about the trainee at the BNB, he's going to work with you guys?"

"Yeah, Dexter. But keep this on the QT, okay? I kinda overheard the Chief talkin' to Faraday about it. They wanna use the young fella as a sort of undercover narc, you know. They wanna bust the ring that's sellin' hard drugs here in town; and, they feel because of his age, that he might have a better chance than us older guys to find out who's behind this. I think he's found the place where some guys are cooking meth. Supposedly it's out in Napan somewhere."

"You don't say," said Dexter. Then, almost as an afterthought, said, "What was his name, again?"

"England, Jacob England. Martin's young fella."

"Oh yeah, now I know who he is. Hell, if he's that good, maybe I can use him at my dealership," and he gave Herb a chuckle. "C'mon! Give me a hand with these drinks, Herb." They made their way back to their table, and Sharpe did not mention the matter again.

At least not that night.

The next morning, Friday, Dexter Sharpe called his new friend and investment partner, Harold Morin, and arranged to have lunch with him. Dexter was pretty sure Harold was 'connected'. Hell, he had to be. The guy was new in town from Montreal, and it was obvious he had access to sizable sums of cash. He had no problem at all coming up with ten big ones for their special project. Look at his recent purchases. The Lincoln would've cost him a minimum of ten grand (come to think of it, why didn't the guy buy one of his new Cadillacs?), and shit, a local realtor had recently told Dexter the vet had bought his new home with cash, no mortgage needed.

There was no question that Morin was certainly knowledgeable about the business deal he and his two banker friends had so far invested $50k in. But Dexter had a sneaky feeling that the venture wasn't totally above board, and it didn't take him long to come up with the type of 'business' they were dealing with.

So, after hearing from Herb Cable about how the Chatham PD were planning to use the BNB employee as an amateur undercover 'agent' in their fight against the town's drug problem, Sharpe thought it wise to sidestep his two bank associates and speak directly to Morin. Both Crawford and Hancock were wussies. He could not rely on them for much more concerning their investment and anyway, he sensed they would soon want out.

That would be just as well, so long as they simply redeemed their original capital plus their guaranteed return of twenty percent, and kept their mouths shut. Dexter was full of ideas as he pulled his Caddy into the parking lot of the Golf & Country Club next to the big black Lincoln.

When Dexter walked into the dining room, he spotted Harold Morin immediately, sitting at a table that was set up for a party of three. With Morin, there was a smaller man, rather unkempt, in Sharpe's opinion. The guy was wearing black jeans, a Montreal Expos tee shirt, and an old pair of black Wellington boots. With a three-day growth on his face and his slicked-back thinning black, greasy hair, he looked all the world to Dexter like he had just arrived from some biker gang convention. When Sharpe reached the table where the two were sitting, he could see the ruffian even sported some kind of tattoo on his right arm. It looked like a cartoon character sitting astride a motorcycle. So, his initial thought was correct. This guy *was* a biker, for Christ's sake.

"Good afternoon, Dexter. Say hello to my friend, Alain. Alain is here giving me a hand with something, and I've asked him to bring me to the club to meet up with you if you don't mind?" In fact, Morin thought it best to have Sharpe introduced to Benoit now, rather than spring him onto the man at a later date.

"No, of course not, Harold. I'm pleased to meet you, Alain." The guy returned Dexter's professional smile with dead, hooded eyes. Despite the man's small stature, he intimidated Sharpe, and once again, Dexter worried somewhat about the nature of the venture they had put money into.

"Alain," said Morin. "Why don't you look after that matter we discussed while I am have lunch with Mr. Sharpe?" He consulted his Rolex watch. "You may pick me up in, say, an hour's time."

Alain tipped his glass to his mouth and swallowed the rest of what appeared to Dexter to be rum and coke. He then left wordlessly, and the two were alone.

"Dexter, I can tell you are not that enamored with my friend." Before Sharpe could counteract that accusation, Morin continued. "That is understandable. His physical appearance does not enhance friendly intercourse, and his manners need improvement. He does, however, possess certain, ah, skills that I need from time to time. I'm sure you understand," he said with a small smile. "So, you mentioned you had something of importance to discuss with me. Something related to our 'investment'?" he asked, stressing the term.

And by taking the approach as he just had, Morin quickly put Sharpe at ease. Dexter noted this social skill that Morin had, this way of, well, almost manipulating people, and he admired the man all the more for it.

"Yes, Harold. I ran across some information last night that I thought I should share with you. And in full transparency, you should also know I have not mentioned what I am about to say to anyone else. Including our two banker associates." Dexter here paused.

"I understand," Morin said. "Continue."

And then Dexter related the business about the police considering Jacob England for help in their 'fight against drug crime' in the town. Sharpe then added, "For what it's worth, I also know that young England and Ronald Doyle were not at all on friendly terms. You recall Doyle was recently the victim of a drug overdose in town. The police, I understand, are now looking at this as a homicide. In fact, for a short time, they were looking at Jacob England as a person of interest for the crime. That has apparently changed, since I am told England has given them the location of some kind of cook house for drugs in Napan!"

"You don't say," said Morin, suddenly very interested in what Sharpe had disclosed.

"Look, Harold. From the outset, I have not asked too many questions concerning this project that the four of us have been putting money into. Call us naïve, but normally Ralph, John, and myself would insist on seeing a history of financial reports, balance sheet info, and a prospectus at the very least, before getting into an investment of this magnitude. We didn't, because we know deep down there is probably a criminal element involved here. Don't give me that look," Dexter said when it appeared that Morin was about to become self-righteous at the very suggestion that he, Morin, was involved in something illegal.

"That's right, Harold. We are not fools. All that aside, we are actually investing in *you*. We think you know what you are doing, and we really don't want to know the nitty-gritty details. But if I am correct in my assumptions, I think you can use this tidbit of info I've just passed on. After all, we just want to protect our investment, right?"

They gave each other knowing looks, thanked each other, and were enjoying a pleasant lunch on grilled salmon steaks when a familiar figure spotted Dexter from across the room and immediately waved his arms to him and began coming their way.

"Ah shit," said Sharpe, unable to avoid Herb Cable. "Don't look up, but the old guy coming to our table is a cop who I met curling. Just a dumb busy body, but just say 'hi' and I'll get rid of him, okay?"

"Hey Dex, how ya doing? Nice to see you here!" Herb then immediately extended his hand to Morin in greeting. They shook hands, Harold being very polite, engaged Herb in some small talk but he didn't leave. In fact, he drew a chair from the empty table beside them and was about to sit down.

"Don't mind if I join you boys for a spell, do ya?" he rudely suggested. However, before he was seated, both Harold and Dexter were up off their seats.

"We've gotta run Herb, you know, meetings, goddamn meetings," he said, and they both rose from their table to walk away.

"Hold up," says Herb. "I'll walk out with you to your car."

Once in his Lincoln, Harold gave a look to Dexter that said, 'get rid of this idiot!' and sped away. Unknown to Dexter, Morin had just been given a pretty good idea who Dexter's source was at the Chatham Police Department. Dexter got in his own car and left the club parking lot, leaving Constable Cable by himself.

Man, that guy must have money! Nice car! Herb says to himself.

Chapter Twenty-four

It was approximately 3:30 pm. Morin and Sharpe had finished lunch at the Country Club, and Benoit had looked after a 'little matter' for Morin. At this time, Faraday, Flynn, and Jake were approaching the secluded structure in Napan that Jake and his friends had earlier spotted.

When they arrived there, the driveway was vacant, and the building also appeared empty. Gone now from the three front windows were the black plastic sheets. They could see inside, but the only thing visible was one large room that was void of everything, save for a large propane stove, several rusted-out steel barrels, and a vast table that covered the far half of the floor area.

Faraday and Flynn both looked questioningly at Jake.

"Detectives, I swear this is the place. Harte had his GMC parked right here." He pointed to the ground in front of them. The driveway, which yesterday held only Harte's GMC half-ton truck, was empty. Also, there was evidence that several vehicles had been here since Jake, and his friends had visited the site.

"Shit, we've missed them," Jake said. "Can we get into the building and have a look around?", he asked Faraday.

"Not without a warrant," Faraday said. "And before you have us chasing down a judge in Chatham to provide us with one, we're going to need more than your word that Darryl Harte's vehicle was here. Besides, you can see for yourself there doesn't appear to be anything criminal happening here." Faraday nodded to the empty building.

"Right," said Jake. "Somebody even removed the black plastic sheets that had been covering the windows."

"C'mon, Jake. Let's roll back to town," Faraday said. "We'll check out Harte's residence, okay?"

Jake got into the back seat of their cruiser and before joining them, Flynn, who had quickly gone to have another look at the empty structure, quietly said to Faraday, "Jack, I spotted some remnants of what looks like black plastic that somebody had tacked to the windows."

"Got it." Faraday just nodded, and they were on their way back to Chatham.

The detectives and Jake arrived at 1704 Shore Road shortly after 4:00 pm. They pulled into the driveway of Harte's residence and went to his front door. There was no other vehicle at his home, and nobody answered their repeated knocks on his door. As a last resort, they checked his single-car detached garage. The door was down and locked, prompting Faraday to go to a side window of the garage and peer through a dirty window. Sitting in the garage was Harte's late model GMC truck. Faraday had a bad feeling about what he saw. After discussing the matter, the detectives decided that under the circumstances, a forced entry on their part was necessary. Faraday grabbed a crowbar from the trunk of their car and, in no time, they had gained entry.

Flynn instructed Jake to stay behind while the two officers approached the vehicle, their handguns drawn. Faraday was the first to notice that somebody had used a makeshift hose from a laundry dryer as an attachment leaving the end of the GMC's tailpipe, running into the passenger side window. The vehicle was not running, but he immediately told Flynn to break any windows he could find, and he quickly opened the garage pull-down door to its full position.

They rushed to the driver's door and opened it to find a body slumped back against the front seat. It was a man in his late forties, his full head of jet-black hair in contrast to his face, which was a bright cherry-red color. His wallet, which contained two hundred dollars, all in bills, also provided Faraday with a license showing the man to be Darrel Harte.

He was quite dead.

Faraday and Flynn were becoming uncomfortably close with Floyd MacNutt, their Chief Medical Officer. Over the past two months, MacNutt had performed three autopsies for the Chatham PD in connection with their search for a suspicious nature of death in each of the three victims. Certainly, he had performed more postmortems in this same time frame during his career, but not for the police. In the summer, there were always drownings, car accidents, even untimely deaths. But homicides in Chatham were a rarity.

Faraday and Flynn now studied MacNutt's third report in less than two months. The cause of death with Darrel Harte was carbon monoxide poisoning. Initially, it appeared as though Harte had taken his own life. They found needle tracks in both of his arms, and there was an abundance of crystal meth in the man's bloodstream.

However, as Faraday said to MacNutt, *fool me once, shame on me; fool me twice, fuck you!* And so, as with Jimmy Whalen, they had a second look. It surprised nobody when MacNutt also located a tiny fresh needle puncture in the back of Harte's neck. Then they found evidence of Pancuronium, the insanely powerful muscle relaxant that was used on animals. This was too similar to Jimmy Whalen's COD to be coincidental, and it gave Faraday another idea. He called MacNutt.

"Yeah, Floyd, Jack here. Look, I just realized something . . . I think we should take a closer look at Ron Doyle's death. He was buried in the Fall, not cremated, right?"

"That's correct. His wife was adamant about both the deceased and his parents not wanting him to be cremated."

"Will there be a problem from next-of-kin in allowing us access to the remains?"

"No, his widow was very co-operative during the entire process at the time. I see no reason for her co-operation to change."

"Perfect. I want you to arrange to have his body exhumed and I want you to check for something. Do you remember what we found in Whalen, and now Harte? I'm thinking the same thing for Doyle, my friend. Please call me when you have your results."

"How did things go for you today?" Harold Morin was with Alain

Benoit who was sitting across from Harold in his posh study. It was late Friday night, and he had invited Benoit over to his house in Newcastle just to get an update of sorts from him. Earlier, he had told Benoit about the police being aware of the location of the cook house, and Benoit said he would come up with something new. The smaller man lit up his ubiquitous Colt cigarillo, much to his host's disdain, and simply looked deadpan at his host, waiting for him to bring an ashtray to the coffee table.

"The problem with the stand-in production manager has been fixed," he said. Morin knew better than to ask for details.

"Then let me just ask you, Alain. I suppose we shall need a new location for the production of our inventory, as well as a new production manager. Let's assume our associate in Montreal can provide me with the latter. Have your local friends given any thought to where we might be able to set up a new shop?"

"The subject was also discussed, and yeah, there's a place closer to Miramichi Bay that would work."

For the next hour, Morin discussed with Benoit his plans to establish a new cookhouse for their lab, the need of close proximity for the proposed site to any local wharf facilities, together with the seclusion and general condition of the building. Benoit assured Morin that he was confident the building he had in mind was more than adequate for their needs and that a deal would likely be made this weekend.

Chapter Twenty-five

The first thing on Monday morning, Faraday and Flynn had a meeting with Chief Bill Young that they had earlier scheduled. They discussed the info about the suspected meth house in Napan they learned from Jake along with the trip Faraday, Flynn, and young England had made to examine the building and what they discovered. They also talked about the discovery of Darrel Harte's body and how they confirmed it was another homicide.

Outside of the Chief's office, Herb Cable was hanging around the water cooler, trying to pick up anything he might hear that would satisfy his nosy appetite.

For some time now, indeed, ever since Faraday had started the investigation into the death of Ronald Doyle, Constable Cable had been feeling snubbed by his superiors. He certainly had seniority over his younger peer, Don Flynn. So, he felt he was quite justified in being more than a little pissed off at Faraday for not picking him as his assistant in the Doyle case. And since that one, there were two new cases that he had not been brought into. Jesus, now to learn that the department was actually thinking of bringing a young *bank trainee* into the precinct. That was just not acceptable.

Cable saw the office door opening and pretended to be busy at the cooler while he listened to what was being discussed by the two officers coming into the general breakout room.

"That went well," said Flynn to Faraday.

"Well, if young England keeps coming up with good intel, we should soon break this wide open. Too bad we couldn't find any evidence in Harte's vehicle with the body."

Herb walked past them on his way back to the front desk where he was assigned for the day, nodded to them on the way, and kept going. When he reached the front desk, he picked up the phone and, on impulse, he looked at the wall clock. It was only 9:00 am, but what the hell, he made the call.

"Yeah, this is Dexter Sharpe speaking."

"Ah, good morning, Dex, this is Herb. Herb Cable."

This took Sharpe by surprise. Why would the police be calling him on a Monday morning? "Ah, good morning, Herb. What can I do for you? Are you in the market for a new vehicle?"

"Nah, Dex. Just thinkin' about our game coming up this week. You're gonna be able to make it, eh?"

"Ah sure, Herb." Dexter knew there was more to Herb's call than a nothing curling game, three days away. He also knew from experience that it was always best to remain silent when he felt the person on the other end of the line had something more to say. Silence in such situations usually acts as a prompt. Sure enough, after a few beats, Herb blurted out, "You know that young fella at the bank? The guy I told ya they were plannin' on hirin' here?" Dexter heard the anger in Herb's voice.

"Yeah, Herb. That must suck, eh? Wouldn't you have seniority over him for that *undercover* job?" He stressed the same word Herb had used the other night.

Herb was pleased his curling buddy understood his feelings. "Sure, Dexter. Man, I wish I had something on that guy. Did I tell you, for a while at first, Faraday and Flynn thought they had him for the murder of Ronald Doyle?"

Christ, this guy! thought Sharpe. He couldn't remember anything from one day to the next! "Ah, yeah, you mentioned that" Dexter said. Again, he held his silence, waiting. Then, Herb again broke their silence. "I guess they just found a body in Darrel's truck. Probably Darrel himself. He was pretty close to Jimmy Whalen, ya know. Anyway, they're lookin' for some kind of evidence."

Wow! Now, this was big news. "I guess so, Herb. Look, I've gotta run, so we'll see you Thursday night at the rink, if not before, okay?" Sharpe hung up and immediately called his vet friend and business associate to set up another quick luncheon meeting. He heard they usually served *Beef*

Wellington on Mondays, a dish he knew Harold Morin favored. Plus, he had a bit of news regarding the Chatham PD that he wanted to pass on. For what it was worth.

When Harold finished his *Beef Wellington,* he thanked Dexter for his hospitality. "Thanks for the lovely lunch, Dexter, I owe you one. Now, what was the news you had for me regarding the police department? It certainly sounds rather mysterious?"

"Right. Harold, earlier today I was thinking about our last conversation, specifically in relation to the news I had heard about the police giving consideration to using Jacob England, a bank trainee, as some kind of civilian undercover agent. I believe they thought he would be useful in infiltrating the local drug culture because of his young age, his being in a 'rock and roll band', and all that." He rolled his eyes at Morin to indicate to him that he very much questioned the wisdom of such a decision on the part of the police, if in fact that had been the case.

"But Dexter, if they have decided to use the services of young England, what do you think *I* should do about it?"

Sharpe studied his associate very carefully. He was almost certain that Morin was testing him. *What the hell*, he thought. *Just go for it!*

"I think, Harold, it would be wise to further protect *our* interests."

"And how would *we* do that?" Morin persisted.

"Well, we know that early on, when the police first determined Ron Doyle's death was a homicide, they were considering England as a suspect. After all, he has admitted to having an affair with a branch employee. A lady that Doyle was also involved with, which created a certain animosity between the two men. Then, he is implicated in a major theft of cash at the branch. Six grand, actually, and it was from his own cash box. He claims Doyle took it and framed him."

"Wait a second. So why would they want to take him on as an employee?"

"Fair question, Harold. Somehow, maybe with the help of his girlfriend, he was successful in convincing them he was innocent. By the way, I am getting this second-hand, from another cop there who I believe trusts me."

"I get it," said Morin. "Okay, so back to England. I don't understand how he comes into play here. How can we use him to help us protect our interests, as you say? He doesn't sound like the guy on our team, Dexter."

"Of course not. But I also just heard something else from my source at the Chatham PD. They discovered a body in Darrel Harte's truck over the weekend. He said it was made to look like a suicide and that they are treating it as another homicide?"

"Get to the goddamn point, Dexter." Now Morin seemed to be getting pissed off. He'd have to choose his words carefully.

"Well, it seems to me, Harold, somehow, maybe we could plant some form of evidence on England?"

"You mean, frame him for this latest homicide?" Morin said.

"Ah, yeah." He made a face like he had just eaten something distasteful. "And then, if that evidence happened to be discovered by my 'friend' at the department, they'd have no choice but to reopen their case against him for the Doyle murder. Am I right? And hey, then they would have more on their hands than they could handle, let alone looking into a drug operation here in town."

"Yes. I see what you mean, Dexter. Well thought out, excellent idea." Morin could see that this praise to his new associate was acting exactly like the product he was intending to put into production. He wasn't sure just how much Sharpe knew. He apparently had a good idea that their 'investment' was actually a drug operation of some type. But did he also have knowledge of the recent homicides and who was behind them? Morin would have to be careful how he handled Sharpe from here on in.

"Okay, leave this with me. It's good info, and worth looking at. Maybe I can do something with it." He looked closely at Sharpe's response, but he was not able to read anything more about the man's motivation. "I'll call you tomorrow, Dexter." He delicately wiped his mouth with a napkin from the table and stood to leave. Lunch was over.

Chapter Twenty-six

Jake and Sharon left the Vogue Theater around ten-thirty on Monday evening. They were of two minds regarding the quality of the movie they had just sat through. It was Elvis Presley's latest attempt at acting, a fluff musical western called Frankie & Johnny. It had Elvis playing the role of a riverboat entertainer. To Jake, Elvis should stick to his original profession as a singer and get the hell out of films. Sharon, on the other hand, didn't care if he wasn't another Richard Burton or Rod Steiger. The man was a *hunk*, and he didn't have to act. Just to watch him move his hips and hear him sing in his movies was pretty cool with Sharon.

After driving her home at her townhouse and staying for a coffee, they both agreed to make it a relatively early night. Since it was a Monday evening, there was only one show playing tonight and it had started at 8:00. Sharon had to get up early for work at least. Besides, Jake had rehearsed most of yesterday afternoon plus today on his own, and he was beat.

On his drive home, he failed to notice a vehicle tailing him. In the town of Chatham, there was seldom a need to keep an eye out for that type of danger, and it simply never occurred to Jake that somebody might be out to cause him harm. Consequently, just as he was casual about his surroundings, he was also carefree concerning his Epic. In any case, if somebody were to later ask him about his carelessness (and they would), his answer was that he had never locked his car doors before, so why start now?

The slight smell of cigar smoke in the Epic the next morning went unnoticed as Jake drove downtown to the precinct just after nine. He was to meet with Faraday following a call he received from Flynn last night. Faraday's assistant sounded somewhat vague about why they wanted to see him, and the cryptic call had caused Jake to become nervous. He was hopeful there would be some news as to any leads in the death of Darrel Harte pursuant to their discovery of his body on Friday. Flynn had made no mention of that to Jake.

When Jake arrived at the precinct he was sent directly to Faraday's office where he was surprised to find a third cop sitting with them at their usual shared table.

"Jacob, please grab a chair and join us," said Faraday. When Jake had a place at the table, he was introduced to Constable Second Class Herbert Cable. Faraday then looked seriously at Jake and continued. "Jacob, Constable Cable has received an anonymous tip that directly concerns you. Indeed, the tip is specifically related to the most recent homicide of Darrel Harte."

"I can't believe this, Faraday. I thought we had already covered all of this bull shit!" Jake shouted. His fear, anguish, and anger were apparent to all in the small room.

"Well, Jacob, we can easily dismiss the accusation. Let's take a quick look inside your vehicle."

"Not until you tell me what, *specifically*, somebody has accused me of supposedly doing in connection with that death. Otherwise, I'm getting a lawyer and I'm betting you will need to have something stronger than an anonymous caller to be able to obtain a search warrant." Jake was now more confident in his demands, but he was still at a total loss regarding the accusation they had just made against him.

"Okay, Jake, calm down. You know that you can save us a lot of time and energy with some cooperation. And I understand your anger. So, here's the thing. Cable received a message on our 911 facility while he was on duty last night. The voice was purposely distorted, probably by the caller speaking through a mask of some sort. We believe it was a male. The caller referred to a syringe that might be found in your vehicle and that it would be wise to have its trace contents analyzed. That's it."

"Jesus, Faraday! Okay, let's have a look in my car. You are right. Eventually, you'll have a subpoena, and you know me enough that I want to know myself what is there. But I'll say this: if we do find something, it was damn-well planted there!"

Five minutes later, Jake and the three officers were examining a large 20-gram, 3 milliliter, 1.5-inch needle and syringe. Jake, who had waited outside his vehicle while the two detectives performed their search, was flabbergasted by the discovery of the object that somebody had placed in the glove box of his Envoy Epic.

After Faraday had carefully placed the implement into an evidence bag for delivery to the Chief Medical Officer Floyd MacNutt, they returned to his office and resumed their discussion. Constable Cable had been dismissed and only the three remained at the table.

"Guys, you have to believe me," Jake pleaded.

Flynn looked directly at Jake, then asked, "Jake, do you smoke cigarillos?"

"Nah., I have the odd cigarette. Like, when I feel like having a beer, why?"

Flynn then turned his attention to Faraday. "It was the same odor, wasn't it, Jack." This was a statement, not a question, to his boss.

"Yeah, it was. Jake, once again I think you've been framed."

Jake could only give a puzzled look to the officers, but he was extremely gratified to hear what Faraday had just said. He let out a long sigh of relief and almost sobbed.

They told Jake about the odor of rum-soaked, wine-dipped Colt cigarillos that Flynn had detected in Harte's truck. At the time, Jake had not been allowed to enter the crime scene. And this morning he had been too preoccupied with Flynn's worrisome call to pick up on the aroma.

"It's difficult to take all of this in. Who would want to frame me for Harte's homicide? And why?"

"If we knew the answer to your first question, Jake, we'd have these crimes solved. As for the second, that is puzzling," said Faraday. "I mean, why *you*, in particular?"

"Exactly," Jake agreed.

Flynn jumped in at this point. "Jack, if somebody is attempting to frame Jake, I think the correct question should be 'why *now*?' I mean, sure, we know, or at least we are willing to make the assumption, that Doyle framed Jake at the outset to cover the theft of the six grand. But that was an entirely different matter. Why wasn't he framed for the deaths of Doyle and Whalen when they occurred? To me, the timing of this is off."

Their discussion was put on hold when Faraday's phone rang. After briefly speaking with somebody, Faraday looked at Jake and Flynn. "That was MacNutt. He just got the results of their secondary tests on the remains of Ronald Doyle. As suspected, there was also evidence of an injection found at the back of his neck. There is no doubt, it was the same drug, Pancuronium." Faraday picked up the evidence bag containing the syringe. "Anyone want to bet what trace evidence we're going to find on this syringe?"

Jake could only shudder at the thought of what was about to be a very bad next few days.

Chapter Twenty-seven

As of late, Dexter Sharpe was not feeling too good about the way Morin was treating him. He was getting the impression that the vet was dealing with some other players, and he was becoming worried that the investment made by him and his banker pals was in some sort of jeopardy.

To Dexter, Morin sounded a tad aloof when he was last talking with him by telephone. Well, too fucking bad if he had caught him at a bad time. Jesus, you'd think Morin would be a little more grateful for the work he had expended in order to gain the confidence of the other two investors. He checked his watch and decided to call his contact at the Chatham PD.

"Hey, Herb. Dexter here. What's new, my friend? Are we on for Thursday night?" He was referring to their weekly curling match.

"Hi Dex', glad you called. I might have to miss the game on Thursday. Things are pretty busy here at the precinct now, you know…"

"No, I don't Herb. Know what?"

"Well, that business I was tellin' you about earlier. You know, about them hirin' on that young banker? Well, I think he's got himself into a whole world of trouble. And now, the last thing the department will be doin' is takin' this guy on as an undercover agent."

"Oh yeah? And why wouldn't they do that?"

"Well, I can't say too much about it, Dex." Cable was practically whispering to him now. "But hell, I think he might be involved in all the shit that's been happenin' around here lately. They just found evidence in England's car that might tie him to the murders."

"Jesus! Okay Herb, I'll let you go. But keep me in the loop, pal. And, say, I hope you get some recognition down there for all you do," Dexter finished. At least he had some good news he could pass on to Morin. He immediately called the vet.

"Yes, hello Harold. This is Dexter Sharpe. Listen Harold, I was just calling to thank you for implementing the suggestion I made to you the other day."

What an idiot! thought Harold Morin. "Ah, yes Dexter. Perhaps we could meet privately to further discuss this matter? I am rather busy at the moment, but how about supper at the club?"

"Sounds fine, Harold. I'm looking forward to it."

Another snide put-down. Maybe it was time to have a man-to-man with the guy and let him know he wasn't happy with the way he was being treated. Sharpe went out to his Cadillac and drove off to the golf clubhouse. He heard from one of the boys that they were serving beef stroganoff this evening. Not his favorite, but it would have to do.

It had been a number of months since Lennie had occasion to meet with Alphonse Cormier, a cousin on his mother's side who lived in Baie Ste. Anne. The community, a fishing village on the east coast of the province, was situated on the south side of Miramichi Bay, only a few miles from where it emptied into the Gulf of St. Lawrence. Cormier was a lobster fisherman who owned his own boat, having inherited it from his deceased father. As a seasonal worker, he was currently receiving Government assistance but made good money when the lobster season was open in their area.

When Lennie and Donnie arrived in the village, they found him at the Crown and Anchor, a local pub. He was sitting by himself, nursing a glass of draft ale, and smoking a cigarette.

"Hey, man, how's the Rebel?", Lennie shouted over to the table where Cormier was sitting when he and Donnie came into the pub. Alphonse Cormier was a young man in his mid-twenties. His full head of black hair was swept back in a duck tail haircut, and he wore a black leather jacket over a white tee shirt. His late-fifties ensemble was replete with tight blue jeans that were tucked over a pair of black leather Wellington boots.

Cormier rose from his seat and gave both his friends fist bumps as he pulled out chairs from the table for them.

"Hey, you guys, have a seat! Donnie, my man, good to see you. And who is 'dis? Jeeze, you look good, dude!" Cormier was elated to see them, and he gave them a shy smile with his close resemblance to the character Jim Stark, played by his idol, James Dean in *Rebel Without a Cause.* "What brings you boys to our fair village?" he asked, at the same time signaling to the waiter who was idling talking to a girl at the bar.

"Trouble, my good cuz', big trouble," answered Lennie seriously.

Lennie and Alphonse shared enormous sadness. When Lennie lost his older brother Frankie to suicide, the bond between the two cousins became cement. This had happened when Alphonse also experienced a similar pain as that encountered by Lennie when his brother Placide came close to dying as the result of overdosing on the same drug that drove Frankie Hachey to take his own life. He had ended up in a psych ward in Saint John for a six-month stretch last year.

"How's Placide these days?" Lennie asked, and by the tone of his voice, Alphonse immediately knew that Lennie's visit was of a serious nature.

"Ah, Placide, he is doing okay. I see him regularly, Len, and I think he's going to be okay. You know, like 'dey say, one day at a time. 'Dere is a group here in the village that gets togedder weekly. 'Dey 'elp each other out and try to mentor de local teens at a club in town. 'Dey do good work, man."

"That's good to hear, cuz'. Look, the reason Donnie and I are in town is a bit related to that. We're wondering what you might know about a meth house that may have just set up shop in the neighborhood? If so, we have a buddy back on the river who is in trouble. He needs some intel to get him out of a bad situation. It goes without saying that anything we can find out stays on the down low."

If there was anyone down this way that had a good ear to the ground, it was The Rebel, and Lennie knew he could trust his cousin by coming to him. They were both on the same team.

"Well, it's funny you should ask, Lennie. Last week 'dere was a guy coming around, wanting to know who might have a boat for sale. But I'm telling you, Lennie, dis dude did not look like a lobster fisherman to me."

"Whaddya mean? He was good looking?" Regardless of the situation, Lennie loved to tease his young cousin.

Alphonse gave his cousin that shy, James Dean look. "Screw you, Leonard. Nah, I mean he was a biker guy. I recognized de tat on his arm from 'Popeye MC', a badass gang from Montreal. And his style of approach matched dat kind of rep. Not a guy you want to introduce to your sister."

"Why would he want a boat?"

"Dere you go. I'd say he has a product to export or import, wouldn't you? It's been 'appening around here, and if he had some kind of legitimate business, say, like a halibut or lobster brokerage, it would be a slick way to launder dirty money."

"I get it. So, what's the end of the story? Did you put this guy on anyone, or do you know if he is still around?"

"You are the first person that I've talked to about dis guy. I can check with some folks, though, Len. Why don't you order some chowder for yourself and Donnie, and I'll make a couple of calls. But not from here, okay?" Cormier made a backward gesture with his eyes to the bartender and waiter who were still talking with each other. "I'll be back in an hour; you guys stay put!"

It was, without a doubt, the best seafood chowder Lennie had ever eaten. Donnie agreed with him, and they ordered another two beers, just after finishing off their lunch. Alphonse, in a timing that Lennie was sure his cousin had rehearsed, landed at that moment, and Lennie yelled out to the waiter requesting an extra draft.

After the waiter set a beer down for Alphonse, the young Frenchman passed a piece of paper with notes on it along with a rough map. Lennie quickly folded the document and placed it in his pocket.

"I think you'll find what you're looking for dere," Alphonse said, keeping his voice low. "But Lennie, if I were you, I'd be extremely careful. Dis place is far off de beaten track and I have a bad feeling about anybody that's associated with it."

"I gather you got some info from reliable sources?" asked Lennie.

"Affirmative. De property belonged to Francois LeBlanc. He retired last year from fishing after his wife died of cancer, and he moved to Moncton to live dere wit' his father. He took a job working in the hospital. His boat, a forty-four foot Cape Cod, called *Sea Witch,* came with the house."

"Well, I guess there would be a record of the mortgage that a lender would have registered?"

"Nope. The word I get is that it was a cash transaction. A quarter of a million."

"All right, Rebel, you be good. Donnie and I are heading back to town, so thanks for all the help. We appreciate it."

"Later, Lennie. Keep your stick on de ice man."

Chapter Twenty-eight

Before driving to Baie Sainte Anne, Lennie had called Jake and told him where he and Donnie were going, and the purpose of their trip. Jake had asked them to drop into Sharon's place on their return into town and meet him there where they would discuss things further.

It was now after four and Jake had introduced his friends to Sharon. They had quickly settled down at her kitchen table to coffee while Jake studied a crude map that Lennie had given him.

"Sharon, could I see your telephone book, please?" Jake asked. After looking at it quickly, then referring to the notes Alphonse had written on the map, he said to the others, "Here we are. Francois LeBlanc, the former owner. He's listed under the Escuminac exchange, at 42 Point Escuminac Road. The place shouldn't be too hard to find, Len."

Jake's memory took him back to a trip he had taken with his parents and their two friends, ironically, Earl and Geraldine Doyle, Ron's parents. They had driven to a lighthouse somewhere in the area of the map that Jake was now holding.

"But your friend was right. It's located at the easternmost tip of central New Brunswick, right on the Atlantic Ocean. I've driven there before, and it's a beautiful area if you like rough seascapes, lighthouses, that kind of thing. More importantly, it's a perfect spot from which to bring in drugs."

"So, what are your thoughts, Jake?" asked Lennie.

"Well, it would be foolish and downright dangerous for us to go there ourselves. I'll call Detective Faraday in the morning and go over this with him, see what he wants to do."

"Okay, my friend. Donnie, let's hit the road," and the two rose to leave.

"Thanks, guys. Lennie, I really appreciate all you and Donnie are doing for us. We'll keep you informed as we hear things." The friends hugged each other, then Sharon and Jake were alone with each other. Jake sat by himself with his own thoughts while Sharon cleared the table. He and Sharon were not really hitting it off very well the past few days. He had chalked it up to stress and hoped things would work out in the long run, but he knew deep down that something serious was bothering her. His drive home was solemn, and he spent an anxious night wondering when all of this business would come to an end.

Herb Cable was a vindictive man. At the moment, the object of his desire for revenge was against the young bank trainee, Jacob England. He was now convinced England was working as an undercover agent for Chatham PD, based on the fact that he had again personally overheard Detective Faraday speaking with Chief Young just a half hour ago. He couldn't believe it, but it was true. He had heard it with his own ears: England was on his way into the precinct to discuss something about the whereabouts of the new meth shop that he had just 'discovered'.

The more he thought about it, the more irate he became. There had to be some way he could prevent this young upstart from finagling his way into the department and taking on a position that should have been given to their own man, himself, Constable Herbert Cable. Herb recalled his last conversation with his curling buddy, Dexter Sharpe, and he made a quick phone call before England arrived.

At ten o'clock, Jake was at the precinct as scheduled, and he was immediately taken into the Chief's office by Faraday with Constable Flynn. After viewing the map and discussing the details of Jake's meeting with Lennie Hachey, the Chief was impressed. At that point, they set about planning a raid on the house in Escuminac Point.

Even though Jake was excited to be involved thus far in the sting that was established by Faraday to take place tomorrow, he was disappointed to learn he was now being pulled off the case, for reasons of his own safety. Then he had an idea.

"Look, Detective, wouldn't it be better for you to catch these guys red-handed, as it were? Like in the middle of bringing in his product from offshore, or selling it to some local dealer. Well, yeah, that would be a bonus, but we don't know exactly when that will happen, do we?"

"Not yet, Detective," said Jake, a smile forming on his face.

Jake was sitting across the kitchen table from Sharon on the Friday afternoon following his meeting with Faraday and Flynn. To Jake, it was a good plan. Bold, but necessary. And after going over it in detail with the two detectives this morning, he was confident it would work. After it was over, Detective Jack Faraday and the Chatham PD could congratulate themselves for bringing down a major drug operation and solving several murders. More important to Jake, both he and Sharon would be able to regain their standing in the community and get on with their lives, whatever that might entail.

Essentially, the plan called for Jake to infiltrate the drug operation at ground level, that is, right at the point where the product was developed, the 'new' cook house in Baie Ste. Anne. He knew where it was located, and since the murder of Jimmy Whalen, he and the police suspected there would probably be a need for a new cook, or at least some other type of help in moving the product. So why not go directly there and apply for the 'job'?

It just might work. Nobody in the small French community of Escuminac knew him. He would have to speak with his buddy Lenny, but he was certain he would assist him. He also knew Lenny had family there who could also come to the party.

Filled as he was with confidence in explaining everything to Sharon, he was quite disappointed to learn she was very much against the whole plan.

"Jake, you simply don't appreciate how dangerous these people are," she pleaded to him. "You are getting into something way over your head here. Please, Jake, just forget the whole thing. We can both go to Moncton, or Saint John, or wherever. I don't care. I'm afraid for you, Jake, for us. Don't you see?" And she broke down and started crying.

Jake stood and pulled her out of her chair, holding her close. "I've got to do this, hon'. It means too much, and if we don't act now, I'm afraid of what else they may try to do to hurt me. The police will be right behind us on every move, and they'll have our backs, I promise."

He kissed her gently. "Look, I've got to run and go over this with Lenny." He left her and quickly drove to Joe's, all the while wondering if he was doing the right thing.

The pool hall was quiet when Jake entered the building just after eight. Lennie and Donnie were each nursing a beer, so Jake picked one up from the bar on his way to their table. It only took him five minutes to explain the plan to his friends, and he was happy when they both bought it. Finishing his beer, and after promising to pick up Lennie and Donnie in the morning, he drove home for an early night's sleep, advising them to do the same.

They'd need to bring their A-game with them tomorrow.

Sharon was beat. Physically and emotionally. When Jake had left earlier to meet with his buddies at the pool hall, she immediately poured a glass of wine for herself and decided to relax in a hot bath, maybe reflect on a number of things.

She had no doubt in her mind concerning her feelings for Jake. Yes, she was six years older than him, but what the hell? If he felt the same way, they would be able to live with an age difference. And yes, he had a tendency to be somewhat naïve about his trust in other people . . . probably not a helpful trait for somebody in the banking business. Maybe he wouldn't even want to stay with the bank when all of this other business was cleared up, then what? How could he make a living in a rock and roll band? Or was she being too judgmental about that part of his character?

Finally, she thought about her mother: a widow for the past three years, Dorothy Donovan was in her mid-sixties, but recently she had been showing signs of dementia, frequently forgetting everyday things in a matter of hours. Sharon often wondered how long it would be before she would have to consider taking her under her care. There was simply no way she would even think about having her go to one of the *old folk's* homes in town.

With these conflicting thoughts in her mind, she realized she was not solving any of her problems, and she decided to go to bed. Despite her feelings of unease surrounding her relationship with Jake, the hot bath and a glass of wine quickly allowed her to fall into a deep sleep.

She did not hear the new Lincoln pull alongside her driveway entrance.

At the time Jake was driving home from the pool hall, Dexter Sharpe was just finishing his beef stroganoff at the Golf and Country Club. The egg noodles were a tad under-cooked, and he made a mental note to mention this to the chef before leaving. The dinner with his investment partner, the new veterinarian Harold Morin, was somewhat of a disappointment, given that Morin had brought along his creepy associate from Montreal.

Why Morin needed to have Benoit with him so often was beyond Sharpe. The guy was downright rude. Just the way he ate his food, for Christ's sake. Slobbering, eating with his mouth open, shoveling his pasta into his mouth right off his fork with his left hand, all the while giving him a snide look, with those hooded eyes. A real nasty man, he was.

"So, Dexter. I wanted to tell you on the phone when you called earlier, but it was not the time. From now on, you should avoid calling me on my land-line telephone." Here, Morin frowned at his associate Benoit, who was continuing to display rude dining etiquette. "My friend has instructed me to tell you, we must start exercising caution in the way we communicate, yes? I am afraid some of our talks may be under scrutiny by the authorities."

"Uh, if you say so, Harold. Look, when do you think we'll be in a position to cash in on our original investment?"

That simple question from Sharpe now convinced Morin he had made a mistake bringing the auto dealer into his project. At least with the other two, the bankers, he rarely heard from them. Which was the way he wanted it. Well, it was something to which he'd have to give a lot of thought. Things had now proceeded too far for some idiot like Sharpe to fuck everything up.

"Soon, my friend. Soon."

Dexter missed the small smile from Benoit.

The three of them finished their supper, and Harold Morin instructed Benoit to run another errand for him, something that involved picking up a package or something; Dexter assumed it was food and groceries. When they were alone, he asked Dexter if he wouldn't mind taking him to his place. He had some important financial projections concerning their joint venture that he wanted to review with him; it shouldn't take too long.

Initially, Sharpe was reluctant to go with him, but Dexter now felt more important and involved in the project. In fact, Morin had even pointed out that he appreciated the optimistic views expressed by Dexter compared to the conservative bankers he had been forced to take on as side partners.

When they arrived at Morin's place, Harold brought Dexter downstairs to his rec room where he proceeded to spread out various cash flow projection sheets on his billiard table. In a matter of minutes, Sharpe was surprised when Benoit came into the room with a tray of canapés and two heavy crystal glasses containing dark rum and ice cubes. Benoit very politely then handed the drinks to the two businessmen and retired upstairs, leaving them to their own business.

The last thing he could recall was the toast the two had made, clinking their heavy crystal glasses together in a sign of success.

When Sharpe regained consciousness, the first feeling he experienced was one of confusion. He simply had no idea where he was, and the fact that he was in total darkness did not help. When he realized both of his hands and feet were bound, a sense of panic quickly established a large part of his ability to think clearly. He could not cry out; his mouth having been gagged. He was cold, and the steady hum of a motor suggested that he was in some type of refrigerated room. But where? How? And why?

In addition, Sharpe was totally unaware of another figure lying some twenty feet from him, also bound and gagged on the floor.

Chapter Twenty-nine

There is nowhere so desolate as the northeast coast of New Brunswick on a stormy, late winter morning. A strong wind blew on shore from the Atlantic, pushing gray clouds which at this point were only a hint of what would surely be coming their way later.

On their right, huge waves violently crashed against mammoth rocks that had been placed along the highway years ago to prevent erosion and flooding. Their vehicle's windshield wipers continued to beat ineffectively in an effort to clear the salt sea spray that constantly threatened to cover their forward view.

It was now approaching eleven o'clock. Earlier, Jake had arrived with Lennie and Donnie in the small French community of Baie Ste. Anne.

Jake had only been to this area a few times, usually in the hot summer months when the open beaches and the cooler winds from the Atlantic were a welcome refuge from the stifling heat further inland. Entering this village, his memory took him back to the night on December 10th, 1958, when he had been across the street from his home in Chatham, watching on TV a world championship light-heavyweight boxing match between the defending title holder, Archie Moore, and 'The Fighting Fisherman', Yvon Durelle, a twenty-seven-year-old contender from this very spot.

Durelle had knocked Moore onto the canvas three times during the first round, a feat which, by today's standards, would have resulted in the fight being stopped by the referee in Durelle's favor (three knockdowns in one round). Moore, however, had held on and managed to win by knocking out Durelle in the eleventh round. It was the stuff of legends in the boxing world.

Six months later, in June 1959, feelings of pride and euphoria in the village were shattered when thirty-five fishermen drowned as they were swept out to sea by forty-foot tidal waves that pounded the wharf of Durelle's village in a freak hurricane.

Jake's thoughts were interrupted when they pulled into the parking lot of the local pub, a tavern supposedly owned by the famous boxer. In minutes they were joined by Lennie's cousin, Alphonse Cormier. Because their group had now grown to four, they decided to take Alphonse's vehicle, a late-model four-wheel-drive Jeep Wagoneer. Jake was grateful for the comfort of the posh SUV, not to mention the much safer conditions its large winter tires provided. According to the rough map that Alphonse had drawn up for Lennie, it was going to be a rough trip once they were on back roads closer to the ocean. They left Jake's Epic in the parking lot and drove East. Approximately one hour later, they had passed through the village of Escuminac. They would soon be running out of highway.

In the distance, Jake spotted a periodic flash of light against the gray background. It was the lighthouse he vaguely remembered, and he grew anxious with the task ahead of them.

Detective Jack Faraday was pissed off. He had made a photocopy of the map that Jake had given him during their meeting with him yesterday. And wouldn't you know, he had left the document in his briefcase back at the precinct. Too embarrassed to admit this to his partner, Faraday desperately tried to recall the directions from his quick look at Jake's map only twelve hours ago.

"How much farther is this place, anyway?" asked Flynn.

"It should be just around the bend here coming up, Don," *I hope!* he thought. So far, they had seen no sign of Jake nor the other boys whom Jake had mentioned would probably be with him. The failure of following the directions properly bothered Faraday to no end and he was concerned for the safety of Jake and his friends. As they made their way around the upcoming turn, a heavy fog seemed to suddenly roll in off the Atlantic from the east.

"Christ, Jack, slow down, man. We can't see anything!" Flynn shouted. Then, "There! See? It's a lighthouse."

"Got it," said Faraday, and he slowly advanced their vehicle down a worn, unpaved lane that led to the ocean. They could see another road to the left of the lighthouse that led to a separate building about a hundred yards from where they were. Acting on a gut feeling, Faraday took the lane past the lighthouse and immediately noticed the tire tracks of another vehicle that had entered the lane before them, and had driven around to the front of the building, the side that faced the open ocean.

The detectives decided to park on the end of the lane at the back of the building and remain hidden, giving themselves a slight advantage over any others that may be inside the structure. They exited their vehicle, handguns drawn, and cautiously circled the property toward the front of the building.

The plan had been for Faraday and Flynn to meet up with Jake and his friends at the designated spot on the map that Faraday had stupidly forgotten back at the precinct. *Maybe this was just as well,* thought Faraday. It was just too risky to involve citizens on an operation of this nature. Flynn and himself would have a look-see, maybe make the bust themselves.

Jake crept stealthily with his three friends along the edge of the steep outcrop of land behind a recently constructed tower of concrete that stood sixty feet tall, a fully automated, state-of-the-art constant beacon for oceanic travel in this part of the country. One hundred feet beneath them, huge waves crashed continuously against a jagged shoreline, spraying sea foam that even reached the boys due to the raging wind that had developed. *Shit!* This was not what they had expected. Unable to see any buildings, they decided to return to Alphonse's Cherokee.

When they were driving away from the lighthouse, Lennie was the first to spot a vehicle about a quarter of a mile further up the road from them. It was a plain grey Ford that Jake immediately recognized as the same vehicle as the one used by Detective Faraday. Obviously they were here, somewhere. When the Jeep Cherokee crept up behind the Ford sedan, they all examined the empty vehicle, then quietly exited the Jeep.

"Lennie, you want to give me a hand with something?" asked Alphonse, after they were all outside of the vehicle. Jake turned around to see

Alphonse had opened the rear of his vehicle and was now laying a large canvas duffle bag out on the tail gate of his Jeep. Lennie came around to examine the items from the bag with Alphonse.

Spread before them was an array of weaponry Jake had never before witnessed: two semi-automatic AR-14 rifles, three handguns, three boxes of ammunition which Jake assumed were for the guns in the bag, and a fourth box full of something else he had only heard or read about but never seen before, sticks of dynamite! One dozen, in all, capable of God knew what destruction!

While the thoughts of what they were seeing leaped through their minds, none of them had heard the silent approach of two men who had managed to sneak up behind them.

"Everybody stand very still! This is the police!" Jake froze in place along with his comrades. The four of them, however, were no more surprised than the two detectives once they were all facing each other.

"Faraday! Flynn! God, where have you guys been?" Jake yelled at them, starting to walk towards the two officers.

"Stay where you are, Jake," warned Faraday. "Who are these men? We need to see ID's quickly, but nothing else! Now!" There was no mistaking the menace in his words when he spotted the display of weaponry laid out before him.

"Detective, I can explain," said Jake and he introduced the other three men to the two detectives. After their drivers' licenses were examined by Flynn and they holstered their handguns. Faraday stood in front of them and folded his arms in an authoritative manner. "Okay, who wants to explain where the war is and who owns all this material?"

Alphonse took the lead. "Yes sir, 'dis is all mine. 'Dese boys 'ere 'ave nutting to do wit' it. I was bringing this in preparation for 'de big fight, if it came to 'dat," Alphonse said, in his heavy French Acadian accent. *The guy is proud of this!* thought Faraday. He took a closer look at everything in front of him spread out on the tail gate of the Jeep.

"Jesus', where did you get all this?"

"The guns are registered to me, all legal. The TNT I bought from my friend in town, he owns a construction company. We just want to make sure dat Jake and his friend get protected, yes?"

Faraday could only shake his head at the weapons laying before him.

"Faraday, when did you get here," asked Jake.

"Just before you. C'mon. Looks like nobody else is here. Let's check this place out."

Once inside the huge building, Alphonse told them it had been a former fish-storage/ packing plant. *It was a perfect building and locale for a drug dealer's cook house,* thought Faraday as they looked around the premises. Faraday surmised the building comprised about three thousand square feet. Aside from one main open area, there were several smaller rooms that served as bedrooms, a couple of washrooms, and a small kitchen/eating area, which presumably were meant to be used by workers. Jake went off by himself into one of the bedrooms.

A mechanical room with a fuse panel, an oil furnace, and a huge hot water heater provided the owners with all the services they would need for their drug setup, as soon as a few large vats and an industrial-sized oven/stove were brought in. They were about to leave the building when Lennie yelled out "Hey Jake, we're going."

Jake appeared from the bedroom where he had been and was carrying something in his right hand. "I found this." he said, holding out a small diamond- studded gold earring. "It belongs to Sharon, Lennie. I gave it to her as a friendship gift last Fall. It was under a cot in that room," he added, gesturing behind him. Lennie knew his friend was having a difficult time holding his emotions in check. "We've got to find her . . ."

Outside, it began snowing again. The group of men soon found a path which led them downhill between large boulders towards the ocean shore and a pier that appeared to have been recently constructed. It was relatively large and to Jake's limited knowledge of the area and such things, he guessed it could probably accommodate lobster boats, and some of the good-sized seiners. He looked closely at the wooden structure which was quickly being covered with fresh snow, searching for footprints or any signs of recent activity.

Lennie walked up beside Jake, loosely placed his arm around his shoulder. "Man, I don't know what to tell you," he said.

"Shit Lennie," Jake said. "Look out there. They could be anywhere."

"Hey, Don! Check this." It was Faraday calling to Flynn, standing at the far end of the wharf, looking down at something. When his partner walked over to him, Lennie and Jake followed him, and they saw what he was looking at. A stub of a cigarillo cigar. Faraday picked it up with his gloves on and smelled it before placing it in a plastic bag he had taken from a side pocket. He looked at Jake and nodded in an unspoken reply. "Yeah, it's one of his, Jake. And it's still soft. So he was here, probably not that long ago."

Lennie called back to Alphonse who had returned to his jeep and was in the process of checking over his weapons. He told him about finding the stogie on the wharf. "These guys were here, Alphonse. You told me this place was owned by a fisherman; a guy named Francoise LeBlanc and you mentioned that a forty-four foot Cape Cod boat was part of the deal. They probably just left here in that boat. You know this area better than any of us, cuz. What's out there that would be a probable destination for these assholes?"

Alphonse looked out at the vastness of the Atlantic and gave it some thought. "Well, depending on what 'dey are looking for, 'dey could maybe go to Prince Edward Island sailing due East. If 'dey went south, 'dey could be headed for Nova Scotia, even the States, maybe Boston. I don' think they would go north …too far to Newfoundland, the nearest port. But you know, I jus' t'ought of something," and he turned his attention to Faraday. "Detective, do you 'ave a two-way radio in your vehicle?"

"I do, and it can also be switched to a UHF band." The Ultra High Frequency would be a better choice than VHF, or Very High Frequency, which is more commonly used.

The big Frenchman gave each of the detectives a hard slap on their backs. "Let's go back to your car, boys. I'd like to make a couple of calls to some friends."

Chapter Thirty

"Yes,'dats de one, t'anks Alfred. We appreciate dat, mon ami! You get all dat, Detective?" Alphonse handed the headset from the UVH system in Faraday's vehicle back to him who in turn shut off the car phone and consulted his notes.

"I did, and this is great stuff, Alphonse. Thank you!" Alphonse had called one of his fishing buddies, Alfred Cormier, who he guessed would have been out on the water over the past few hours. He guessed correctly. Cormier had run across the *Sea Witch* two hours earlier when she was tied up at the wharf in Point Sapin, gassing up. They were approximately eight miles south of their present location.

"Let's see," said Faraday, again referring to his legal pad. We're looking for a Cape Cod tuna boat, a forty-four foot vessel called the *Sea Witch*, last seen heading due south off the coast from Pointe Sapin, New Brunswick. Shit! That means they could be headed for Nova Scotia, or even the U.S."

"Detective, you've got to place an APB out for them," Jake said to Faraday. "It's not too late. Alphonse, what speed would a forty-footer normally run at, and where would that put them now?"

Alphonse thought for a few seconds and to Faraday, he was surprisingly quick in his calculations.

"Ah, d'ese boats do about twenty to twenty-five knots, so dat would get them to, oh, around Richibucto, close to fifty miles from us." Faraday looked at Don Flynn and raised his eyebrows, then jerked his thumb at Alphonse, but basically indicating to Flynn, *See, Don, you're not the only one!*

In a matter of minutes, Faraday was again on his car phone, this time

172

speaking with an old chum of his with the RCMP detachment in Moncton, N.B., Captain Norman Hilchey. The two had spent the better part of October 1944 in Antwerp while they were with the Canadian First Army during the Liberation of Holland. Since then, they managed to get together once or twice annually for a few beers.

"Norm, I have a big favor to ask of you, my friend. We have a situation here on the Miramichi that involves a major drug bust, three homicides, and a kidnapping, which, with your assistance, we may still be able to thwart. It's going to mean getting your air-born people involved, the use of a chopper perhaps, to sight a boat that by this point may be somewhere off the coast of Shediac."

"Jesus, Jack, you don't want much, do you," was the sarcastic response he received from Hilchey. Faraday then went on to explain in more detail the fact that the life of a young lady was probably in jeopardy, and oh yes, how much excellent PR his detachment in Moncton would receive. Jack knew Hilchey's weaknesses.

"Okay, Jack, but really what you should be looking for is assistance from the Canadian Coast Guard."

"There you go, Norm. Know anybody in that outfit?"

"Well, I __ "

"Great, Captain," Jack cut his friend short. "When can you let me know how you made out? It's important, Norman." He said the last statement in a very serious, almost pleading manner.

"You know you're gonna owe me big on this, Jack."

Faraday knew he would have to take a dressing down for acting as he did without the pre-approval of his Chief. It couldn't be helped.

The drive home was uneventful. Going through Baie Ste. Anne, Alphonse dropped Lennie Hachey, Donnie Mitchell, and Jake off at the pub and the three drove from there to Chatham in Jake's Epic. Jake was frantic, his mind constantly thinking about Sharon, and what she must be going through. Faraday had told Jack before they left Escuminac that he would be calling Mrs. Donovan to tell her about the situation her daughter now found herself in. So, on top of the worry, he could not stop the feelings of guilt which continued to flood his thoughts. If anything terrible happened, how would he ever live with himself?

That night, Jake was able to bring both his parents completely up to date regarding the situation with himself, the police, and Sharon Donovan. They were so grateful for his safety that chastisement for his actions were not even considered.

The following morning Jake was in Faraday's office, hounding the detective for any up-to-date information he could get on the status of the search for Sharon Donovan and her captors.

"Detective, it's been over twelve hours," begged Jake. "Come on Jack, give your buddy with the RCMP another call. He must have something to tell us."

Faraday was getting exasperated with the young man's persistence, and yet, he couldn't blame him. He checked his watch, it was now 8:15 and he reluctantly dialed the number he knew by rote. Captain Hilchey picked up on the first ring.

"Your ears must have been burning, Jack. I was just about to call you. Get your pen and take some details, I think you're gonna like what we have to say."

Twenty minutes later, and four full pages of notes on his legal pad, Jack called Don Flynn and the three of them marched into the Chief's office to discuss their findings.

Chief Bill Young had no idea of the magnitude of the law enforcement network that had recently been created by his investigative team. Included in the personnel and equipment recruited by Faraday's colleague, Cpt. Norman Hilchey, were an aviation team of a pilot and navigator with a Sikorsky helicopter from the Chatham air base; an ERT (Emergency Response Team) from Moncton of four armed, seasoned constables who were currently on their way to Shediac, N.B.; a summer tourist town renowned for its beautiful beaches and fresh lobster; and the *piece de resistance*, a team of five men from the recently established Canadian Coast Guard: four ensigns and their captain in a Cape Class rescue boat, the HMS *Cap Breton,* from Shippegan, N.B.

Chief Young had not yet discussed the cost of the venture with Faraday, how it was to be split, and who reported to whom. One thing he knew: the sheer size of the group was definitely more than he had bargained for, and they had better get him the results he was expecting. He mentioned this fact in an aside with Faraday. There was no point arguing about something of an administrative nature at this juncture in their operation in front of the detective's subordinates.

"So where do things stand at the moment?" asked Young.

"Sir, like I outlined to you, my contact with the RCMP in Moncton has really got the ball rolling. We were informed earlier this morning that his colleagues with the CCG spotted the *Sea Witch*. She is tied up at the Shediac Marina. I understand the Captain of the Coast Guard vessel, in a piece of very good foresight, I might add, had put out an alert to all of the local marinas, asking to be advised if and when they were to come across any info. It paid off.

"As per my earlier instructions, they have not approached anybody from the *Sea Witch*, but they are lying in watch offshore for any signs of movement. We are to be advised if and when that happens. In lieu of this, I have asked my friend Hilchey at the RCMP Moncton detachment to confirm that request and as well, to have his folks in the Sikorsky H-34 Choctaw 'copter stationed at CFB Chatham stand down until further word from us here. He has also contacted his ERT who were en route from Moncton to Shediac. Same deal, everybody's waiting for the word from us."

Chief Young took all of this into account and made a quick decision. "I like what you've done, Jack. Unfortunately, there's not much else we can do at this time. I think the most rational move we have is to wait for these guys to make their play. There are plenty of resources at our disposal for the moment, so let's give it one hour to see what takes place."

To Jake, trying every second not to think about Sharon's situation was like an eternity in hell. The best they could tell, Sharon had been taken from her residence some time Friday night. It was now Sunday; she'd been gone for a day and a half!

Chapter Thirty-one

At 10:15 a.m. the telephone on Faraday's desk rang and it was quickly grabbed by the impatient detective.

"Faraday here," he spoke into the mouthpiece. "Yes sir, go ahead." In his office with him at this time were two others, Jake, and Don Flynn, who both stared at Faraday, waiting for some signal as to whom he was addressing and what was being said. Faraday hung up his phone, a small smile on his face.

"That was Captain James Ross with the Coast Guard calling from the HMS *Cap Breton* off the coast of Shediac. They've just heard from their source at the marina there that two men came out of The Busy Brig, a local watering hole there, and they have now gone aboard the *Sea Witch*, tied up at the marina on the far north side of the wharf."

Faraday hung up his phone and sat looking out the lone window in his office, watching the snow picking up once again, swirling around the vehicles parked outside. The two others could sense something was on his mind.

"Shit!", he yelled to himself, retrieving his phone as he dialed up the Chief on his intercom.

"Sir, I just heard from the CCG. Things are happening and here's what I'd like to do."

On the drive from town out to the Air Base, a short distance of only two miles, Faraday was berating himself to the two passengers with him. Every now and then he hit his closed fist against the steering wheel.

"I can't believe I never noticed that" he said. "Christ, I distinctly remember seeing their vehicle's tracks leading into the driveway of the new cookhouse when we were in Escuminac yesterday. And yet I never gave any thought to the fact that no vehicle was there when we landed. So, one or more people were probably picked up by the *Sea Witch* and one or more drove off before we came. Shit!", and he slammed his fist again on the steering wheel of his cruiser.

A quick call was made to Hilchey after their meeting with Chief Young, and Faraday along with Flynn and Jake were all given permission to fly with Captain Nigel Dryden and his co-pilot John Wilks on board the H-34 Sikorsky helicopter to Shediac. They were to meet with Hilchey's ERT of four officers at the Shore's Inn and Hotel, a four-star favorite for folks going to Parlee Beach, a five-minute walk from them.

More to their needs, it was also only a five-minute drive in the opposite direction down Highway 133 to the Shediac Marina. Faraday, Flynn, and Jake had been dropped off from the Sikorsky at the Moncton International Airport where they rented a new Chevy Impala which Faraday drove to the pre-arranged meet with the Emergency Response Team already waiting for them at the Shore's Inn.

Jake was very impressed with how smooth everything was going since Faraday had gotten the RCMP involved. The flight in the helicopter from Chatham was amazing. It was his first flight ever! Now, meeting the four-man team of professional responders he felt very much out of his league. Man, these guys were like something out of a James Bond movie. They were huge men, clean cut, all in excellent shape. And quiet as house mice. They had each only said their first names and shook hands when Faraday introduced himself, and then Don and Jake as his aides.

The team then popped their four semi-automatic AR-14's into the trunk of their unit, an unmarked late model Plymouth, and the two vehicles left the Shore's Inn in tandem for the Shediac Marina. When they drove onto the main pier, they spotted the HMS Cap Breton. As prearranged with Capt. Ross on board the Coast Guard ship, Constable Dave Flemming and his three ERT specialists slowly drove by the ship, followed by Faraday. The two vehicles were noted by Capt. Ross as he stood on the prow of the *Cap Breton* and gave them a slight nod of his head in acknowledgment of the arrival of the two teams. They had pre-arranged to meet in the Busy Brig.

Minutes later, Capt. Ross was sitting with Faraday and his six colleagues. To an undiscerning eye they would look like a group of tourists, albeit this was not the normal time of year for such activity. To their benefit, the pub was quiet at this time. In any case, they assumed the two men they were seeking were already holed up on the *Sea Witch*, which Ross now confirmed had not left the marina.

Faraday took control of the meeting. This seemed to go over fine with the rest of the men, who had probably already been made aware of this link in the chain of command. Faraday made a point of thanking Hilchey for that little favor.

"Gentlemen, the way I see this happening is a straight-out confrontation with these people. Jim, we can all go with you on your ship and quietly run alongside the *Sea Witch*. With this much manpower suddenly showing up broadside them, and jumping on their decks, they'll be overwhelmed. Agreed?"

"Yes sir," said Ross.

"Very well, men. We'll drive down to the *Cap Breton* in my rental and Dave, you and your guys, follow us down. Once there, we'll arm ourselves and get this operation underway." Constable Flemming just gave Faraday a thumbs-up and they all went to their vehicles. When Faraday was in his rental with Jake in the front and Flynn sitting in the back with Ross, he spoke to the two behind him. "Just in case there are people on board the *Witch* who may get a little overzealous with this unwanted company boarding their boat, I want you, Don, to hang back a bit with Jake here. Got it?"

"Understood, sir," Flynn said.

This was serious shit, thought Faraday. *He didn't call me Jack.*

In no time, they were all on board the HMS *Cap Breton* and Capt. Ross introduced them to his four subordinate ensigns. All men were now wearing Kevlar vests. Just in case.

'Okay boys, let's rock and roll!" Faraday intoned, a glint in his eyes known too well by Flynn. The *Cap Breton* set out for the short ride to the north side of the pier, its two Caterpillar diesel engines quietly chugging in the calm waters, for all intents and purposes silently approaching the *Sea Witch* now only a hundred yards away.

The forty-four foot Cape Cod fishing boat sat tied up on the north side of the marina as they had expected. It was now dark, no other boats were near them, nor was there any sign of activity on the *Sea Witch* when Capt. Ross navigated the *Cap Breton* alongside her. The Coast Guard sat two feet higher in the water than the seiner, and in no time a dozen men in black-face camouflage hopped onto her decks, fully armed and ten of them surrounded the entry to the hold below decks.

Faraday nodded to Dave Flemming who then rammed the butt of his AR-14 against the thin door.

"This is the police! Everybody on deck, now! I repeat! Police!

They all stood back, waiting for a response. In under a minute, the door opened, and a chubby face with a two-day growth of grey stubble appeared. The man, red-eyed and clearly shit-faced on some form of narcotic, could only stare and grin at the army of law enforcement people confronting him.

"Whoa, man. What's happening?" he exclaimed.

Chapter Thirty-two

Ronnie Walsh was having problems understanding things. The minute he had responded to the loud crash on the door leading down to his cabin, he had been quickly handcuffed by the giant standing in front of him. And in another few seconds he was pushed aside while a second behemoth ran down the short flight of stairs and returned with his buddy, Lloyd Fanjoy, who was also hand-cuffed, and just as stoned as he was. What the hell was going on? All these bad-ass dudes on the boat? It finally dawned on his drugged mind that they were cops. Man, this was not part of his job description!

The two hapless druggies were roughly taken on board the HMS *Cap Breton* by Flynn and Jake while the rest of Faraday's squad stayed on the *Sea Witch* to conduct a thorough search of the vessel.

Flynn was able to find a supply of cups and some instant coffee in the ship's galley, and he asked Jake to heat up some water. He then took the role of the 'bad cop' and shoved their captives into two available chairs, hands cuffed to the back arms of the seats.

"I want to see some IDs, and I want some answers, no bull shit. Am I clear?"

The two told them to check their wallets and when he had their drivers' licenses in hand, he began his interrogation.

"Okay, let's see," Flynn said. "You, Ronald Joseph Walsh," he continued, looking at the license. "This is your current address, 15 Pleasant Street, Bathurst, N.B.?"

"Yeah, but__", Ronnie started to reply, and he was quickly cut off by Flynn.

"I am the only one asking questions Mr. Walsh. We are investigating a serious situation which involves drug trafficking, kidnapping, and possibly three homicides. If you guys cooperate with us, maybe we can go easy on some of these alleged charges which surely will be coming your way." At that point, Jake came back to the small table bearing a tray with four coffees, the 'good cop' of the two.

"Watch these assholes for a while, Jake. I've gotta go to the head," Flynn said, rising from the table, leaving his keys to Jake. Instinctively, Jake knew this was his cue to get into his role.

"You guys want a coffee?" he asked. "You both look like you can use one!" He laid two cups of java in front of them, giving them a small grin. Not getting any response, just vacant looks from the two, he pretended to look stupid, then added. "Aw, shit, sorry, guys," and he used Don's keys to remove the handcuffs. "Kinda hard to drink with these things on, eh?"

When he saw what looked like a small indication of gratitude from Ron Walsh, he focused on him.

"So, Ron. You're from Bathurst. What's knew at the Lounge?" LeBlanc's Lounge was a favorite hang-out for many of the young crowd in that city. Ron rubbed his wrists where the cuffs had chafed them. "Same old," he said.

"What the hell are you guys doing here, man?" Jake asked outright. He said this almost in a conspiratorial way, giving a side glance to the bathroom door where Flynn had gone.

Walsh took a second sip of his coffee, gave a questioning look to his friend Lloyd Fanjoy who simply shrugged, returned a sorry look then shifted his eyes down to the floor, more or less in resignation.

It only took Jake another three minutes for him to gather what he felt to be the majority of data they were seeking. Apparently, Walsh had been staying for a few days at his buddy Lloyd's place in Baie Ste. Anne. Fanjoy had received a call yesterday from some guy whom they both only knew as 'Alain', who had recently hired them to do some work on a building in Point Escuminac. According to the boys, all they did for this 'Alain' dude so far was some cleanup work in the building.

Jake thought Fanjoy was choosing his words carefully, but he did not press him for further information.

Fanjoy told Jake that Alain had later arranged to meet the both of them at the dock in Escuminac where they were then given the keys to the *Sea Witch* and told to sail her to this marina, here in Shediac, that Alain would meet up with them later today. Their new boss had arrived as arranged, paid them each a hundred bucks for their trouble and also gave them a couple of joints of 'really heavy' pot. Then he left, telling them to hang around and they'd be back later tonight or first thing in the morning.

No, as far as they knew there was no woman with him. Yeah, there *was* another dude, they were driving a new black Lincoln.

At this point in the narrative, Flynn appeared from the bathroom, his gun in hand, covering the two druggies while seemingly very pissed off at Jake. "Hey! What's going on Partner? You okay? "He grabbed the cuffs off the table and in no time had replaced them on Walsh and Fanjoy. "Jeeze, man, you can be so naïve at times!" he said, giving his partner a glare, then a backwards wink as he headed the two off the boat.

"Let's get these jerks in our rental where they won't need babysitting."

As they were putting the two in their Chevy rental, Faraday arrived with his comrades, each carrying canvas bags which they placed in the trunk. Outside of the vehicle, Faraday gave Flynn and Jake a huge grin, saying, "Pay load! I'll explain in a minute."

Flynn looked at his watch. "We don't have a lot of time, sir." He jerked his thumb towards the two sitting in their back seat. "Their boss, somebody named 'Alain', might be returning here later tonight or in the morning. He was with another male, somebody driving a new Lincoln."

"Oh yeah?" Faraday suddenly seemed to realize something. "Captain Ross, okay if we use your comms system to make a couple of calls? We have to be quick, though. If the guy in the Lincoln is who I think it is, things should be falling in place for us, finally." Again, Faraday berated himself. *It must be my age,* he thought. *Maybe it's time I gave this shit a rest.*

In minutes, they had all poured back onto the HMS *Cap Breton.* They were sitting around the pilot's cabin, making small talk while their two captives sat cuffed in the rear of Faraday's rental, the wharf beside them. Their discussions were halted by a static break from Ross's ship-to-shore communication speakers. It was the voice of Jenny Olsen with NB Tel., getting back to her friend Don Flynn with some very important information.

"Could you please spell that for me, Jen?" Don was writing on a legal pad, hands-free, wearing a set of headphones. "Got it," he said. "Here you are sir," he said to Faraday, passing the pad and pen to Jack. "We are now looking for one Dr. Harold Morin. A new veterinarian in Chatham."

Jennie had supplied the name they couldn't remember from the more recent calls showing up on Ralph Crawford's phone. It belonged to Dexter Sharpe, owner of a small construction business, also a member of the Golf and Country Club. After getting that info from Jennifer, he quickly had her obtain the remainder of calls made on Sharpe's phone in the last few days.

It took a few minutes, but Jenny was very helpful. A new name and number came to light, one Harold Morin. And now, headset on, Jack was speaking through the mic to his contact at the Provincial Motor Vehicle department.

"Thanks a lot Michele," he said, and he passed the info to Don Flynn who got on the system to call in an APB to their Chatham precinct for one Harold Morin, said to be driving his new black Lincoln Mark IV, plate NB 314 NTY. Don clapped his hands together, a grin on his face.

"That's done, folks. The APB will be going out on the network as we speak."

Both of the Chatham PD officers soon heard the All-Points Bulletin being sent by Herb Cable, yet neither of them thought to question why old Herb would be working OT on a Saturday night.

Constable Cable *never* worked overtime. Tonight, he was at the precinct, not working, but hanging out. Herb was bored, he was looking for some dirt to gossip about when out of the blue a call came in from Constable Don Flynn asking him to put out an APB for one Mr. Harold Morin driving a new, black Lincoln Mark IV. Flynn had asked him to look up Morin's address and check it out. *Yeah, yeah, I know, it's a long shot, but just do it, okay Herb! And let me know!* The young punk telling him what to do, it really pissed Herb off!

He immediately consulted Morin's address in the telephone directory: 18 Riverview Drive, next to the golf course. Only a five-minute drive . . . *Why not?* he muttered to himself and left the precinct. There had to be some mistake. He'd take the initiative, make a short drive, and earn some recognition in the process. How many Harold Morin's who drove a new black Lincoln could there be, anyway?

This *had* to be the same guy he met the other day at the Club with Dexter Sharpe.

Chapter Thirty-three

When Herb arrived at the Morin residence, he noted all the lights were off. He thought it a bit strange, nevertheless, and decided to make a quick check and shut off his cruiser. He walked up the short entrance pathway and knocked lightly on the veterinarian's door. A light came on and shit, there was Harold Morin standing in front of him. What the hell?

"Hey! Mr. Morin, it's you! Uh, sorry to bother you. Herb Cable. Ah, *Constable* Herb Cable, Chatham PD. We met the other day, you were with Dex Sharpe, remember?"

Morin looked behind Herb, saw his empty cruiser, then looked behind himself, and seemingly satisfied, he invited the busy-body cop into his home.

"Yes, yes, Constable. Please come in. Uh, what brings you to my house this evening?" Again, he looked behind Herb as he closed the door and led him into his den.

"Well, it's a bit strange, Harold. Okay if I call you Harold?"

"No, no problem, ah, Herb." He waited for the idiot's explanation for his visit here in the middle of the night.

After an awkward pause, Herb seemed to remember why he was here.

"Right. I just received a request from one of my people to send out an All-Points Bulletin for you. In fact, I ran the broadcast. But then I realized, *Hey! I know this fella!* So, while a whole crew of men are down in Shediac, I figured I'd run over here to make sure you are home and that everything's fine. I guess my gut feeling was right, and I'll be pleased to tell them that, so . . ." Herb was getting up to leave, and Morin's mind was busy weighing various options.

Once again, he looked around the corner of the den where an open door could be seen, beyond which a set of stairs led down to his rec room. He quickly came to a decision and brought his attention back to the policeman.

"Well, that's quite the story, Herb. Do they suspect me of something?"

"Hell, not that I'm aware of, Hal'. I'm pretty sure they probably just want to make sure you are not in any harm, you know. That's why I thought I'd confirm that, being as I know you, I'd save them a lot of work and everything and let them know I had the whole thing straightened out."

Man, this guy! thought Morin. *How stupid could one get?*

"Herb, I know it's getting late, and I suppose you are now off duty. But maybe you could share a small night-cap with me?" Harold Morin was a good judge of character and knew he had correctly pegged Cable as the type of guy who was eager to rub elbows with the rich.

Herb gave his host a big smile and sat back in his seat. "Why, that would be very sociable, Hal'. Sure, why not?" He would call Flynn right after he had a drink with his new friend.

Hal'? Give me a break! thought Morin. He made a quick trip to his rec room where a color TV was on, a slight male figure was lying spread out on a sofa. He was wearing ratty old jeans that had seen better days, and a stained T-shirt that stretched over his pot belly. It was Alain Benoit, watching The Ed Sullivan Show, slopping a bowl of some kind of cereal into his mouth, and now and then laughing hilariously at some kind of stupid mouse puppet called Topo Gigio.

When Morin entered the room, he told Benoit to get properly dressed, that they had company in the form of a *policeman* upstairs and he wanted Morin to fix a couple of drinks for them. He said this with a serious wink.

The hit man from Montreal almost upset his bowl of cereal upon hearing Morin use the word 'policeman'. Morin had to quickly assure his associate that he had little to worry about. Hell, the guy was about as sharp as a boiled egg. Morin told Benoit, however, that they might be able to get some information about where things stood on the drug investigation they believed was going on. He went on to quickly tell him what he knew so far, that is, about the APB that the cop upstairs told him had been put out on him.

More importantly, Benoit was all ears when Morin mentioned their guest had just told him a large contingency of law enforcement officers were currently in the Shediac area.

"We've got to do something with this guy, Alain. I'm sure he hasn't yet radioed info as to his present whereabouts. His trip here was just something he decided to do on his way home off his shift. But if the others are on their way back from Shediac, they may land here for all I know." He left Benoit and returned upstairs.

Benoit hurried to one of the two guest rooms downstairs he had been using, careful to quietly check on the other one that was also in use. Everything in that room was quiet. He returned to his own and put on a pair of dress slacks and a white shirt, badly in need of ironing, but it would suffice. He was getting tired of this shit with Morin. It was time to have a talk with him. First though, he decided to look after this other business.

While Benoit was changing clothes, Morin had returned to his 'guest'. From what Cable had just mentioned, it appeared their little ploy had worked. When Morin and Benoit became aware the police had knowledge of the cook house in Napan, they began the set-up of their new operation in Escuminac. As a precaution to keep the new shop hidden, and suspecting the police were getting intel from a source in town, it was decided to use Benoit's two new recruits, Ron Walsh and Lloyd Fanjoy, a couple of local flunkies, to take his boat to Shediac unwittingly on a 'fishing trip'.

The two druggies didn't know it, but they were being used by Benoit to 'fish' for some law enforcement folks if they were to show up in Escuminac.

"No problem," Morin had said. "Let them chase the *Sea Witch* down to Shediac. Those two druggies know nothing about what we have on the go." *Bingo!* They had landed some fish by what Cable was saying. He was now about to gather some more information from his 'guest'.

"Sorry to keep you waiting, Herb. Had to use the little boys' room," Harold said to the cop who had decided to take a look around the room, checking out some pictures taken of Harold with various dignitaries in other places while he lived and worked in Montreal.

"Nice place ya have here, Hal'," Cable said.

"Yeah, I try,' Harold replied. He turned around and yelled out to somebody through the downstairs doorway, "Hey! Alain, how are those drinks coming?"

Alain Benoit was carrying two crystal glasses filled with rum and cokes up the stairs to Harold's den. One of them was a tad stronger than the other, having been doctored with a healthy hit of methamphetamine, or meth, the same shit Jimmy Whalen had been using as an additive on his special joints.

When he entered the den, Morin introduced him to Herb Cable. Herb was instantly intimidated by the man, but figured, hell, he'd seen plenty of weirdos in his days. He'd have just this one drink, then get back to the precinct and call Flynn. Herb accepted the drink offered to him by the guy with a reptilian smile who was now lighting up a fancy cigar, for Christ's sake, even in defiance of a stern glare that the owner was giving him.

"Well, Herb, here's to your health!", Harold said, and they each took a drink. It was weird, but he saw that Morin was now giving the small creep a big smile, just after that menacing glare.

Unheard by those upstairs, a figure down in one of the guest bedrooms was coming to life. Dexter Sharpe awoke with a tremendous headache, moaned softly and looked all around the room while lying on his back. The last thing he recalled was waking up in a different room. It had been totally dark, and cold. At least this room was warm, and he was lying in a nice bed. But then he realized his hands were tied behind his back, his feet were bound, and he had been gagged. Same as before.

He managed to lift himself into a sitting position, and it was then that he saw the girl lying on the floor in front of the bed. She too was bound, also wearing a gag.

She was beautiful.

Dexter slowly edged his body closer to the end of the bed, dragging a heavy pillow with him by maneuvering it forward with his bound feet until he reached the footboard directly over the head of the girl on the floor. He released the pillow from his feet, and it landed on her head.

For a moment, Dexter thought she might be dead. Given the

circumstances he was in himself, anything was possible. Then a moan escaped from behind her gagged mouth, and she lifted that beautiful face. She screamed, but of course, nothing came out. Her eyes betrayed the horror her mind was experiencing as she looked at Dexter. He could only return a look that he hoped resembled something like pity, maybe consolation, when he rolled his body over and showed his bound hands to her.

Chapter Thirty-four

After Don Flynn had arranged with Herb Cable to have the APB dispatched on Harold Morin, there was not a whole lot to do but wait. Faraday decided their time could best be spent at the precinct back in Chatham, so he contacted his colleague Capt. Hilchey and told him it was time for Norm to call back the cavalry.

The ERT boys drove back to report to Hilchey in Moncton, Capt. Ross returned to the HMS *Cap Breton* with the Coast Guard crew, and the two druggies were escorted to the RCMP station in Shediac for the arraignment on their charges. Any felonies laid against them would fall under the jurisdiction of that county. Faraday told the locals about the cooperation given by the two boys, and he put in his recommendation for leniency, if possible, once all the facts were uncovered.

In a gesture of gratitude for the quantity of methamphetamine Faraday's team had recovered through his raid on the *Sea Witch*, Hilchey arranged to have Faraday, Flynn, and Jake flown back to the Chatham Air Force base. All Jack had to do was return their rental vehicle to the Moncton airport where he met up with the pilot of the Sikorsky helicopter and they were off.

On the quick flight back to Chatham, Jake's thoughts continued to center on Sharon. It was now Sunday evening, closing on ten o'clock, and he was extremely worried about her safety. She had been gone now for at least forty-eight hours.

Since her abduction on the Friday evening just past, so much had happened, yet very little of a tangible nature. Yes, they were now quite certain of where the new drug cookhouse was situated; they had reason to suspect one of the heads of the operation was Harold Morin, the new veterinarian in town; and they *did* have possession of the *Sea Witch,* which was now under the surveillance of the Shediac RCMP.

Jake was amazed at the volume of drugs Faraday's colleagues had seized from the ship when they had boarded her. Flynn had told him it was in the vicinity of fifty kilos of meth, a nice haul which would make their Chief happy, and probably more or less compensate for the expense of the raid.

Yet, with all of these positive rewards for their activity, Jake was heartsick.

Where was Sharon?

The first thing he was going to do when they landed in Chatham would be to make a quick trip to her place.

"Tell me, Herb, how do you like your work with the town police?" asked Morin.

"Well, it's not horrible," replied Herb. "Just that it gets kinda boring. I'd prefer to be more involved in actual crime fighting."

"Yeah, I suppose you don't get to shoot that gun too often, eh?" said Morin, pointing at Herb's service revolver, an Enfield.

Herb looked at Morin, with a grin. *What an odd thing to say,* he thought. "Nope, wanna have a look at her?" Herb was on his second *special* rum and coke, his mind awhirl, and he was having difficulty understanding things. This disorientation, however, did not seem to give him any concern. Herb's mind was simply in a state of bliss. He was…happy!

"Not my kinda thing, but maybe Alain here might," Harold suggested. Out of nowhere, the creepy little guy with the cigar was standing beside him.

"Hey, dat's a nice machine," Benoit said. "Why don't you show me how it works, 'erb? We can go out da back yard, shoot at a target, okay?" The next thing Herb knew, they were walking through the house toward the back, Herb stumbling, laughing, taking a few more sips of his drink along the way.

When they had reached the door to Harold's bedroom, Benoit stepped inside and came back out with a pillow. "I'm just gonna bring 'dis wit' me," he said. "You know, to keep da' noise down, okay?"

By this time Herb was shit-faced. He gave Alain a nod with a big stupid grin. They walked off the back deck and across the lawn up to a large oak tree. "Okay, Herb, you stand 'dere a second," he said, pointing to a spot about a foot from the trunk of the tree. "Now, you look over 'dere at dat ting sitting on da pole," he said. Herb was thinking they were going to have some kind of target- shooting game. He was a pretty good shot, old Herb was. *Hey, maybe they would shoot for a few bucks.*

In a stupor, Herb was looking at an ornamental bird house on the opposite side of the lawn, and very calmly, Alain simply walked up beside him and shot him in the right side of his head while holding Harold's pillow pressed against the barrel of the Enfield.

Alain was impressed; it was the first time he had ever tried that. The sound of the gun going off was actually not as loud as he imagined it would be. He wiped Herb's revolver of any prints, replaced it in his lifeless right hand, and fired off another round through the bloodied pillow into the darkness.

Sharon heard a scraping sound and heavy breathing coming near her as she lay on the floor of the bedroom. She had no idea where she was, only that she had just woken up with a terrible headache and a feeling of nausea in the pit of her stomach. She turned toward the sounds and saw it was a man inching toward her while lying on his back. The same man she had just seen looking down at her from the foot of the bed. His hands and feet, however, were also bound as were her own, and his mouth was filled with a rag tied around his mouth and knotted at the back of his neck. Accordingly, she immediately considered him an ally.

As Dexter neared the woman, he maneuvered his body, so his hands came up against the back of her neck, and with difficulty he was able to undo the knot holding the gag over her mouth. He quickly repositioned his body, so the back of his neck was touching her bound hands, and she was able to undo his gag. At least, now they were able to communicate, if only in whispers.

"My name is Dexter Sharpe," he began. "I own a new car Pontiac Oldsmobile franchise dealership in Chatham. I don't know exactly where we are, but I have an idea we're in the home of the new animal doctor from

Montreal. His name is Harold Morin, and he is with a psycho named Alain. Somehow, we have got to get out of here. Our lives are in great danger."

Sharon took all of this in and gave him her name. Oddly, she remembered the talks she and Jake had last Monday evening with Detective Faraday and his assistant, Don Flynn. She then told Sharpe of her work with the bank, and the death of her supervisor, Ron Doyle. She even decided to tell this man about her involvement with Jacob England, and how he was assisting the police in some kind of undercover work that probably involved the guy's Dexter just told her about.

Wham! Suddenly it hit Sharpe! She was talking about the young guy Dexter had set up to be framed by Morin and his wacko buddy, Alain. Not to be killed, but just to be at least investigated for the murder of Darrel Harte *Jesus!* He said nothing about that to her, but suddenly he harbored feelings of guilt for what he had done, and he vowed to himself that from this point on, he would do whatever he could to protect her.

"This is going to be awkward, but I think in the long run, it will be the quickest way to get ourselves out of these ropes. The gags were not that much of a problem since the knots were loose and made of cotton, right?", he explained to Sharon.

"Yes, I understand. So?"

"So, I want you to turn over on your back and push yourself backwards with your legs so your hands behind you are closer to my mouth." This brought a look of skepticism, or maybe it was a quick, odd smile.

If it had not been for the seriousness of their situation, Harold would have had problems containing his embarrassment. There was something sensual about their positions.

As she moved against him, however, another part of Harold's body reacted involuntarily. Sharon was not able to see the result of Harold's state of arousal as her back was to him during her endeavors, but she *did* feel him.

"Okay, you're almost there, just move about a foot closer." Dexter was directing Sharon backwards to his face. He was intending to undo the knot that was binding her wrists together by using his teeth. From his experience, he always found this to be a more effective method of getting the job done quickly than using his awkward fingers or thumbs. In a few seconds he had accomplished the task, and Sharon's hands were free.

He watched her as she quickly went to work on the rope around her feet. There! She was finally able to stand and walk around. *What a wonderful feeling!* Then she looked down at the man lying on the floor. For a minute, Dexter had the feeling she might have second thoughts, and bolt from the room.

Relief came over him when Sharon knelt beside him and quickly freed his hands and feet. He stood, not knowing what to say, then acting on impulse, he gave her a long, tight hug. It was probably the fact that they were comrades together in jeopardy, and having survived the terror of it thus far, he acted as he did.

He quickly pulled away from her, exclaiming, "Oh, I'm sorry. I didn't mean to, you know, please forgive me."

"Forget it," she said. She quietly walked on her new-found legs to the bedroom door and opened it, surprised to find a large, empty recreation room that contained a billiards table that appeared to have been recently occupied, abandoned. A number of balls and a sole pool cue lay scattered on the green felt table. A strong aroma of cigar smoke assaulted her nose. She turned to face Dexter, and said, "Let's get out of this place. There may still be people around __".

Her words were suddenly interrupted by a loud thump coming from above them.

Chapter Thirty-five

"So, now what?", asked Jake of the two officers when they got off the Sikorsky at the Chatham Air Base. It was Sunday evening, around 7:00.

"Not much we can do," said Faraday. "I expect Morin is headed for Shediac to meet up with the two bad apples who were hired by his buddy Alain. We have arranged with the RCMP there to keep the *Sea Witch* under surveillance. Come to think of it, they wouldn't know that both those kids have been arrested. They will be very pissed off when they find out."

"Go home and get some rest, Jake," added Flynn. "You can give us a call at the precinct in the morning."

"Man, I hate just sitting around knowing she's out there somewhere."

"Yeah, that sucks," said Flynn. "But hopefully, we'll hear something in the morning, maybe even later tonight. We'll call you if we do, okay?"

Not okay, thought Jake. *I'm going to make a visit to someone.*

Earlier, when they heard Flynn place the APB with Herb Cable, Jake was certain that Flynn told Herb to advise them ASAP if Morin was located at home, and he would have done that, wouldn't he? It was really grasping at straws, but Jake decided to check it out, just to be sure. First though, he wanted to catch up with his buddies Lennie and Donnie and bring them up to date on where things stood. He made a quick side trip to *Joe's*.

"Do you have the guy's address Jake?" asked Lennie.

"Not exactly. Do you have a telephone directory?"

"Shit! Some detective, eh Donnie?" He pulled a book from a phone booth in the corner of the building. "So, let's see. Morin, Harold…here we are. 18 Riverview Drive. Want us to join you?"

Jake drove his Epic west on Wellington Street under the newly constructed Centennial Bridge that spanned the Miramichi River, then took a sharp left on Riverview Drive. He was looking for the number 18 on the houses to his left. He had Lennie beside him in the front and Donnie in the back. It was now dark, and Jake had turned off his headlights, not wanting to give themselves away should that be of any advantage over who or what they were hoping to find.

As they came to an intersection, they had to brake at the four-way stop. A town black and white Chatham police cruiser was stopped opposite them. Jake yielded to the cruiser since it had arrived at the intersection before him, but first he but his lights back on. The police car slowly passed by him, and the driver was not known by Jake. He did not have the look of a cop, and they eyed each other closely as he drove by. The guy had weird, hooded eyes.

When Sharon and her unlikely ally heard the noise from upstairs, they warily left the bedroom and tiptoed through the rec room up the stairwell to a closed door. Dexter put his ear to the door in front of him and listened intently. In a matter of less than a minute, the sound of a car engine revving up could be heard and they both opened the upstairs door leading to the den and ran into the room.

Dexter was the first to view the body lying on the floor. It was his former venture partner, Harold Morin. An iron poker was protruding from the top of his head and the man's lifeless eyes gave no doubt as to the condition of his health. Dexter turned to see Sharon attempting to see around him while standing in the doorway that led downstairs.

"Sharon, you do *not* want to see this," he said, standing between her and Morin's body, shielding it from her view. Because he was a bit late, she did see a fraction of the scene, and it was enough to allow her to be pushed by Sharpe into the kitchen.

"Oh my God, Dexter, is he __?"

"Yes, Sharon. He's dead. He is, make that, *was,* a prominent businessman in our community. He was the new vet in town who came here from Montreal. Unfortunately, I now believe he was involved in a drug ring- - A couple of bankers and I. Shit, I am just getting it all. Sharon, do you know John Hancock or Ralph Crawford?"

"Uh, yes. I work for Mr. Crawford. He's the manager at the Bank of

New Brunswick. My God, is he involved in this, this…?" She couldn't even say the word, as she looked toward the door that led to the den and what lay unseen on the floor behind it.

"Very indirectly, yes. The both of them are, Sharon, including myself, dammit! I want to tell you something." Dexter then began to relate how, in a moment of greed, he had become involved with the bankers and the veterinarian. How he had very stupidly suggested to Morin that they could frame the young bank trainee. He tried to explain that Jacob was only supposed to be investigated for the murder of Darrel Harte, not physically hurt; that Jacob was getting too close to what was happening, and it was supposed to take the police away from them.

Just before he got to that point, however, their discussion was cut short by the ringing of the front doorbell.

"Wait here. Do *not* go into the den, okay?" He gave her a pleading look, and she sat in one of the chairs at the kitchen table. Everything was so damn *surreal!* She felt like she was about to faint.

The Epic slowly crept up to a two-story Cape Cod style home with the number 18 in wrought iron figures affixed to the front door casing. There was a light showing from a large living room picture window, otherwise, nothing else to indicate anybody was in the residence. Jake and his two friends climbed out of his vehicle and cautiously approached the front door. Jake rang the doorbell and as they waited, he thought he saw a drape being pulled back at the edge of the living room window. Just then, the door opened, and a figure appeared before them.

The man looked somewhat familiar to Jake, like somebody he had seen around town, maybe a customer at the bank? When Sharpe saw Jake standing in front of him, he instinctively knew it was Jacob England. He also looked familiar to Dexter. Dexter had a small personal loan at the bank where Jake worked, his business account for the dealership was at the Bank of Toronto, so maybe he spotted him at the bank.

"Yes sir, my name is Jake England. These are my friends, Len and Don. We are looking for the owner of the residence, a Mr. Harold Morin." Jake immediately picked up on the man's nervous state. *He definitely knows something,* thought Jake.

"Er, Jake England, you say. Do you happen to work at the Bank of New Brunswick?"

"I do," said Jake. "Is everything okay?"

"Why are you here? Is this some kind of collection call? Does Harold owe you guys money?" Dexter was having a hard time getting his nerves settled. Christ, Morin's body was lying on the floor only twenty feet from them in the den. Sharpe didn't know what to do, and he was about to slam the door in Jake's face, when Sharon suddenly appeared behind him.

She and Jake saw each other at the same instant, and Jake roughly pushed Dexter aside, ran to Sharon and wrapped his arms around her.

"Sharon, my God! Are you okay?"

"Oh, Jake, I am! This man and I were drugged and brought here by the owner of the place who we think has been murdered by somebody! Jake, we need to contact the police. Just this minute we were able to free ourselves after being drugged by these guys and held captive for the past two days and—

Jake interrupted her. "Whoa, slow down, Sharon. Let's go inside, is it safe?"

"Yes, but…", she began and was again cut short.

"Lennie, Donnie, have a look. I'll take Sharon and, uh, Dexter here, into the kitchen." Jake got Sharon and Dexter seated and grabbed a couple of glasses from a shelf, filled them with cold water, and gave them to his girlfriend and the other guy. "Drink these! Calm down, both of you. You're both in shock," he explained. He was about to start asking questions when Lennie came into the kitchen from the den.

"Jake, have a look in the den, but you better prepare yourself. It is bad. I'm calling Detective Faraday to tell him what we have here. I'm sure he'll want to bring his partner Don Flynn and call in his forensic people. Jesus! This is crazy!" He used the landline phone over the kitchen counter to call the precinct.

"Okay, thanks, Lennie." Donnie was now with them in the kitchen, and Jake thought quickly. "Everybody sit right here, do not touch anything else, the police arrive soon. Donnie, make a mental note of where you were in the house so far, and what you may have touched.

"Sharon, when the police come, try to be calm and tell them everything you know. Just start from last Friday night and try to recall anybody else, aside from Dexter here, who you may have had contact with." As he said this, she averted her eyes from his, which up until then had been locked with hers. Jake picked up on this, and he felt weird.

Concerned? Yes.

Hurt? *Definitely!*

Chapter Thirty-six

9:15 pm

Faraday, Flynn, and the Medical Examiner, Floyd MacNutt, and his two aides had arrived. The two detectives had just finished checking out the premises and Faraday told Don to look around the backyard for anything of note, while he began to obtain statements from Dexter and Sharon. He had not even put his note pad in order when Flynn came running back into the house.

"Sir, you have to come with me. Jake, could you please stay with these folks, and we'll be right back." On their way back outside, Flynn first went into the den and spoke quietly with MacNutt who dropped what he was doing and followed the two detectives onto the back lawn.

In minutes, two ambulances had been called. Not that they would have been of any help to the two bodies at the scene of the crime, but they would still need to be bagged and transported. While the manner of Herb Cable's death was still debatable, the method of Harold Morin's death was definitely not. So, Faraday was now immediately referring to this previously peaceful residence as the scene of the crime.

At one point, Jake called Faraday aside. "Detective," he said. "On our way here, we stopped at the intersection where Riverview Drive crosses Cedar Ave. I had a good look at a black and white cruiser, and it was definitely not poor Herb. Some very sketchy looking hood was driving, nobody else in the car. He saw me, we locked eyes, and I won't ever forget his look. I'm sure it was the guy Alain, who was mentioned by one of the druggies, Fanjoy, I think his name was. You know, one of those guys who sailed the *Sea Witch* down to Shediac from Escuminac."

"You're right, Jake! Of course, but let's make sure. Let me see," he said, looking around the kitchen. He opened another side door beside the one that led into the den. This took him into Morin's garage, and sitting there was Harold's brand new, black Lincoln.

Up to this point, Faraday had only interviewed Sharon, he had not yet spoken with Dexter who was sitting by himself, looking vacantly at a wall in the kitchen. *Poor guy,* thought Jack, *this business was definitely not in the same league as selling Pontiacs.*

Faraday went back to the kitchen and pulled up a chair beside Dexter Sharpe. "Mr. Sharpe, okay if I call you Dexter? I need to ask you a few questions about your relationship with the owner of the residence, a Mr. Harold Morin. Perhaps, though, before we start, ah, Miss Donovan, are you in need of any medical assistance? The same goes for yourself, Dexter. We can certainly arrange to have you both seen by the appropriate officials." Faraday looked at Dexter and Sharon, then receiving assurances from them both that they were okay, Faraday added, "Jake, could you please give Miss Donovan a drive home. I'm sure she is anxious to get back to her own surroundings."

Jake and Sharon stood to leave, Faraday said to her, "Miss Donovan, I am truly sorry this business had to happen. You may not agree, but, in a sense, you are lucky things worked out for you and Mr. Sharpe as they did. Nevertheless, please let us know if there is anything we can do to help you get your life back in order. Also, if you think of anything you would like to add to your statement that you have given to us tonight, please call me. And Jake, I'll see that your friends Lennie and Donnie get a ride home. Thanks, son."

"Just drop them off at *Joe's Billiards*, Detective. I'll get them home." He said this to Faraday, not as a request, but more as an instruction, an expectation on Jake's part. First of all, he was a bit pissed off with how Sharon and this Dexter guy happened to be together. He needed to talk to his friends about it after he dropped Sharon off at her place.

Jake and Sharon were on their way out of the house when she stopped mid-stride and turned around to speak to Faraday.

"Detective, there *is* one thing you should know before you question

Mr. Sharpe. In case I didn't mention this in my statement, I was ready to run upstairs the moment he untied my wrists, and I was then able to complete the job myself. Had I done that, I would have surely entered the den right when that man was being killed. Dexter displayed an act of unselfishness by freeing up my hands first. Then his honesty after that persuaded me to listen to him. He undoubtedly saved both of our lives."

Jake and Sharon left the house on Riverview Drive and Faraday returned to his interrogation of Dexter Sharpe. They heard the sirens of police cars in the distance, approaching their area from downtown. The sounds reminded Faraday to call the precinct, cancel the APB earlier issued for Harold Morin and put out a new one for Alain Benoit, thought to be driving Herb's cruiser.

It was going to be a long night.

The Chatham PD cruiser slowly entered an unlit dirt road at the east end of town. Only a few houses were on the street. A pair of carelessly strewn older bicycles had been left in the middle of one of the weed-filled lawns beside an old mobile home where Alain brought the stolen vehicle to a halt. He did a quick survey of the vicinity, then quietly walked up a sketchy set of wooden steps and tried the aluminum-frame door. It was open, and he entered the structure.

As Benoit expected, Lloyd Fanjoy was home, 'entertaining' his guest Ron Walsh. They had a joint on the go, watching a rental movie that Benoit immediately recognized as one he had recently watched and loved, called *In Cold Blood,* a film based on Truman Capote's portrayal of the true killing of the Clutter family…a man, his wife, and their two teenagers, that occurred in rural Kansas in the Fall of 1959.

Sensing Benoit's presence, Lloyd turned to face him, his heart suddenly racing. *Shit!* It was the dude who had hired them to sail the *Sea Witch* from Escuminac down to Shediac. Although Fanjoy was not fully aware of everything that Alain Benoit had done in the past week, he did not need to know what it was to cause the fear now flooding his veins. After being allowed to go home after explaining things to the police in Shediac, they thought they were done with the weirdo. One look at this psycho, however, was enough to convince him that was not the case.

"Uh, hey, Alain. What's going on, man?" Lloyd asked. Alain didn't seem to hear him. His full attention was on the screen in front of them. Ron Walsh was also transfixed to the scene on the twenty-six-inch black and white RCA television. Then, as if nothing had been said to him, Benoit walked over to the TV and turned it off. Walsh seemed to come out of some kind of trance. He jumped off the beat-up old sofa and was about to yell at Fanjoy when he realized who was with them. He meekly sat back where he had been and nodded to Benoit. "Hello, Alain," he muttered.

The two druggies were only wearing jeans and tee shirts. "Get your jackets and boots on. We're goin' for a drive." That was all it took. No questions were asked by either of them, and they quickly did as they were told.

"Are your kids at home?" Alain asked Lloyd. For a moment, Lloyd was unsure of how to answer the maniac. Why did he need this information? He decided to play it straight. "Ah, yes, they're in bed," he said to Alain. He looked blankly at the two boys standing in front of him, then shifted his awful stare toward the back room of the trailer, presumably Lloyd's bedroom. "Oh. Okay then, let's go."

The guy was definitely weird, thought Lloyd as he zippered up his parka and the three of them left the trailer to go to the cruiser. Lloyd thought about it, but he was unwilling to try and take the maniac down by force. He had seen the bulge of what had to be a handgun inside Alain's jacket pocket. If he had the balls to somehow take possession of a cop car, God only knew what else he might do.

As the three of them approached the car, Alain threw the cruiser's keys to Walsh. "You drive," he said. "Lloyd, you get in da back seat." He then proceeded to tell them where he wanted to go, and what he wanted them to do.

Chapter Thirty-seven

The drive from Riverview Drive to Sharon's condo was like an eternity, and it was not pleasant. Jake had turned on Epic's radio when they were leaving the terrible scene behind them. Their local station in Newcastle was playing their late- night hits, but Sharon had abruptly turned it off. She sat in the seat beside him, not talking, her shoulders shaking as she quietly sobbed to herself.

"Sharon, I'm sorry," he said. "Did that Sharpe guy, you know, do anything to you?"

She stopped crying and looked angrily at him. For a second, he thought she might slap him. "Oh Jacob! God no! Dexter did nothing of that kind. He was a perfect gentleman. I just feel so sorry for what he must be going through with all of this, this…oh God, I don't believe this has happened right here in Chatham! It's something that I thought only took place in the big cities." Again, she started to cry. He noted with anguish that she had used his first name in a formal context, yet she was now on a first name basis with Sharpe.

By this time, he had reached and pulled into her driveway. He brought his arm across the mid-consul area to put around her, maybe kiss her goodnight, but she made a quick exit from the Epic before he was half-way there and ran to her door. When she had it open, she turned back to him and in a serious tone, said, "I'm sorry, Jacob." Again, the formal use of his name gave him anguish. "I'm not feeling well, I just want to be by myself. I need to call my mother and tell her I'm home. Things are *different* now," she said. "I'll call you tomorrow. Goodbye, Jacob." She closed the door and left Jake with many unanswered questions running through his mind.

All he heard was the phrase she had used: *'Goodbye'*, not *'goodnight'*.

10:30 p.m.

"Hey, Jake, there you are," shouted Lennie when he and Donnie Mitchell spotted their buddy at a lone table at the back of Joe's pool room, shooting a game of eight-ball by himself. "You winning?" teased Donnie.

"Nowhere close to it," mumbled Jake, more to himself. Lennie, who was always very intuitive to Jake's moods, now asked him. "What's the problem, Jake?"

"Aw, girl problems, Len. You don't need to know about it. Tell me, how did things go with Faraday?" Jake asked, changing the subject.

"Good, I'd say. Right, Donnie?" and his friend nodded in agreement. "It was mainly a rehash of what we did when we came here, what we saw. You know, the usual. Comparing statements between you, Donnie, and myself after interviewing us separately. I assume the same went for your lady and the guy she was with. Oh! Sorry, Jake. I didn't mean that like it sounded." Lennie saw the scowl appear on Jake's face as soon as he inferred Sharon had 'been with' Dexter.

"Well, she *was* with the dude, wasn't she? And for basically forty-eight hours," Jake exclaimed.

"C'mon, man! They were both drugged and tied up. What could they have done about it? I think you're overreacting, not that I blame you. But man, the guy you should be pissed off at, though, is that creep, Benoit."

"Yeah, as usual, you're right," Jake sighed in frustration. "Speaking of, where do you think the asshole went?"

"Well, he has poor Herb's cruiser, and if he has any smarts, he'll certainly be able to figure out how the com system in the vehicle works. He'll know where the cops are, all that stuff."

"You think he is going to head for Montreal?"

"Yeah, probably, lose himself in the hordes of bad asses in the city. Still, these guys have invested a lot of money in our area. It's hard to imagine Benoit going back to his boss sort of empty-handed. They bought and paid for the property in Escuminac as the perfect set-up for their drug business."

"Plus, the *boat* that came with the building there," Jake said to himself, thinking about something. He looked at Lennie.

Lennie, sensing Jake was going to come up with another whacky idea, said, "I don't want to hear it, Jake. It's late."

"I'd just like you to call Alphonse in Escuminac, that's all. No biggie, okay?" He was giving Lennie his 'trust me' smile, it usually worked.

11:30 pm.

Constable Gerard Rossignol had been with the Shediac detachment of the RCMP for three years, having completed his basic training with the Canadian law enforcement group in Depot Division located in southwest Regina, Saskatchewan. It was the best twenty-six weeks of his young life, having gone there upon graduating from high school in the small rural community of Maple Creek, some 230 miles away from the training facilities.

Gerard was a big boy, a Metis native, and he had no problems mixing it up during any of the hockey games he had played in over the years. However, since receiving his posting to Shediac two years earlier, he had not encountered any incidents rowdier than the odd drunk needing to be removed from one of the local pubs in the busier summer months. The past week was particularly a real drag, keeping watch on a damned boat. It was a converted lobster boat called the *Sea Witch,* they had recently confiscated during a drug bust. Unfortunately, young Rossignol had not participated in the raid which had been organized by an out-of-town *cop* from the Miramichi area, for Christ's sakes.

They even had the damned Coast Guard involved, plus a team of *special-ops* RCMP officers from Moncton. *Give me a break!* he muttered to himself as he sat in his cruiser and sipped the remainder of the first coffee of the night, he had purchased from Tim Horton's just two blocks down from the Shediac Marina where the *Sea Witch* was moored. *Shit, this stuff goes right through me!* he thought.

Against all his hard-earned normal work ethics, Gerard decided to make a second trip down to Tim's, use their washroom and have a quick leak. And sure, why not pick up another large double-double and give the cute little waitress there a smile. Her name tag told him she was Yvette LeBlanc, a local *belle jeune dame.* He would impress her with his native Metis/Francais. Tossing the empty coffee carton into a waste bag he carried in the front with him, he took off.

He failed to spot the black and white police cruiser that had just pulled into the shadows of a side street, sitting only fifty yards from him. It was even close enough to him that he would have detected the strong sweet-sick aroma of a wine-dipped, rum-soaked, Old Port cigarillo, had he decided to take his leak off the pier. *Sometimes, fate can be cruel.*

Chapter Thirty-eight

Benoit couldn't believe his good luck. For some reason, the lone RCMP officer sitting in his cruiser had just decided to leave the scene and drive back toward the downtown area.

"Here's our chance," he said, watching in his rear-view mirror as Constable Rossignol left the marina. To make sure he wasn't seen by the departing cop, or that they were definitely going to be alone, Alain waited a full five minutes. Satisfied, he then drove alongside the *Sea Witch* and deftly pulled another set of keys out of his jacket pocket. "Ron, Lloyd, follow me. We're gonna reclaim my goddamn boat!" In a matter of minutes, Alain and Lloyd were aboard the *Sea Witch* while Ronnie prepared to untie her from the dock.

As Constable Rossignol was rounding the corner to return him onto the pier, he saw the black and white vehicle sitting close to the *Sea Witch* and somebody was wrestling with a rope that ran from the boat and was tied to a cleat on the dock, obviously in a great hurry to release her moorings.

Son of a bitch! Gerard muttered to himself as he turned off his cruiser's engine and lights. The boat's twin diesels suddenly came to life. Quietly, he exited his vehicle and crept toward the figure who was scrambling to untie a final rope. Due to his haste and the sound from the boat's motors, Walsh never heard Rossignol approaching. Too late, he felt the constable's weapon in his back and the harsh whisper coming from behind him. "This is the police, do not move a muscle."

The young Metis RCMP constable from Maple Creek, Saskatchewan was in his glory. This was what he was meant to do. "Now," he whispered, "Do exactly as I say, and you will not be shot. You are going to precede me onto the boat and not make a sound. How many others are here with you?

Hold up your fingers to tell me, no talking," and Walsh showed him the first two fingers of his left hand behind his back.

"Okay, you are doing good. Now, up the gangway, *quietly,*" he said, and Rossignol prodded Walsh up the slip onto the deck of the *Sea Witch,* his service revolver behind the druggy's back.

Saskatchewan is a landlocked province. Most people who reside there, or who are from there, are not overly familiar with things of a nautical nature. This included Constable Rossignol, and as the two young men plodded up the gangway, Gerard paid no heed to the tell-tale effect their combined weight was having on the stability of the boat. Certainly, Alain noted the obvious swaying immediately as he was waiting for Ron Marsh to come back aboard. Ron was not *that* heavy.

Constable Rossignol was looking for two men when he entered the captain's cabin, but he only saw one figure, that of Lloyd Fanjoy who was standing at the helm with a worried look on his face. Gerard was about to ask where the other party was when he felt a sting on the back of his neck. *Jesus!* He thought it was a wasp, but he knew there were no wasps in Shediac, N.B. in the wintertime. Then his legs grew numb, and he collapsed.

"Hey, Alphonse! *Comment ca va*? asked Jake, after Lennie quickly passed the telephone to him. They were in *Joe's Billiards* shooting pool, and Lennie had finally agreed to call his cousin Alphonse Cormier after Jake's third request. It was late, almost midnight, and Alphonse would probably be pissed off to be aroused at this ungodly hour. Lennie, however, was surprised to see a smile appear on Jake's face as he talked to the fisherman in Baie Ste. Anne. Their conversation continued for another five minutes.

"I know, my friend," said Jake. "I agree. We have to do something about it. Placide would want us to be more involved." At this point in their talk, Jake winked at Lennie and gave him a thumb's up sign. After a few minutes of what was apparently a one-way discussion, all from Alphonse, Jake said, "No problem, we can leave immediately!" He gave the phone back to Lennie. "Let's go, man. Hey, Donnie!" he shouted to their close friend who was at a lone table practicing his 'three-in-the-side' bank shot. "Come on, we gotta go!"

Donnie, his back to them, held his hand up signaling 'one second', and struck the cue ball across the table at a forty-five-degree angle, aiming at and hitting the eight-ball at the perfect spot. It was nestled tight against the rail directly opposite him, about a foot from the back rear pocket, and now it flew back at the rear rail, continued at an angle close to where Donnie was standing, hit the rail in front of him, and caromed back across the table, directly into the side pocket.

"Yesss!" said Donnie, making an imaginary fist bump, and proudly strutting to his buddies, taking a slight bow.

"What's up?" he asked. Jake just looked at him and was about to explain, then he looked back at Lennie and quickly shook his head.

After piling into Jake's Epic and getting on their way, Jake began to explain what had happened so far this evening to his buddies:

Since leaving Sharpe's residence at Riverside Drive, Jake had been giving a lot of thought to where things stood. He knew Herb Cable had probably gone there to seek out Harold Morin once he received the APB from Flynn. He would have done this wanting to grab some recognition from the Chief. He probably knows Morin from the Curling Club, so he comes here, finds Morin is with the crazy guy, Alain Benoit. Benoit kills Herb, takes his vehicle because Herb has stupidly told them about the APB being issued on Morin's Lincoln. The two hoods are unable to leave in the Lincoln because of the APB, so now their problem is solved.

Where would they want to go? Jake had asked himself. The most likely spot was Montreal, it would be easy to blend in with the organized crime people there, the bikers, etc. But as Lennie had pointed out, Benoit would not want to displease his capo in Montreal by returning empty-handed. So, yeah, he'd first go to Shediac. Somehow, he would try to regain possession of the Sea Witch, then sail to the Quebec metropolis. First though, he'd get rid of Morin. The guy was no longer of any use. The Miramichi area started off as a good idea, but face it, now it was a no-go. No problem, there would be other places.

So, with that destination in mind, Jake figured the best guy to call and find out if anything like that was happening in Shediac would be the one person they knew who had friends there, Alphonse Cormier. Besides, back in Escuminac, Alphonse had already seen a preview of what this Benoit freak was into. Also, Alphonse sincerely wanted to do what he could to help rid the area of scum like Benoit. It was the least he could do to avenge his brother, Placide.

It was nothing less than a miracle the way it all worked out. While putting Jake on hold, Alphonse called his friend, Maurice Poirier. Maurice lived in a one-room apartment above The Happy Clam, a seafood restaurant at the end of the Shediac Marina. Prompted by Alphonse, Maurice had looked out his bedroom window and he was amazed by the activity taking place on the wharf. There were a number of police cars there, lights flashing, cops milling about, and an ambulance had just arrived. 'No.' Maurice had told Alphonse There were no lobster boats tied up at the wharf. Definitely not one called the Sea Witch.'

Benoit was not much of a sailor. Tonight, however, he had the fortune of a calm sea on which to navigate. Already, he could see shore lights from a community some five or six miles ahead of him. He consulted a map he had found earlier in a desk drawer. *It had to be Tracadie,* he thought to himself. On further examining the chart, he could see where he needed to go if he wanted to get to Montreal. Even if he could make it as far as Three Rivers or Quebec City, he'd be happy. Hell, if he could make it to the Gaspe coast, he'd call a few friends. No sweat!

First things first, though. He turned on his running lights and made for the nearest marina in the coastal town. He was also starving, so he needed to get something to eat, then he'd gas up the *Witch*.

It was close to midnight. They were entering Baie Ste. Anne, the small fishing village of northeast New Brunswick that had been afforded world recognition in December 1959 by its famous boxing athlete, Yvon Durelle.

"Take your next right," said Lennie. "Here we are," he added, pointing at a nice three-bedroom split-level bungalow situated on a well-kept lawn, bordered by a three-foot hedge. Jake was impressed. Alphonse was standing beside his sparkling almost-new Jeep Wagoneer, waving them over to his garage.

"Eh, you guys. We meet again!" said Alphonse. They greeted each other warmly and the five of them jumped into the Wagoneer.

"I t'ink da bes' move we make at dis time, boys, is to go look for some fish, what you t'ink?" Alphonse asked, a huge grin on his face. "Some bad, rotten fish! Besides, you guys have never been on my boat, an' I'm sorry 'bout dat. But we gonna fix dat now!"

They drove further out of the village toward Escuminac Point where he told them his boat was moored. It was a private dock, not far, maybe five miles, from the site they had earlier visited where Benoit and Morin had intended to set up their now abandoned meth cook house.

Alphonse's boat was a beauty. He had purchased it last summer from a down-and-out lobster fisherman in Maine. Initially a lobster boat, Alphonse had her rigged out for tuna fishing by SW Boat Works in Lamoine. He told Jake there was more money in sport fishing for tuna, and from what Jake had so far seen, he believed him.

The boat, named *Reel Therapy,* sported a 575 hp John Deere diesel engine which soon proved to be of great help for what they were attempting to do. As soon as they had boarded the *Reel Therapy*, Alphonse got on his ship-to-shore comms system and once again he amazed Jake with his ability for finding out things they never would have found on their own, even with the help of Faraday and Flynn.

As it turned out, another friend and fellow tuna fisherman, a guy from Prince Edward Island, his name Jean Paul Hachey, was visiting the Shediac area on a business trip. Cormier was aware of this and after contacting him they learned some more interesting data.

Hachey had heard about the commotion at the Shediac Marina only ten or fifteen minutes ago on his boat radio while cruising offshore not far from the site. Oddly, he thought he had come across the very boat that was the subject of all the uproar, the *Sea Witch,* a Cape Cod class forty-four footer. In fact, she had been running without her port and starboard lights on, and the fool had nearly run into him! She had been headed in a due north-easterly direction and based on the info given to Alphonse by Hachey, along with the estimated speed of the *Sea Witch* and the time he saw them, Alphonse was now able to make some calculations.

It only took the experienced seaman a matter of minutes, and as the result of his reckoning, he felt he would find the *Witch* in the vicinity of Tracadie, a town of 16,000 situated on the Northeast coast of New Brunswick. It was a fair-sized town, suitable for Benoit's needs, and Alphonse figured the chances of Benoit stopping in Tracadie were quite favorable, since the town lay directly in line with the route Alphonse had chartered from the data supplied by his friend Jean Paul. As well, if Benoit was going to Montreal as they all assumed, there were no other towns close by that met these specs.

Alphonse again got on his marine VHF radio. "One more call to make," he said to Jake. So far today, they had been extremely lucky in their search for the psycho hit man from Montreal. Jake hoped their good fortune would prevail for just a bit longer. His hopes were answered when Alphonse closed his comms down and started up his John Deere diesel engine.

"We are in lucky," he said to Jake, who did not bother to correct his English. "Dat guy I was jus' talking wit'. He tell me he jus' 'ad a weird guy come to his station, fill up his boat wit' gas, and he tol' him where he could get something to eat. I jus' ask my friend to try and keep him busy for a while if he comes back before we get 'dere!"

The question now was, could they get to Tracadie before Benoit returned to the *Sea Witch*?

Chapter Thirty-nine

Chaos reigned at the Shediac Marina. An EMT who had been administering aid to Constable Gerard Rossignol for the past twenty minutes finally left his side. "You can talk to him now," he said to Capt. Norman Hilchey from the Moncton detachment of the RCMP. Hilchey had been called to the scene by his colleague Capt. Michel Leblanc when they had received an 'Officer Down' alert from Rossignol. Rushing there, they were surprised to find two individuals sitting in Rossignol's squad cruiser, trying to revive the constable.

They were the same two delinquents they had earlier released, Fanjoy and Walsh. The two had been released on their own recognizance only after a lengthy discussion with Don Flynn, with the Chatham PD, who spoke highly on their behalf. According to statements given by the young pair, they had been forced by Benoit to assist him in bringing him here in the police car previously owned by Herb Cable, from the Chatham Police Department. They did not know where Cable was, only that Benoit had shown up at Fanjoy's place driving Herb's car, demanding that they take him here. After that, they were forced to assist in the abduction of Constable Rossignol, and that's when things got very scary for them and Rossignol.

"Benoit surprised Rossignol when he came aboard *the Sea Witch*, leading Ron with a gun against his back. He came up behind officer Rossignol and stabbed him in the back of his neck with a bbbig syringe," said Lloyd. He ordered us to ppput him____ " Lloyd was now stuttering badly, losing control, "in the back of his cruiser and drive it down to the slip at the end of the wharf. We were supppposed to push it into the water. We cccould not do th-th-that!"

Lloyd struggled, but he was eventually able to describe how Benoit had drawn a gun and came after them, getting off several shots at them but missing. They ran, and Benoit had fled back onto the *Witch* when he heard the siren's coming and took to sea. By the time he had finished, Rossignol had regained his senses and was able to corroborate the boys' statements. They would later confirm the drug used on Constable Rossignol was the same substance involved in the homicides of Jimmy Whalen and Ron Doyle: Pancuronium.

With the return of the two boys, Cable's vehicle, and the heist of the *Sea Witch,* Hilchey decided to bring Faraday and the Chatham PD back into the investigation.

Who knew where this thing was headed?

Faraday returned his telephone to its cradle after finishing his call with his friend, Captain Norman Hilchey. *Hot damn! The case was still active!* When he learned from Hilchey that Benoit was probably somewhere at sea, he urged his friend to once again make arrangements with his associates, Captain Dryden and Lieutenant Wilks, and most importantly their Sikorsky helicopter. With no hesitation, he then called Flynn, and with no apologies whatever, even at this late hour, he was out the door on his way to Flynn's apartment. Faraday felt like a teenager on his first date.

The *Reel Therapy* slid over the glass-like water in an ultra-smooth fashion, her 525 hp motor getting Cormier and his friends to their destination at the Marina de Tracadie in one hour flat. On the way, Alphonse had again called his friend Francoise at the marina and confirmed that Benoit, as far as his friend knew, was still at the Dixie Lee Tracadie fried chicken haven.

It was just after 1:00 a.m. when Alphonse quietly entered the furthest possible mooring berth he could find away from the *Sea Witch* where they spotted it, obviously very sloppily tied up at Francoise's station. The foursome walked back to Francoise's place, Alphonse carrying a small pack strapped to his back.

They hopped onto the floating marine fuel dock where a large, semi-bald figure in a tight-fitting parka greeted them warmly, all the while looking behind and around his visitors. Introductions were made, hot coffees were quickly poured, and setting his aside, Alphonse got up to leave.

"I'll be right back," he said.

Only three minutes after his return, they all felt the platform heave a couple of times and a slight figure came into the store. As soon as Jake saw the man, he knew who it was. The look of concern now showing on Francoise's face confirmed it was Alain Benoit, the object of their search, the direct murderer of at least four people in Chatham, the indirect killer of God-knew how many others in their town and elsewhere.

Benoit, never having met Jake nor any of his three friends with him, gave them all a menacing look and walked up to Francoise, who was standing behind his cash till. "How much?" was all he asked.

"Ah, dat' would be thirty," said Francoise. Benoit gave him two twenties, waited for his change.

"Not leaving a tip?" asked Jake. Benoit was annoyed at the insulting remark from some local.

"Who the fuck are you?" was Benoit's come-back. He rudely grabbed the ten-spot that Francoise was holding out to him, still glaring at Jake. "Here's a tip for you, asshole. Be very careful what you say to me. I don't have the time to screw around with kids!" and he started to leave.

Jake got up to exit the table where he was sitting, fire in his brain, and just as he was about to leave his chair, Alphonse pushed him back into it. Jake saw a look of warning come from Alphonse as their eyes met, Alphonse, with his back to Benoit. He was holding both his arms high against Jake, silently telling him, *Let the guy go.* Jake got the message.

Holy shit! Jake thought. *What had he just done?*

Benoit only gave Jake a pitiful sneer. "Fucking kids . . . think you are so macho! You are nothing, little boy!" he smirked as he slammed the door and left. They all walked slowly off the fuel station and watched as Benoit untied the *Sea Witch* and hopped aboard her, now and then giving them all an evil smile. Alphonse made sure Benoit saw the AR-14 semi-automatic rifle he was carrying by his side.

Benoit had entered the boat's cabin, and he had fired up its twin engines, leaving them idle while he came back out onto her decks. From the pier's overhead light, Jake could discern a different look appearing on the face of the little man who was finally seeing Jake from a different time and situation, now remembering the four-way stop on Riverview Drive in Chatham.

At that realization, he gave Jake a slow nod. He pulled out one of his Colt cigarillos and gave the others a smirk as he quickly returned to the helm. The boat's engines dropped into gear and the *Sea Witch* took off into the night, a three-quarter moon shining on the open sea as she sped north toward the Gaspe Peninsula.

Several things then occurred that Jake would remember for a while. The first was the distinctive *whump-whump* sound from the Sikorsky's blades as it approached them, maybe a mile away; secondly, Jake briefly saw Alphonse check his watch, and at that exact moment there was a bright flash of light three or four miles on the water to the north. It was instantly followed by the sound of a huge explosion.

They were all still staring at the ocean in awe when the 'copter carrying Faraday and Flynn landed on the pier. Jake noted Alphonse giving Lennie a quick serious nod, and the group walked over to meet up with the cops.

"Jake! What's going on!?" Faraday yelled as he ran over to them, followed by Flynn, both ducking under the spinning blades of the Sikorsky helicopter.

"Let's go in Francoise's station where we can talk!" Jake had to yell back at Faraday over the noise of the 'copter's props.

Once inside the fuel house, fresh coffees were served up, introductions were made all around, and Jake explained how they were able to determine the whereabouts of Alain Benoit with the help of his friend Alphonse and his colleague Francoise. For his part, Faraday told Jake and his party of the abduction of the two youths by Benoit, their rationale for coming to Shediac, and the role of the Shediac RCMP and the two boys in helping to break up what was about to be the tragic death of Constable Gerard Rossignol in their detachment.

The RCMP had determined that Ron Walsh and Lloyd Fanjoy, the two boys from Chatham, had aided Benoit but only because they were under great duress. Indeed, when Rossignol had been drugged by Benoit, they refused to carry out his orders. When they were told to push the constable off the wharf while he was lying in a state of paralysis in his cruiser, the boys ran, and Benoit attempted to shoot them. He was forced to flee the scene in the *Sea Witch* when he heard the sirens of Capt. Michel LeBlanc and his team arriving, responding to an 'officer down' call from the boys in Rossignol's cruiser.

"Was that Benoit's boat that just exploded in the harbor?"

"It was, Detective. He came in to pay for his fuel while we were here, and then he left. We watched him leave after a few words were exchanged, then he was gone. Like, forever." Jake said no more, just looked at Faraday.

"You said a few words were exchanged. What did he say?"

"I don't remember, exactly." Jake looked over at Alphonse and Lenny. "Something derogative about *kids*, he was talking about me, I guess."

"Weird…," said Faraday, then turned his attention to the marine fuel shop owner. "Francoise, you filled his tank. You see anything amiss around the engine that might have triggered such an explosion?"

"No, Sir," replied Francoise. "I will say though, d'at d'is man, he was not an experienced seaman. He was a heavy smoker, an when he lef' he was lighting up one of d'ose small cigars, you know, da smelly ones! Not a smart t'ing to do around so much fuel!"

Faraday nodded in agreement, looked at the group of men, all of them stone silent. "Yeah, I guess that could be the answer," he said. He now singled out Alphonse, said, "So, there would be no need for us to go out there searching for evidence of, oh, I don't know, maybe some chemical traces of nitro or fragments of switches floating about?"

"You could, but it would be a waste of time, Detective. Really." Alphonse said and left it at that.

Faraday looked at Flynn, his eyebrows raised. Flynn nodded. They left the fuel shop and the group of men watched in silence as the two policemen returned to the waiting helicopter. In minutes, the props of the Sikorsky were roaring, and it flew into the night.

Alphonse shook hands with Francoise and picked up his AR-14 with his backpack. Jake, Lennie, and Donnie walked back to the *Reel Therapy* with him. Like the 'copter they were quickly on their way. Several residents of Tracadie had started to appear on the wharf, all talking at once trying to figure out what had just happened.

Francoise stood alone on the dock and waved goodbye to Alphonse and his friends. It had been a long and exciting night, and it was clouding over. Snow was in the air. He was looking forward to a nice warm bed.

Chapter Forty

It was after 3:00 a.m. by the time Alphonse had returned to Escuminac with his three passengers, and before leaving the poolroom yesterday evening, Jake had made a point of calling his parents and telling them he would probably be staying overnight at Len's place.

"So, what now, Jake? Are you still going to Moncton?" asked Lennie. They were sitting in Lennie's small kitchen drinking a beer. It had started snowing about half-way home from Alphonse's and the roads were a little too slick for the hill Jake would have to navigate in order to reach his house, so he decided to stay where he was. Besides, he felt he needed to have a talk with his friend in any case.

"Good question, Len. At this point, I'm not sure what the bank thinks of me. All this business with the police, the drugs, the killings. You *know* it will be in the papers tomorrow. Sorry, today," he said, correcting himself as he looked at the clock on the kitchen wall. "Regional Office will not be looking at this as good PR material, I wouldn't think."

"You never know," countered Len. "A lot will depend on how Faraday presents it to the press. Actually, Jake, I was thinking more about you and your relationship with Sharon?"

"Well, *that* is another story, isn't it. I really don't have an answer for it either," he said. "You know, Len, even if she still wants us to be a couple, if the bank transfer is on, then I'll be going to Moncton. I've got to do something meaningful with my life, and Sharon knows that. So, we'll see."

They decided to call it a night, and Lenny showed Jake to the spare room he had used on many occasions. As his head was still spinning with the events of the night, he said to his friend, "Len, I saw Alphonse check his watch tonight, *the very second* the *Sea Witch* exploded. He knew that was

220

going to happen. I also saw him winking at you . . ." *It was in the open. Now what?*

Lennie couldn't meet Jake's gaze. His eyes drifted to a picture on the wall beside Jake of a young boy, maybe in his late teens. The teen wore a smile that hid the sorrow, fear, and pain, perhaps a thousand other emotions, none of them healthy, that the boy would struggle with in later years. Frank Hachey was one of many young men in the past few years to get way over his head into meth. Last year he had found out the hard way that he couldn't fly off Centennial Bridge.

"I guess I told you earlier about Frankie," Len said, nodding to the wall picture behind Jake. "I loved that guy, Jake. I would have done anything for him, but believe me, no matter what you're thinking, I was not in on that with Al," he said. "Yeah, I sort of guessed when he winked at me, that he might have been behind it. But, like he said to Faraday, it would never be proven. Besides, the world is a better place with that creep no longer in it."

"Yeah, you are right, Len. Good night, man."

"Good night, Jake."

Their talk was over.

In the morning, Jake arrived home to find his mother on the telephone. She held her hand out to Jake, speaking to somebody on the other end of the line, "Hold on one second please, he just arrived. Jake, it's for you."

"This is Jacob." He decided to use his formal name.

"Hi Jacob. I'm sorry to bother you. This is John Jackson, Human Resources manager at BNB in Saint John. Do you have a minute?"

"Yes, sir. Certainly."

"Well, I just wanted to let you know that your transfer to Moncton is still open, if you are interested?"

"Yes, definitely, sir. When should I report? I am to see Mr. Gray down there, correct?"

"Correct. You can go there tomorrow morning, weather permitting. By the way, just so there are no surprises when you get there, Mr. Crawford at your branch in Chatham has decided to take early retirement. Oh, and you will be pleased to know that we have decided to have your colleague, Miss

Donovan, replace him as the branch manager."

"Wow! I mean, wonderful for Sharon, um, I mean, Miss Donovan. She will be very happy with that, and I know she deserves it!"

Jake hung up the phone, ecstatic with the news. He related everything to his mother. "Jake, your father will be so proud to hear this," Meg said. "Martin is working at a job he recently took on at the Morrison's place on Wellington Street. He'll be home for supper."

"I'll be here, Mom. Right now, I need to get some sleep and pack up a week's supply of clothing to take with me to Moncton."

That evening, Sharon Donovan was having Dexter Sharpe over for supper. She was still on cloud nine after getting the call from HR about her new appointment, and she was eager to share this news with him. She had not been speaking with Jacob since he had brought her home after everything she had been through with those terrible people. And to think her own boss and the manager of the Bank of Toronto were prepared to do business with those others.

Her doorbell sounded and she jumped to greet the new man in her life, the guy who was more level-headed about where he wanted to go. She was shocked when she opened the door and Jake was standing there.

"Oh, it's you!" she exclaimed.

"I should have called you first, Sharon," he said. "I'm sorry. Do you have a few minutes?" he asked, pleasantly.

"Er, no, Jacob, not really. In fact, I am expecting Dexter at any minute for supper. Ah, this is a little awkward," she tried explaining, constantly looking out to the street.

Suddenly, it all fell into place for Jake. Oddly, he was not angry, not even sad, for that matter. He felt, *relieved. Yes, that was the feeling,* he thought to himself. Then he quickly backed away from her. "Aw, look, Sharon. I understand. No hard feelings. I'm sure everything will work out for you and, uh, Dexter. I've gotta go get my stuff together for the move to Moncton. So, look, all the best, okay?" He opened his arms, approached her and they briefly hugged. Jake jumped into his little Epic and he was gone.

Sharon slowly turned to go back into her townhouse. Her eye was caught by the vacant hummingbird feeder she had neglected to put away for the winter last fall. It looked so incongruous, and forlorn. She should have taken it in with her but decided for some unknown reason to leave it where it was.

A reminder.

Also, by the author
at
Rogue Phoenix Press

Iggy & Jake

It is 1969. Iggy and Jake are two rock musicians who decide to leave their mundane jobs and travel west in search of finding that elusive record label. Their journey takes them to Calgary where they plan to hook up with an old-time buddy, only to discover he has been the victim of foul play. Two jaded Calgary PD detectives utilize the talents of the streetwise musicians, and they are soon involved in an international drug bust in which their lives and those of their friends are at great risk.

Ogopogo

A former GI vet from the Vietnam war, suffering from PTSD, has made his way to the peaceful Okanagan area of B.C. Here he chooses to target young Asian female victims who will serve his purpose as he assumes the persona of Ogopogo, a Canadian folk lore lake serpent who was said to inhabit Okanagan Lake.

Ignatius (Iggy) Myles and Jacob (Jake) England, two Kelowna streetwise detectives are nearing retirement, but their plans are put on hold as the killer's prey becomes personal, and they are forced to pursue the monster through the mountainous wilds of British Columbia.

Martin's War

July 1945. Martin England arrives home from war-torn Europe. His flashbacks are increasing, threatening his fragile marriage and his ability to function normally. When he is involved in the death of a war comrade and charged with homicide, he seeks the help of his captain and closest ally, Reginald Jacobs, Q.C. Jacobs takes temporary leave from his law practice in Montreal to defend his friend and in the process of the trial, he realizes Martin is suffering from PTSD. He obtains the help of a friend, Dr. Michel LeBlanc, a specialist in hypnotherapy. Together, they determine they must confront Martin with the truth of what happened one day during the war in a Tuscany vineyard. Other powerful people, however, will go to extreme lengths to prevent Jacobs from uncovering the facts, and a deadly plot is set in place to ensure the truth is kept buried.

About the Author

Thomas Jardine is a late bloomer as crime novelists go. He is retired from the Canadian financial services industry, and a part-time musician. He lives with his wife Alexandra and Biewer Yorky Clancy in the Annapolis Valley of Nova Scotia.

www.ingramcontent.com/pod-product-compliance
Lightning Source LLC
Chambersburg PA
CBHW071503170626
46811CB00007B/2705